GHOR
Kin-Slayer

The Saga of Genseric's Fifth-Born Son

Necronomicon Press

Cover art by Robert H. Knox
First printing — August 1997
Published by Necronomicon Press, P. O. Box 1304, West Warwick, RI 02893

Copyright © 1997 by Necronomicon Press

"Genseric's Son" by Robert E. Howard, copyright © 1977 by Jonathan Bacon for *Fantasy Crossroads*, reprinted by permission of Jack W. Baum for Robert E. Howard Properties

"The Coming of Ghor" by Karl Edward Wagner, copyright © 1977 by Jonathan Bacon for *Fantasy Crossroads*, reprinted by permission of the author's estate

"Ghor's Revenge" by Joseph Payne Brennan, copyright © 1977 by Jonathan Bacon for *Fantasy Crossroads*, reprinted by permission of the author's estate

"The Ice Woman's Prophecy" by Richard L. Tierney, copyright © 1977 by Jonathan Bacon for *Fantasy Crossroads*, reprinted by permission of the author

"The Nemedians" by Michael Moorcock, copyright © 1977 by Jonathan Bacon for *Fantasy Crossroads*, reprinted by permission of the author

"Betrayal in Belverus" by Charles R. Saunders, copyright © 1977 by Jonathan Bacon for *Fantasy Crossroads*, reprinted by permission of the author

"Lord General of Nemedia" by Andrew J. Offutt, copyright © 1978 by Jonathan Bacon for *Fantasy Crossroads*, reprinted by permission of the author

"The Oath of Agha Junghaz" by Manly Wade Wellman, copyright © 1978 by Jonathan Bacon for *Fantasy Crossroads*, reprinted by permission of the author's estate

"The Mouth of the Earth" by Darrell Schweitzer, copyright © 1978 by Jonathan Bacon for *Fantasy Crossroads*, reprinted by permission of the author

"The Gods Defied" by A. E. Van Vogt, copyright © 1978 by Jonathan Bacon for *Fantasy Crossroads*, reprinted by permission of the author's representative, the Ashley Grayson Literary Agency

"Swordsmith and Sorcerer" by Brian Lumley, copyright © 1979 by Jonathan Bacon for *Fantasy Crossroads*, reprinted by permission of the author

"The Gift of Lycanthropy" by Frank Belknap Long, copyright © 1979 by Jonathan Bacon for *Fantasy Crossroads*, reprinted by permission of representatives of the author's estate, the Pimlico Agency

"The War Among the Gods" by Adrian Cole, copyright © 1997 by Adrian Cole and original to this collection

"The Ways of Chaos" by Ramsey Campbell, copyright © 1996 by Ramsey Campbell for *Far Away & Never*, reprinted by permission of the author

"The Caves of Stygia" by H. Warner Munn, copyright © 1997 by the author's estate and original to this collection

"Doom of the Thrice-Cursed" by Marion Zimmer Bradley, copyright © 1997 by Marion Zimmer Bradley and original to this collection. By permission of the Scovil, Chichak, Galen Literary Agency, Inc., representatives of the author

"The River of Fog" by Richard A. Lupoff, copyright © 1997 by Richard A. Lupoff and original to this collection

ISBN 0-940884-91-7

Ghor, Kin-Slayer
The Saga of Genseric's Fifth-Born Son

I.	Genseric's Son *by Robert E. Howard*	7
II.	The Coming of Ghor *by Karl Edward Wagner*	11
III.	Ghor's Revenge *by Joseph Payne Brennan*	19
IV.	The Ice Woman's Prophecy *by Richard L. Tierney*	29
V.	The Nemedians *by Michael Moorcock*	37
VI.	Betrayal in Belverus *by Charles R. Saunders*	43
VII.	Lord General of Nemedia *by andrew j. offutt*	55
VIII.	The Oath of Agha Junghaz *by Manly Wade Wellman*	65
IX.	The Mouth of the Earth *by Darrell Schweitzer*	77
X.	The Gods Defied *by A. E. Van Vogt*	88
XI.	Swordsmith and Sorcerer *by Brian Lumley*	94
XII.	The Gift of Lycanthropy *by Frank Belknap Long*	105
XIII.	The War Among the Gods *by Adrian Cole*	122
XIV.	The Ways of Chaos *by Ramsey Campbell*	133
XV.	The Caves of Stygia *by H. Warner Munn*	141
XVI.	Doom of the Thrice-Cursed *by Marion Zimmer Bradley*	152
XVII.	The River of Fog *by Richard A. Lupoff*	163
	Publisher's Note	176

Chapter I
Genseric's Son
Robert E. Howard

Long, long ago an infant son was born to Gudrun of the Shining Locks, the wife of Genseric the Sworder, in their horse-hide lodge on the frozen snows of Vanaheim. When the man-child's first wail of life broke upon the icy waste, Genseric lifted him in his mighty hand and searched him for any blemish, as was the custom of the Vanir and their brothers the Æsir. And he frowned, for the infant's left leg was crooked.

Immemorial custom had decreed that only the perfect should live; but Genseric turned to Gudrun questioningly, for hers was the last word in the matter. But Gudrun, with the rack of her throes still upon her, threw back fiercely and proudly her thick shining tresses, and said harshly: "I have four sons of fair straight limbs; shall I give them a crippled frog for a brother?"

So Genseric went from the tent into the chill grey dawn, carrying the man-child naked. The smoke of his breath clotted his beard, and his shod feet crunched in the frozen crust. There was frost upon his sword hilt, and the icy air bit through his furs and the mail beneath.

Far out on the misty waste he laid the infant, its body turning blue in the wind that wailed out of the murky depths that veiled the horizons. He laid his hand on his sword, then blown to his ears from afar came the long howling of the great grey wolves. So he turned and strode back across the waste, like a dark phantom of the indefinite dawn, and behind him the cry of the pack rose to a crescendo of exultation and died away.

But even before the sun had thrust its way through the icy mists and low-lying clouds to turn the snow fields to a floating plain of blinding fire, old Bragi came to Genseric's tent, with his grey beard and his haunted eyes and the strangeness in his soul that an ancient sword-cut upon his head had made his.

"I saw you lay the child upon the snow," quoth old Bragi. "I saw as I returned across the chill wastes in the grey birth of dawn. I heard the howling of the wolves as you turned away, and soon the swift patter of their feet over the crust. Their eyes were green in the murk, and their tongues lolled red as hunger between their white fangs. They came about the infant where it lay upon the snow, and stirred its limbs with their muzzles, yet harmed it not. By the icy blood of Ymir, they howled like the fiends of the wastes about it, and a great grey she-wolf lay down beside it and gave it her teats. Its fingers clutched at her stiff grey ice-clotted hair, and it sucked at her dugs as a wolf cub suckles. Then fear fell upon me, and I fled swiftly. Yet it is the truth I speak."

So Genseric and his brothers went forth into the waste, until they came to the spot where the babe was left. But the infant was gone, and all about the spot where it had lain were the tracks of wolves. There was no blood on the snow, but the tracks of many wolves led westward into the plains of eternal ice and snow. And afterwards, in the horse-hide tents of Vanaheim and of Asgard, over the flickering fires was told the tale of Genseric's fifth born, the man-child who was taken by the wolves.

I was the man-child. I, whom men now call James Allison, in another, weaker, softer age and clime. I can not tell you how I possess this knowledge, any more than you can tell me how it is that the events of yesterday, and the days before, and the years before remain indelibly impressed upon that part of your consciousness we call memory, so that you can call them into life again by speech and writing. You know, that is all; aye, and I *know*. As you remember your days, I remember my lives. Your memory of your days is unbroken by the nights of sleep which separate them, nor is the memory of my lives broken by the alternating nights of deeper sleep we call death. In that night I have gone ten thousand times, and out of that night ten thousand times have I wakened, as I shall awake again and again throughout the long ages until the destruction of the planet that spawned it shall at last and ultimately break the chain of flesh and blood and bone figments which have successively cloaked the undying spirit that is *I*.

Even the destruction of the planet can not kill that spirit, whether its end be blackening frost under a dead, icy sun, or the melting wrath of cosmic fires. Let the earth burst like an iridescent bubble floating in the gulf of infinity, yet *life* is not destroyed. I have seen visions, vast and terrible and wonderful, of the cataclysm that shall not destroy the spirit that is me, but hurl it into unguessed infinities, into undreamed oceans of suns and stars beyond the ken of man, to take up the endless succession anew in gorgeous, weird worlds beyond the echoing voids.

But I have no lust to plumb those dreaming deeps. I am of the earth earthly. Out of the dust I have sprung, and into the dust I have returned, not once, but a million times, to rise in eternal resurrection, clothed in a new flesh and burning youth, like fresh and shining raiment. I look not beyond the horizons of the planet that gave me birth. My feet are deep in the mysteries of her grasses and her pools; her dew is in my hair, and her sun is hot gold on my naked

I. Genseric's Son

shoulders; under my hands the warm earth pulses with life that gave the races of man being, and my arms embrace the living trunks of her trees; they are no less her children than am I: the speech of their leaves no less articulate than mine.

Oh, I have been many men in many lands! As I lay here waiting for death to free me from this broken, unsound body, I do not see the dingy walls, the cobwebbed ceiling, the cheap prints that pass for pictures; they do not limit my vision, nor the houses and the oak groves and the hills beyond; not the horizons themselves are my boundaries. I see the flaming dawns I have known of old, the far lands, the broad, foaming seas—white cliffs against the clear cold blue, with a smother of sparkling froth about their foot, and the cry of gulls. I see pageantry, and pride, and glory, the shine of the sun on golden corselets, the breaking of spears, the spreading of purple sails, and the dark eyes of women who have loved me.

Oh, I see all the men that have been I! The brave, the fearful, the strong, the weak, the kind, the cruel, the living, loving, hating, lusting, swilling, gorging, fighting, betraying, swaggering figures that have borne equally with one another the transient, restless spirit that now animates the frail and sickly frame that men call James Allison.

What have I not been? King, warrior, slave. I died at Marathon, at Arbela, at Cannae, at Chalons, at Clontarf, at Hastings, at Agincourt, at Austerlitz, at San Jacinto, and at Gettysburg. I was a nameless, yellow-haired chieftain riding a half-wild stallion when we brought bronze into western Europe; I bore spear and shield in the Macedonian phalanx when the plains of India shook to the tread of Alexander; I pulled a strong bow at Poitiers, when our whistling clouds of arrows broke the chivalry of France; and I heard the creak of leather, the tinkling of spurs and the singing of the night-riders when we drove the lowing herds of longhorns up the dim trail men call the Chisholm to build a new young empire of leather and beef and steel.

What could I not tell you of this planet, and the life that teems upon it; how could I not refute the chroniclers and the sages, and laugh to scorn the historians and the philosophers!

But I will rather go back beyond their ken, into an age of which they have no cognizance. I will tell you of the man-child of Genseric and of Gudrun of the Shining Locks, who was suckled by wolves.

Oh, the tale is no new one. Every race has its legends of a babe who tugged at the breasts of a she-wolf. It is the heritage of all Aryan peoples, and from them other races have borrowed.

But it was from the actuality of the son of Genseric and Gudrun that all these tales sprang. Romulus was suckled by a harlot, and his sons called her a wolf through courtesy and evasion. But the milk of the grey she-wolf was the only sustenance the son of Genseric knew.

I never had a name, as men are named, though in the years of my life I was called many things by many tribes. I was The Strong One. That was what my many names signified, in whatever tongue they were framed. I remember that a tribe of the Æsir called me Ghor, and since that is as good a name as another I will call the son of Genseric and of Gudrun by that name.

Chapter II
The Coming of Ghor
Karl Edward Wagner

Of the first years of my life, only the most nebulous impressions remain etched into my memory. Most vividly penetrates the image of endless ice and snow, the memory of the cold—the relentless cold winds and crystalline nights when the chill stars shimmered through the frozen haze of my breath.

Even among the savage races of that age, I think no other infant could have survived a single night of that frozen wasteland. I survived.

I remember the sour warmth of the she-wolf's fur, the panting caress of her tongue, the sharp sting of her fangs. Dimly comes the remembrance of the acrid milk that I suckled from her dugs. Sharper comes the memory of the hotter sustenance I drank as it gushed from the torn veins of some fallen prey, of sweet raw flesh stripped from yet thrashing flanks—before the cold transformed our kill into a broken statue of crimson marble and tattered fur. Nor were all our prey clad in their natural furs.

I say there was not another man-child who could have lived through my savage childhood. In the light of another age, I realize there was something about me that made me different from the tribe of Vanir from which I sprang. The pack sensed this, else they would have devoured me in that first instant: Some atavistic heritage in my soul, that called back to a lost age when man's apish forebears coupled with certain creatures who only mimicked the shape of man.

At times I think my father did well to cast my naked body onto the icy drifts, that his fault was rather to stay his hand from swordhilt as I squalled an answering cry to the oncoming wolfpack.

From the first dawning of conscious thought, I was aware that I was different from the she-wolf whose dugs nourished me, from my swift grey-furred brothers and sisters. The white fur that lay upon my childish limbs was no more than the down of a newborn cub, so that instinctively I wrapped about myself the half-rotted pelts of old kills. In the space of a few seasons, the cubs amongst whom I gamboled chased across the ice fields on powerful limbs—as bold and savage killers as their sires—while I scrambled clumsily about our den, too slow to join with the others.

I cannot say how many frozen seasons drifted past before I began to pull myself painfully erect, began to understand that I could stand unaided on my hind legs, realized that I could dash about in this strange upright posture. The crooked left leg that had condemned me to the icy waste had slowly straightened in the interim—whether from the rigors of my existence, or because it bore no weight while my infant bones elongated and hardened, I cannot guess. In time I ran across the tundra as swiftly and relentlessly as my brothers of the pack, with only a slight twist at my ankle to evidence my old deformity.

It was now that I began to sense a certain kinship to the strange two-legged prey we sometimes stalked. Before, seeing only a torn and mangled kill, I gave no more thought to what meal I shared than I did to the carcass of an elk or reindeer.

But now, running with the pack, for the first time I beheld another living man—a lone hunter, half-dead from the sudden blizzard that had separated him from his fellows. I held back, fascinated, as he made a desperate stand. He had neither fangs and claws, nor hooves and antlers—no more than did I. But as the pack ringed him in, he bent back the curved stick he carried, released its taut cord with an angry *thrumm*. A howl of agony, and the nearest wolf of the circle bounded high with a wooden shaft through his heart. The hunter drew a second shaft from the sling at his back, fitted it to his bow, sped it full into the throat of a second grey brother—all in the space of a heartbeat. Then the pack closed over him.

For a moment his limbs thrashed beneath the press of snarling slayers, and I saw that my first impression was mistaken, for one paw was armed with a single long, sharp talon. One ripping stroke of that silver-grey talon disemboweled one of those who tore at his throat. Then his struggles ceased.

Despite my own hunger, I watched in thought while my brothers fought over the steaming carcass. The curved stick and the shafts it hurled were beyond my understanding. The silver-grey talon had been torn from the man's forepaw. I examined it curiously, saw that the sharp grey sliver was fitted with a haft of bone that my own smaller forepaw could grip in the same manner as had the hunter. It felt good in my grip.

Standing there, the knife in my hand, looking down as the pack snarled over the flesh that so resembled my own—I recognized that I was not, as I had assumed when I thought about it at all, some ludicrously misshapen freak of nature, tolerated by my swifter and stronger brothers. I knew then that I was a man. At least in form.

With that understanding, a strange unrest claimed my soul. If I were a man, why did I not dwell among men—why was I brother to those whose enemy was man?

The mystery became an obsession with me. In fascination I crouched in the shadows beyond the campfires of men, studying

II. The Coming of Ghor

their inconceivable actions and incoherent barks and cries. On moonless nights when the frost hung invisibly upon my stealthy breaths, I slunk down almost within confines of their camps and villages. While my grey brothers kept a safe distance, I crept along unnoticed behind roving packs of hunters—mused upon their strange weapons, the pelts they wrapped their hairless flesh in, and the flashing devil of heat and light they shared their meat with.

As season followed bleak season, with but a fleeting thaw between the deadly chill of winter's return, I spent less time with the pack and ever more hours in contemplation of man and his ways. I recognized that his yelps and grunts were a pattern of speech far more complex than that of my wolf brothers. By long study I found I could form some of their cries in my own throat; that the bright devil-thing was called "fire", that the curved stick that hurled sharp-fanged shafts was called "bow". The silver-grey talon was "knife", and knife had an older, deadlier brother called "sword"— longer and sharper far than any tusk or talon. I coveted sword as I had desired no other thing in all my grim youth.

There came a day when the sun was a cold red disc lost beneath the lowering clouds of a gathering ice storm. My grey brothers had slunk into the shelter of their dens, while I, a wild thing of little more than ten winters, crouched along beneath the leaden skies to watch a scene beyond all marvels.

Two packs of men had come together in the storm-fraught waste. Their encounter was a bloody clash—a battle fought without quarter. The reason of their conflict was beyond my understanding, but the savage ferocity of that battle made my heart leap within my young chest. My blood throbbed in my veins, and I gnashed my teeth and trembled with a lust to throw myself into the slaughter. Some final instinct held me back, and the snarls and howls that escaped my frothing lips were drowned in the shouts and death cries of the combatants.

There were perhaps twenty men in one group and little more than half as many in the other. Despite the odds, the smaller pack held their ground gamely—because of the deadly prowess of one warrior. That one man, a mighty figure whose blond mane towered over the others, held my attention despite the moan of the approaching storm. Gripped in his huge hands, a sword as long as my own thin body wove a murderous pattern of red-streaked death. All about him men struggled together—locked in death embraces, battering steel against steel—until death brought a gory close to their separate battles.

The battle was too savagely fought to long endure. One by one those of the tall swordsman's pack died beneath the blades of the others. Then for a space he stood alone, ringed by four of his enemies—all that still lived of their band. One he clove from shoulder to belly—but before he could recover from that furious stroke, the others surged upon him. What followed was too fast for my eye. Blades clashed against blades—flesh tore apart with gouts of scarlet spray—bodies reeled brokenly as fierce shouts died in sudden groans. Then only the tall swordsman was standing.

As I watched, entranced by the tableau, he slowly sank to his knees, surveying the silent field of carnage. The snow was trampled and streaked with crimson, and the stream of blood that flowed from a dozen wounds in his flesh added its steaming portion to the spreading stain. His head sagged onto his chest.

The first crystals of ice were spitting down upon the broken bodies of the slain, when at last I dared leave my place of concealment. In silent awe I crept among the slaughtered corpses, drawn to the motionless figure who slumped amidst the dead. The storm would soon bury slayers and slain, I knew from its deepening moan. But more urgently I knew that I must have that great sword for my own.

I had thought the man dead. As I reached for the sword, his eyes snapped open. I recoiled. The huge blade rose menacingly in the blood-caked fist.

"Æsir dog..." his voice snarled, then fell. Dying eyes beheld me in wonder.

Stinging needles of ice rattled against the still bodies. A rising wind tore away our cloudy breaths. I stood before him—a tall thin youth, seeming older than my years for my rearing in the wild—even as my sinewy frame was ice-hard with the tempered muscles of the wild. Gusts of icy wind tossed my snow-white mane, rippled the beard I had already grown and the wiry hairs that matted limbs and trunk. Ill-fitting tatters of hide and fur were bound to my body, in crude mimicry of the hunters I had seen.

I snarled low in my throat, advanced when I saw he did not rise. "Sword!" I grated awkwardly, and growled as does one wolf who demands a joint of meat from a weaker brother.

As I started forward, his eyes fell upon my twisted left ankle. I snarled again, and his face showed stark wonder.

"By Ymir!" he swore. "You!"

But now on the howling wind I heard voices of other men. I must have the sword now.

With a sudden lunge I avoided his clumsy guard and wrenched at the swordhilt. He bellowed in rage, staggered upright with me clinging to his arm. My strength and my quickness surprised him, and I set my fangs into his arm before he quite realized I was upon him. Mortally wounded, he was still stronger than I, and knew the ways in which man fights man. A blow of his fist on my head all but cracked my skull. I hung on grimly, biting and evading his clumsy efforts to grip with me.

His swordarm pinioned, he then released his sword, caught its hilt in his free hand. Dazed from his pummelling, I remembered the knife I kept thrust in my furs. As he held me with his gashed swordarm and raised his sword on high with his other arm, I reached swiftly with my knife and drew it across his throat.

Blood choked his sudden cry of agony. Even a heart's beat from death, he had strength left to slash downward with his upraised sword. Slippery with gore, I already was tearing away from his weakened grasp. I spun under his arm, and the sword's massive hilt smashed against my skull, its blade grazing across my shoulder.

Then the dead giant had slumped over me. Waves of pain blurred my vision, but I triumphantly wrenched the sword from his dead fist, started away with my prize. I staggered only a few strides.

Now there were new figures to bar my way. Through the clawing ice-storm, another band of warriors had rushed upon the scarlet-streaked patch of snow. They gazed at me in astonishment as I drew away from the toppled corpse. Snarling, I reeled toward them, thinking to break past them and disappear into the storm.

My legs would not hold my weight. Blackness swallowed my brain, and I never felt my body strike the trampled snow.

• • •

I lay in a stupor for some days. The warrior's dying blow would have shattered any other youth's skull. As it was, I must have sustained a severe concussion, for my scalp was laid open to the bone, and it was days before my vision focused and I could stand without the roaring of black winds spinning through my brain.

Any other would have died. I was not like any other.

I awoke in a camp of the Æsir, where they cared for my wounds and gave me food. The Æsir treated me with a mingling of respect and of fear. I was the slayer of Genseric the Sworder.

Over the ensuing months I was made to understand. The Vanir and the Æsir were at war—not that there were ever extended intervals of peace. The tribe I had fallen in with was part of a new drift of the Æsir into Vanaheim. Many and bloody were their savage conflicts, for upon the loss or gaining of hunting grounds in that frozen waste balanced death or survival. Chief among the Vanir warriors was Genseric the Sworder. A band of Æsir warriors had overtaken Genseric, as he and the other Vanir returned from an earlier battle. Before the presence of these Æsir, I had slain their fiercest enemy.

At first they wondered at my strange ways, at my ignorance of their speech and customs. But the wound to my head was one that should have slain, and the Æsir quickly assumed that the blow had driven all my wits from me. Beyond that, their speculation was simply that I was a youth of some other Æsir clan, whose kinsmen had all perished in that battle with Genseric. Later they would know different. For now they cared for my needs, according me the same consideration they would to any hero of their race, blinded or crippled in battle.

Despite the death of Genseric, the tide of war ran against the Æsir, so that for a space the tribal drift was driven back into the snowfields of Asgard. I went with them, although at any moment I might have clipped away and returned to the pack. But with the years I had slowly drawn away from my grey brothers, increasingly caught up in my obsession with man. At last, so it seemed to me, fate had given me a chance to live among men, to learn the ways of man. I would learn now whether I was indeed man, or some freak of the wild who only mimicked the shape of man.

I had no name, so the Æsir called me Ghor, meaning the Strong. And strong I was—strong with muscle and sinew honed by the merciless wild—and quick with the instant reflexes of a hungry wolf. A stripling in years, unskilled in the use of weapons—yet not even the boldest of their warriors cared to test my ready temper. They were all savage warriors, the least of them more than a match for any dozen men of James Allison's day. But they were reared in horse-hide tents and suckled at their mothers' breasts, while I had crawled naked in the snow to wrest a portion of the kill from my yellow-eyed brothers.

For all the strangeness of man's ways, I learned quickly. At times I frightened those about me, for I was a thing of the wild, and even their rude existence seemed to me soft, and contrary to the law of kill or be killed, that was my only law. But I wished to become as men, so I made myself learn their speech and their pointless customs. Had I fallen in with a tribe of the Vanir, I am certain I would have been recognized for what I was. But this tribe had migrated from far within Asgard, where no Æsir had yet heard the tale of Genseric's fifth son who ran with the wolves and haunted the darkness beyond the firelight.

Four years and more crept past, while I dwelt with the Æsir and learned the ways of men. By the time the scars of Genseric's blows had faded, I could speak their tongue fluently, could eat their burned meat, wear their stifling garments, and sleep within a tent without fear of smothering. My fear of fire was slow in leaving me, and not a few brows were darkly furrowed at this.

No man disputed my possession of Genseric's great sword. In their eyes the sword was mine by law of combat. Indeed, I should have killed any who sought to contest my prize. The blade was huge, and while I had the strength to wield it, my movements were clumsy

II. The Coming of Ghor

and untutored. Again my awkwardness with weaponry was laid to the wound I had suffered. Patiently the Æsir trained me in the use of sword and knife, axe and shield, bow and arrow. My natural strength and feral quickness made me learn such arts in a fraction of the time another youth would have required. Not many seasons had passed before my skill with the sword excelled that of my tutors, and I could speed an arrow through the eye of a reindeer as it fled in vain.

And yet, for all the respect my strength and skill in arms gained for me, I knew I was still as much an outsider among the Æsir as I had been among my brothers of the pack. There was a strangeness about me that no veneer could conceal. Most shrugged and said my wound had left me with a streak of madness. Some, who remembered my savagery in those first months, might scowl at my crooked ankle and the white hair that matted my body more thickly than seemed good, but out of fear of my anger they held their suspicions to themselves.

At length the Æsir again looked hungrily upon the lands of the Vanir. Once more the war horns bellowed, and the tribe with whom I dwelt heeded its summons. With a high heart I marched with them, for lately existence within their village had grown stale, and I was eager to turn to other things.

As before, the borders of Asgard and Vanaheim resounded with countless deadly battles and individual duels. Our wars were not a great massing of army against army, but rather a long series of chance encounters between raiding parties, of ambushes and pillaged camps. We had no cities to burn, no kings or generals to command great armies—only the savage ferocity of desperate men who followed their clans to seize or to defend the frozen expanses whose bounty meant life or starvation. We fought not for princes nor for ideals, but for our bellies and our lives.

This time the scales of war favored the Æsir. Some said it was because of Ghor, the white-maned berserker whose reckless strength and mighty blade tore a gory swath through the Vanir ranks. Be that as it may, I found my prowess in battle and zeal for slaughter did little to overcome the indefinable barrier that separated me from my Æsir comrades.

The sun was falling beneath the ice-locked horizon, when we overtook a handful of stragglers from the Vanir retreat. A dismal lot, they were, aged and infirm, and scarcely worth the dulling of our blades. I raised my sword over a fallen man, grey-bearded and too ancient to fight. Briefly I noticed the scars on his thinning scalp from an old wound, saw the haunted look in his eyes as he awaited death. I knew then that he was fey, and held my blade to hear his words.

"That sword," the greybeard rasped. "How did you get it?"

"I took it from the Vanir chief who carried it not five years past," I laughed. "And paid him for it with a knife for his throat."

"Who are you?" he queried, staring at me strangely.

"I am called Ghor."

"But you are not Æsir!" the old man swore, his eyes looking beyond me. "I saw you as a babe, laid out on the ice. You were suckled by wolves, and you are a child of evil—but I know you for Genseric's fifth son, and your father's blood is on your hands!"

"Better than for mine to be on his hands," I sneered. "Say on old one. How do you know of such matters?"

"I am Bragi," he whispered. "Of the Vanir clan to which you were born. Your mother is Gudrun of the Shining Locks, and your father was Genseric the Sworder. You are the fifth of their sons, but because your leg was crooked, Gudrun bade Genseric to leave you upon the ice, saying she had already four strong sons with fine straight limbs. Ymir curse that day, for you have proven Genseric's bane, and now you turn upon your own people! "

"I have no people!" I growled. "And of Gudrun's four strong sons? How fared they?"

"They are their mother's pride. Raki the Swift, Sigismund the Bear, Obri the Cunning, and Alwin the Silent. Hear their names and tremble, for they shall avenge their father and sweeten the snows of Vanaheim with Æsir blood!"

I laughed and placed the point of my sword to his throat. "It is Ghor the Strong who craves vengeance, Bragi! Vengeance on my brothers who usurped my place at the fire! Vengeance on my mother who condemned her own babe to death! The gods favor my vengeance, else they would not have given my father into my hands for the killing. Let Gudrun and her sons beware the vengeance of Ghor! I am what I am because of their crime against me!"

"You are a child of evil!" Bragi swore fiercely. "There is evil in your blood and in your soul—I see it! I saw it then, as I fled from the vision of the wolves who suckled a human babe!"

"And what else do you now see, old one?"

"I see death," Bragi whispered.

"You see truly," I told him, and drove home the blade.

Chapter III
Ghor's Revenge
Joseph Payne Brennan

The Æsir tribe I fought among had had a successful sword reaping that icy day. In the evening they squatted around their fires and roasted succulent bits of hoarded meat to celebrate but I brooded alone in my horse-hide tent.

The dying words of Bragi echoed in my ears: "Hear their names and tremble!" I did tremble, but not with fear—with rage. Fury swept through me like a fiery fever. I repeated the names of my hated brothers over and over again: "Raki the Swift," "Sigismund the Bear," "Obri the Cunning," "Alwin the Silent." And then there was Gudrun, at whose bidding I had been left on the frozen snows to await the fangs of the wolf pack. "Gudrun of the Shining Locks"! The day was not far off, I vowed, when those locks would lie entangled in a welter of blood and brain fragments!

More than once that night the killing madness overcame me to such an extent that I gripped Genseric's great sword and started to leave the tent. Ice stung my face and the wind howled like a hundred demons as I stared into the outside blackness. Each time I turned back, shaking with the savagery of my own blood hunger. The fierce desire for revenge was like an inward fire burning away at my very bone marrow.

But the white heat of hatred did not completely blot out my common sense. There was work to be done before I wreaked my vengeance. I would have to learn which tribe of the Vanir my kinsmen led. And I would have to find out where in Vanaheim their chief camp was located.

If I rushed out blindly, thirsting for blood, I might indeed kill dozens of Vanir clansmen—but I myself might be cut down before I found my hated brothers and mother.

As I sat alone in the darkness of my tent, I decided that I would adopt the tactics of the great grey wasteland wolves. I would prowl the perimeters of the Vanir outposts; I would lie in the shadows just beyond the light of their campfires. Sooner or later I would learn all I needed to know.

Shortly before a frigid dawn threw scattered light about the Æsir camp, I slipped away. Guards had been posted, but I had no trouble evading them. Belly-down, I crept through the brittle-cold brush and not even the snap of a single twig betrayed my presence.

By the time a fog-shrouded disc of sun arose above the bleak barrens, I was miles from the Æsir camp. Stopping briefly where a fringe of tundra grass provided cover, I ate a piece of dried venison which I carried in an improvised pouch.

I was confident that the Æsir would shrug off my absence. Most of them believed I was half-mad anyway. If and when I needed their help, I felt sure they would welcome me back. In their deadly war with the Vanir, the great sword of Genseric would be sorely missed!

From that morning on, for over a fortnight, I lived like a wolf. If hunger became unbearable, I took time out to hunt. I could run a deer to earth. Not for nothing had I been raised with those tireless roving wraiths of the northern wilderness!

I headed north and slightly east, where I judged the main Vanir encampments lay. On several occasions I spotted heavily armed Vanir war parties, but I avoided them, even though my hand tightened on the hilt of Genseric's mighty sword. Wholesale tribal killing would have to wait; first, I had personal blood debts to pay!

In my mind, I repeated the names of my brothers and mother over and over. Raki the Swift, Sigismund the Bear, Obri the Cunning, Alwin the Silent—and Gudrun of the Shining Locks.

Their names became a refrain, rushing through my head even while I slept. Sometimes I sat bolt upright, roused from sleep, my hand convulsively tightening on Genseric's sword. Momentarily, I was sure they were nearby, awaiting my vengeance. Then I would settle back and sleep again, but the names, like some sort of evil insistent chant, went on ringing in my head.

I slept under the shelter of rocks, or stunted trees, or even on bare unyielding ice with snow falling heavily from starless skies. A plain shoulder tunic, consisting of scraped animal skins, covered my back and belly. Deerskin covered my feet. I wore nothing else save a hide belt to which were attached scabbards for my huge sword and a bone-handled knife, plus a small but powerful bow and a few arrows. I sometimes awoke buried in snow, but, like a wolf, I simply shook it off and roved on, none the worse.

One morning, the third week after I left the Æsir camp, I noticed a feather of smoke float out above a small stand of larch trees a mile away.

There was little cover, but I made the most of it. Squirming over the frozen ground, scarcely more than a layer of gravel-laced ice, I inched toward the larches, taking advantage of every contour of the terrain which gave concealment.

It took me nearly a half hour to reach the larch grove but I was not too late. A small band of Vanir—stragglers from a much larger group, I gathered—were picking the bones of some burnt animal as they hunkered over a tiny fire.

III. Ghor's Revenge

"Hell's traces!" one of them exclaimed. "Raki may have our heads for this!"

I shivered as I heard the name, but I dared not make a sound. Instinctively my hand squeezed the hilt of Genseric's thirsty sword.

Another Vanir tossed a bone over his shoulder. He shrugged and growled. "Let him rave. We got cut off. What could we do? Don't worry. Raki and his brothers need every fighting man they can muster."

He leaned forward over the fire. "With Ghor leading them, the Æsir may drive us into the Death Lands. Eternal night and not even moss to chew on!"

Skulking only yards away, I started at the sound of my own name. In the mouth of this Vanir, it sounded strange.

Another arose from the fire with an oath. "Ghor is blood and bone like the rest of us! We'll drive the Æsir back to Asgard—and glad to get there they'll be!"

Presently they all stood up, kicked snow over the campfire and headed northeast. Like a gaunt, ravenous wolf, I followed. Once one of them turned around, scowling, but I was already flat on the ice by the time his eyes swung in my direction. He looked right over me. Shrugging, he turned and went on.

There were five of them but I felt confident that I could have killed the whole lot, if I attacked while they were off guard. I had other plans.

They would lead me to Raki — Raki the Swift, Sigismund the Bear, Obri the Cunning, Alwin the Silent — and Gudrun of the Shining Locks.

The five Vanir traveled with deliberation. It was obvious that they were in no great rush to rejoin their comrades. I raged with impatience but there was no way that I could hurry them along. Above all, I wanted them to remain ignorant of my presence.

It took them nearly three days to reach their main camp. Meanwhile I followed in their footsteps, famished, savage, implacable. I crouched outside the circle of the firelight while they ate, my own belly grinding with hunger, my eyes burning. They became uneasy and subdued, as if they sensed they were being followed, but not once did they catch a glimpse of me. I crept over the ice fields and through the sparse thickets like a wolf—like the shadow of a wolf. Occasionally I ran across small game but I ignored it in spite of my ravenous hunger. I could not take the time, I felt, to run down game and eat it. I had only one driving purpose and nothing short of death itself would deter me.

At last the Vanir reached the outposts of the main camp. After a brief confab, the sentries let them pass and they disappeared from my sight.

For an hour or more I watched from a nearby point of trees. At length I decided to circle the entire camp. It was no easy task. Guards had been doubled; they were wary and alert. But my long years with the wolf pack paid off; I prowled the entire perimeter of the camp and not a sentry the wiser.

It was a large clan assemblage, gathered and geared for war. There seemed to be an incessant whetting of sword blades, a notching of arrows, a repair and reinforcement of the heavy hide shields.

Time after time I had the opportunity to slit the throat of some isolated Vanir guard, but I desisted, even though the fingers of my knife hand itched. The killing of a sentry would arouse the entire camp. That was the last thing I wanted.

Early on the morning of the second day I found what I sought: a large skin tent set somewhat apart from the others and closely guarded by two powerful Vanir. They kept constant patrol, hands on sword hilts, eyes searching. From time to time single Vanir, whom I judged to be sub-chieftains, strode toward the tent and were admitted after a close scrutiny by the guards. One of these visitors was let in only after he had lain his sword, knife and arrows outside the tent. He cursed the guards but complied.

War strategy was being planned within the tent and that could mean only one thing: inside were my hated brothers. My heart hammered against my ribs but I managed to restrain myself.

Just to the rear of the large tent was another, smaller one. I could not be sure but I felt convinced that this was the tent of Gudrun of the Shining Locks.

It was late morning before one of the brothers emerged. There was no doubt in my mind that it was Raki the Swift. I had heard that he bore a striking resemblance to Genseric, whose prowess had become a legend. Raki was a huge man, far over six feet in height, muscular yet rangy, with gleaming blue eyes and long yellow hair. He carried an oversize sword and I noticed that his shield was not made of animal hides but hammered metal—rare in these parts.

The sweat burst out on me as I gripped the hilt of Genseric's fabled sword. I felt no fear of this swaggering giant—only a hatred so intense I seemed to be on fire.

I needed every ounce of self-control I possessed to keep to my place of concealment in the fringe of woods and brush. But I forced myself to remain silent and motionless. I was confident that I could kill Raki in open combat, but I was sure there were three more of Genseric's sons in the tent behind him. And Gudrun, probably, in the small tent to the rear.

I wanted to make a clean sweep. It would be necessary for me to pick my own place and time, if I hoped to succeed.

After striding about a bit, and exchanging some words with the

III. Ghor's Revenge

guards, Raki reentered the tent.

All day, at intervals, sub-chiefs and leading fighters visited the tent. I surmised that a massive attack was being prepared against the Æsir. Genseric's sons were planning carefully. I sensed that the old days—small war parties, hit-and-run tactics—were drawing to a close. Soon there would be all-out war, with extermination the goal.

During the course of the day, as they ventured out at intervals I got a good look at my other three brothers: Sigismund the Bear, shorter and broader than Raki, a veritable barrel of a body, with a thick neck and rather small head; Obri the Cunning, thin and lean, with crafty eyes and an expression of open contempt permanently etched on his unpleasant features; Alwin the Silent, another giant of a man, with hooded, enigmatic eyes and compressed lips which seldom opened for speech.

Towards late afternoon a tall amazon strode around the side of the tent and spoke to the guards. I knew at once it was Gudrun of the Shining Locks. She had become somewhat heavy-bodied, but her thick plaited hair still gleamed yellow in the afternoon sun and, had I been able to retain any sense of objectivity, I would have been forced to admit that she remained an attractive woman.

But I glared at her with a loathing which no words could encompass. I think she actually felt the withering blast of my hatred. She turned, frowning, and stared toward the brush where I lay concealed. One of the guards made some comment and started toward the woods but she shook her head and called him back.

I looked away, afraid that if I stared at her longer, she would indeed order the guards to beat through the scrub where I crouched.

Presently she returned to the small tent at the rear of the larger one.

As shadows fell over the camp, I made my plans. I would wait until the middle of the night before I struck. Disposing of the two guards should present no great problem. When they were safely out of the way, I would glide into the large tent with Genseric's great sword held at the ready....

I reasoned that it would be easier to fight inside the tent, than out. I would have the advantage of surprise for one thing, and in the relatively small confines of the tent there would be less room for four fighting men to maneuver. Outside the tent, on the other hand, I would be surrounded at once and attacked from all sides. If I could kill the guards and steal into the tent while my brothers still slept, the odds would be more in my favor.

In addition, I foresaw, the ring of sword blades and the clamor of raised voices would be at least partially muffled inside the tent. Outside, the racket might rouse the entire camp.

Although I felt no fear, I was well aware that the sons of Genseric the Sworder would fight savagely and to the death. My only fear, however—if fear it might be called—was that I could be wounded or driven off before my revenge was complete. The thought gnawed at me. My own attack, I therefore determined, must be swift, merciless and efficient. The guards must make no outcry and the camp must under no conditions be aroused. I would have to strike with the speed and silence of Death itself.

The hours dragged. At first half a moon hung in the sky, but soon heavy cloud banks covered it completely. As full darkness closed in, the guards paced restlessly. Once a snow owl hooted somewhere in the nearby thickets.

Inch by inch, foot by foot, I squirmed out of the woods. I made no more sound than a shadow makes as it falls on frozen ground. No creeping tundra wolf could have advanced more silently than I.

At last I slid within sword range of the nearest guard. I bided my time. Leaving Genseric's gleaming sword in its scabbard, I drew my short bone-handled knife and waited.

The unsuspecting guard came within two feet, paused, turned and started to retrace his footsteps. I left the ground like an arrow sped from the bow. While one arm circled the guard's mouth to stifle any cries, the other whipped the knife blade across his throat, severing the jugular. Even with his life-blood spurting out, he tried to fight back. It was useless. Only death could have broken my grip. When his body grew limp, I eased it to the icy ground and wriggled along through the darkness toward the second guard like a deadly night adder.

He was standing still, staring off into the blackness, when my knife slashed across his throat. He twisted about and attempted to draw his sword but never managed to lift it more than an inch or two out of the scabbard. When his struggles ended, I drew my arm away from his face and very carefully tipped him backwards to the ground.

Then I started for the tent of Genseric's sons.

I paused at the flap and listened. Heavy snoring came from within. I forced myself to wait a full five minutes, hand on sword hilt, but no other sound save that of snoring reached my ears. Drawing Genseric's heavy sword, I stepped just inside the tent, letting my eyes adjust to the interior. In spite of the unrelieved darkness, I could presently make out the shadowy forms of four sleeping figures.

Lifting the massive sword high over my head, I crept toward the skin bed of the nearest. In spite of my stealth, something—some obscure unspoken warning, some mental image of danger—must have reached the brain of the sleeping man. He sat up suddenly,

III. Ghor's Revenge

with a soft grunt. I judged it was Sigismund the Bear.

Waiting no longer, I lunged toward the pile of skins. The legendary sword of Genseric swung downward in a mighty sweeping arc, cleaving through skull, rib-cage, and spine. The Bear toppled backwards, split apart like a pine riven by a lightning bolt.

I had scarcely drawn the sword clear when someone bounded from an adjacent bed of skins. It was Raki and I knew now why he was known as the Swift. He must have slept sword in hand, because the blade of his slashing weapon whistled within a half inch of my face as I leaped backwards toward the side of the tent.

Confident, he came on, but luck was with me. As he was about to slash again, he slipped on one of the skin blankets. Momentarily, he was thrown slightly off balance. It was all the opening I needed. Genseric's sword licked out, thrust forward with all my strength, and buried itself halfway to the hilt in Raki's chest. To my amazement, he held onto his own sword and slashed at me again. But it was the last instinctive movement of a dying man.

Two more figures were coming at me now and I saw there was no time to be lost. With a tremendous heave, I tore Genseric's sword out of Raki's breast and turned to meet Obri the Cunning and Alwin the Silent.

As Raki crashed to the ground, Alwin, the other giant, jumped forward, hacking at my head. I felt the tip of his blade cut through my scalp and scrape against bone and I laughed.

The fabled sword of Genseric became like a live thing in my hand. It leaped and slashed and parried and although Alwin fought with great skill, his efforts seemed clumsy and ponderous compared with my own.

As we fought, Obri the Cunning circled about, dagger in hand, striking at me like a coiled snake as I came within range. Once I felt his knife slice through my left forearm but I paid no attention.

Muttering with rage and exasperation, Alwin made a ferocious lunge with his oversize sword. It was his last. He was just a fraction of a second too slow in recovering. The great sword of Genseric, his father, sang through the air and Alwin's head spun off.

Grinning, I turned toward Obri. Quickly sheathing his knife, he backed off and drew, not his sword as I had expected, but a bow. An arrow smashed into my right shoulder and I knew more would be streaking toward me before I could reach him. Lifting Genseric's sword in both hands, by hilt and tip, I hurled it straight at him.

The impact of the heavy blade knocked him off his feet as another arrow hissed past my head. With a great bound, I sprang across the tent. My hands found Obri's throat before he could draw his knife. As I squeezed, I could see his bulging eyes shine wildly in the darkness. Bones cracked; his tongue protruded. Blood poured out his mouth and he went limp.

Flinging his body aside, I recovered Genseric's sword, strode to the tent flap and listened. I heard nothing. I surmised, correctly, that the brief sound of clashing sword blades had been effectively muffled by the horse-hide tent.

Blood was flowing out of my scalp, forearm and shoulder, but I paid no attention.

Pausing only momentarily as I slipped outside, I hurried through the darkness to the small tent at the back.

The sound of heavy, regular breathing reached me as I approached the tent flap. Without stopping, I stepped inside. Like a wolf, I could now see well in the darkness and I had no trouble making out a bulky form lying on skins toward the rear of the tent.

Slipping out my bone-handled knife, I held it by the blade, judged the blow carefully and swung the handle of the knife against Gudrun's temple. She jerked once but made no sound. Her breathing became harsh and irregular.

Hoping I had not struck too hard, I threw her over my shoulder like the carcass of a deer and hurried out of the tent.

Twenty minutes later I was well away from the camp and deep in scrub woods which covered much of the area. I walked swiftly, in spite of my burden, stopping only long enough to ram a crumpled piece of rabbit skin inside the woman's mouth. If she revived and tried to scream, the gag would turn her cries into little more than whimpers.

I estimated that I still had several hours before the bodies were discovered and the alarm sounded. But I could not be positive. I could not be sure that the two guards had been put on station for the entire night. They might be relieved. In that case, I would have only a few more minutes.

The night remained quiet. I heard no sounds save the occasional hoot of a snow owl, or the scutter of tiny feet as some small animal scurried away.

In spite of my wounds and the weight I carried, I was not even winded when I finally stopped.

Dumping Gudrun on the icy-covered ground, I wiped the blood from my face. Then I bent, ripped the gag from her mouth and stripped off every last shred of her clothes—skin garments made doubly soft by the patient gums of elderly Vanir women.

At length she stirred, groaned and opened her eyes. I grinned down at her. She recognized me at once, in spite of my blood-smeared face, and sat up, snarling.

I prodded her with my foot. "Well, old hag, your crippled frog has hopped back to play a little game!"

Swaying, she stood up and beat at me with both fists. Dodging,

III. Ghor's Revenge

I stuck out my foot and she crashed to the ground again.

"Frogs never forget," I told her, "nor does Ghor the Strong whom you had set out for the wolves to devour!"

She sat up again, glaring at me. "A pity they didn't! I should have strangled you myself! Give me a knife and we shall see who is left for the wolves!"

"I don't fight females," I said. "Besides, I have other plans for you!"

She sneered. "You are afraid to fight me with cold steel!"

I shrugged and laughed. "Ask your four sons if Ghor the Strong is afraid to fight. They lie back in their tent, still as in sleep—but no longer do they snore!"

I saw her face whiten. She remained silent.

"Enough of this," I growled. "Get up, hag, and walk."

She got up without another word and started off, barefooted, across the ice. She staggered and I saw that already she was starting to turn blue with the cold.

When we reached the middle of a wide expanse, open to the frigid winds, I reached out and sent her crashing to earth again.

Shivering, half-dead with the cold, she continued to glare up at me.

I stared down without pity. "You will be warm soon enough, Gudrun of the Shining Locks," I assured her. "Warm in the hungry bellies of the wolf pack!"

She made no reply and I walked away. When I reached the edge of a ragged fringe of fir trees, I stopped, turned and lifted my head. From my throat issued the long-drawn, eerie howl of the hunting wolf. I repeated the call three times. Then I squatted on my haunches and waited.

Answering howls rose in the night air. I could tell by the sounds that the pack was famished. They came on swiftly.

Gudrun had struggled to her knees. She knelt motionless, like an image carved out of blue stone.

Soon enough the pack swung into view, long, lean hunters of the night with lolling tongues and glinting green-yellow eyes. Their grey coats looked mangy and thin. The hunting had not been good.

Paying no attention to me, they headed straight for Gudrun, who remained kneeling motionless.

I thought she was already frozen to death, but as the lead wolf leaped for her throat, she dodged aside, gripped it by the hind legs and swung it like a scythe.

In spite of my passionate hatred, I felt a brief flash of grudging admiration for the doomed woman.

Her maneuver held off death only for minutes however. The lead wolf finally wrenched itself from her freezing hands and the pack closed in for the kill.

Even then she fought on. As she went down under the ravenous, threshing grey shapes, I saw her sink her teeth into one of the wolves' throats.

That was her final act. Seconds later she was being torn to pieces.

I sat and watched as the pack fed, snarling and fighting among themselves. A few minutes later there was nothing left on the ice except smears of blood and a few of the larger bones.

The pack gathered together, swung in my direction, stopped, sat back on their haunches, howled in unison and trotted off into the night.

I walked out where the wolves had fed. The shining locks of Gudrun lay gleaming on the ice, tangled together with stiffening blood and bits of brain stuff. The great jaws of the starving beasts had even cracked open Gudrun's skull.

My blood debt was finally paid.

I strode off, across the expanse of ice, into the fir trees. From far away, over the freezing plains, I heard the subdued but growing murmur of many voices.

My night's earlier handiwork, I assumed, had been discovered.

Chapter IV
The Ice Woman's Prophecy
Richard L. Tierney

For a long time I stood silent amid the firs, while the voices of the approaching Vanir grew louder. I watched as the warriors emerged from the trees and gathered about the torn flesh and scattered bones of their former chieftainess. Another man than I might have fled, but a weird mood was upon me and I cared no more for life. With my deed of revenge completed, it seemed to me that no reason for living remained. Perhaps my wounds, too, had sapped vitality from my body and contributed to my feeling of indifferent lethargy.

The warriors' gestures became less excited, and it seemed to me that a tone of subdued fear gradually dampened their distant voices. I was ready to fight them to my inevitable death when they should track me—but instead of following my trail, they finally clustered together more closely and, after gathering up Gudrun's remains and wrapping them in a great fur mantle, hurried away toward their camp with excited and fearful mutterings. Then I realized what had struck fear into their hearts, for they had seen my tracks amid those of the wolves and knew in their barbaric, superstitious souls that one of those half-human "wolves of the waste" had stolen into their camp—one of those monstrous beings whose normally human body and soul become those of a wolf when the winter moon shines down upon the snows.

When they had gone, I turned wearily and made my way into the forested hills, vaguely following the track of the wolves. But my weakness increased, and after some time I turned aside and found a small cave under a low hillside. It had once been used by wild beasts, but their smell was weak and I knew they had gone elsewhere long ago. The arrow that protruded from my right shoulder hampered me in these close quarters, and I tore at it impatiently. It was not barbed, and came free easily, followed by a great gush of blood. I stared for a while at the dark fluid running down my arm; then, feeling dizzy and light-headed, I lay down upon the dirt and litter and was soon asleep.

I remember waking once, briefly, I know not how long after. A large grey wolf stood in the cave entrance, gazing at me with feral yellow eyes, and I sat up weakly and snarled at him. Evidently he had been attracted by the blood from my wound, which lay puddled and congealed where I had lain. He did not attack—whether because he sensed my kinship to him or because he was gorged on the flesh of Gudrun, I do not know—but presently turned about and trotted away. My wound, I saw, had ceased to bleed, but it throbbed more than ever and I was sick and chilled. At that time I do not think I was even a man at all—for a man, in my extremity, would have gone back to the Æsir tribe to seek aid, whereas I had turned instinctively to the ways of a wolf. Those Vanir had been right, after all, in thinking they had to deal with a half-human "wolf of the waste."

I slept again, for how long I know not, and as I slumbered I dreamed—if indeed it was a dream.

It seemed to me that I woke in the night. The air was still and there was a strange singing in my ears—not a singing such as the fever of my wound might have caused, but a tinkling music as of clouds of tiny ice-crystals swirling together. A dim light was streaming into the mouth of my cave. I rose softly, cautiously, feeling no pain from my wounds, and crawled forth.

It seemed to me that the light emanated from a tall, white figure, twice as tall as a warrior, that stood at the edge of the small clearing before my cave. It was the figure of a woman—a woman of supreme beauty, cold and hard of countenance and clad in a misty, shifting veil composed partly of wraps of snow-crystals and partly of her long, silvery tresses. Then she spoke to me, and her voice was as the whisper of winds amid caverns of fluted ice-pillars.

"Accursed art thou, man called Ghor," she said, and I thought her eyes seemed to flash like the points of ice-daggers. "Accursed art thou, mother-slayer!"

For an instant I had the illusion that her face was that of Gudrun—but then I saw this was not so, for the face of this beautiful, terrible being was also like that of every Æsir and Vanir woman I had ever seen. One after another I was reminded subtly of all the tribeswomen I had known, though none of these quite resembled the strange, beautiful entity that stood before me. And then I knew that this was Ythillin, the Ice Woman, about whom the northern tribesmen speak so fearfully as they huddle around their fires in the cold northern night—Ythillin, the first daughter of those Ice Gods who also sired the Frost Giants and, through them, the Vanir and Æsir races!

For an instant I knew a human fear; but then, snarling like a wolf, I drew both sword and dagger.

"Seek you to avenge Gudrun?" I snarled. "I'll strew your flesh for the beasts even as I did hers!"

"Fool!" Ythillin's voice was like the shriek of wind among barren ice-crags. "You cannot slay me, nor I you. The Ice Gods have

IV. The Ice Woman's Prophecy

decreed otherwise. They have bidden me to bear a prophecy unto you. But before I deliver it, you shall hear my own curse upon you for the death of Gudrun, who was my worshipper. Danger and strife shall be your lot for all the years of your life, and never shall you sire children of your own to aid you in age or carry on a line in your name!"

I laughed harshly—for what had wolves such as I ever known save danger and strife? And as for dynasties, what cared a wolf for such human concerns?

"Since you are too weak to slay me, then," I shouted, "give me the prophecy of the gods!"

"Idiot mortal!" Ythillin's eyes were like sparks of frozen fire that for an instant swelled to a blazing glare. "Tempt me not to disregard their decree. Hear me: the Ice Gods have chosen you to aid them in their struggle against the gods of the South and their worshippers, since you are the only man ever to survive the ordeal of cold. You, who are wolf as much as man, shall yet save a civilization from destruction, and give it into the hands of an Æsir king and his tribe. And they shall reap its benefits, and rule it, and offer their thanks unto the Ice Gods.

"So say those gods. But to their prophecy is my curse added: strife and childlessness in punishment for slaying father, mother, and brothers. Nor shall you, who are half man and half beast, ever find peace in either wolf-pack or human nation."

"Ice bitch," I snarled, "I ask no boons nor curses from you or those above you!"

And I charged at her with sword and dagger in hand. But she laughed and began to fade from my view, and when I slashed at her fading form, my body grew cold and numb and consciousness left me once more.

I woke later within the cave, not knowing whether I had crawled back there in a stupor or whether the whole episode had been a dream. I sensed that at least a day had passed. My shoulder still ached terribly, but it was partly healed and was not infected. I still possessed a wild beast's vitality, even after having lived so long among men.

Then I heard human voices outside.

I sprang up, my lips twisted in a silent snarl, and peered out. Several Vanir warriors were approaching through the trees, apparently following my trail, and I realized that daylight had diminished their fear of the "wolf of the waste"—or, more likely, that certain ones who had heard of me, such as the guard I had overheard the day before, had convinced the rest of my non-supernatural identity.

They saw me as I darted forth from the cave, and their arrows whistled about me amid the trees as I fled. But I was too much of a wolf for them, even in my weakened condition, and soon left them far behind.

For many days I lived in the forest, subsisting on such small wild game as I could catch with my hands. And as my wounds healed, a measure of my human curiosity began to return and my prowlings took me back toward the camp of the Vanir. I may have had some notion of skirting that camp and spying on it, then making my way onward to rejoin the Æsir tribe; I do not know.

I remember that one night, when the moon was full, I strode to that open expanse where I had fed my mother Gudrun to the wolves. The northern lights were flickering more wildly than ever I had seen them before, so that their light, combined with that of the moon, made the landscape nearly as distinct as by day. The snow lay only in isolated patches now, most of it melted away by the mild winds of early spring. A cold night breeze moaned in the sparse shrubbery and stirred my beard. A weird mood grew upon me, and I felt the flesh on the back of my neck begin to prickle . . .

Then my keen nostrils detected man-scent. I turned, crouching—and spied a figure advancing slowly into the open, some distance off. It was a man—probably a warrior from the Vanir tribe. He had not seen me. Slowly I drew my great sword and stood motionless as he continued to advance. Soon he was very close to me—so close that I could have rushed forth and cut him down in the space of a second, which it was nearly in my mind to do. But even as I clutched my sword hilt more tightly, tense and undecided, the man spoke:

"Ho, Ice Woman—I am here! But where is the war-chief you promised me? I think you have used me for dream-sport, cold goddess!—and with your leave, I will return now to my warm bed."

He chuckled and began to walk back the way he had come; but I, recognizing him now as a young warrior of the Æsir tribe I had lived among, strode forth boldly and called out: "Hialmar!"

He whirled, his sword half-drawn. I sheathed mine deliberately, in his plain view; seeing which, he sheathed his also after a brief hesitation. Then he approached me closely and stood staring with an expression of disbelief on his youthful features.

"Ghor!" he exclaimed finally. "Did the Ice Woman send you here also?"

"I come from the wastes, like a wolf," said I, evading his question. "What's this talk about the Ice Woman?"

"She came to me this night in a dream! She told me to walk out to this place—that here I would meet one who would lead our tribe to such conquests as no tribe of Nordheim has ever enjoyed before, and that he would establish me as king on the throne of a southern nation. I woke in fear—but laughed when I knew it was but a dream.

IV. The Ice Woman's Prophecy

Yet I could not sleep again, so I finally donned my garb and went forth... Ghor, what does this mean?"

"It means your brains are still fuddled with sleep," I said, despite a strange fear that had stolen over me at his words. "How did you walk so far from your camp in one night? And do you not know that a large force of the Vanir are camped not far from here?"

"Ha! Were camped, you mean." Hialmar's eyes sparkled, and he threw back his head and laughed. "Their camp is now ours, and they are food for the ravens. When we found you missing, I led a small party on your trail. You are a crafty wolf, Ghor!—but I've tracked wolves often, and I didn't lose your trail till we were close enough to the Vanir to see the smoke of their cooking fires. So in the night I stole close and heard two of their sentries talking. They were frightened because all of their leaders had been slain by a wolf-of-the-waste and the camp was divided between tracking it down and retiring from the border country toward Vanaheim. I took my scouting party away as fast as I could, and returned the next day with my whole tribe of Æsir at my back. We caught the Vanir while they were still quarreling among themselves. Then was there a feasting of the swords! We slew them all, save for the women—and perhaps a dozen warriors whose blood shall redden the altars of the Ice Gods on the morrow." He laughed again; but then he looked at me once more, and wonder crept anew over his face. "What does this mean, Ghor? Did you also dream of the Ice Woman?"

"Let us go to the camp," I said.

• • •

I slept long in the tent of Hialmar, and none disturbed me; for there had been a revel to celebrate the overcoming of the Vanir, and it had lasted many days, but now it was ended and the entire camp slumbered late into the day.

Many were surprised to see me walking among them the next afternoon, for they had thought me dead or perhaps gone to join the Vanir. But they were even more surprised when Hialmar told them of his dream.

"The Ice Woman has returned Ghor the Strong to us," he said, "to lead us to conquests such as no tribe of Nordheim has ever known before."

Most were pleased to hear such things, but a few were not—notably Harolf the chieftain and his stepson Hetlund, who commanded the tribe's fighting men. Before the day was out, these two had ordered a tribe council, and had summoned Hialmar and I to appear before it. It was convened in the central space of the camp, surrounded by the tents. Most of the warriors squatted on the ground, but Harolf and Hetlund sat before their tent in chairs of finely carved wood, together with the head priest, Tjarvakka, who occupied a chair of ivory plundered from a southern Vanir tribe.

"What's this gossip about Ghor and the Ice Woman, Hialmar?" roared Harolf, rising. "Let's have it out in the open. The rumors I have heard smack of insurrection."

"I know only what the Ice Woman told me," said Hialmar; and ho related his dream once more, and told of how he then went forth in the night and met with me in the wasteland.

"Ythillin has not spoken to me!" shouted Tjarvakka, shaking his bead-ornamented staff. "Why then should she speak to this young upstart? Trust him not, great chief—this is some plot that aims at your overthrow."

"A cowardly plot!" growled Harolf, drawing his great axe. "If indeed you seek to supplant me, Hialmar, let us decide it now as warriors should—with steel."

"I hatch no plots," said Hialmar, "yet neither do I allow any to call me a coward. If steel is your wish, so be it!"

Harolf grinned, and I knew that in his mind he had doomed Hialmar who, though a fine warrior, was scarcely more than a youth. Hialmar came of a line that had ruled the tribe aforetime, and I think Harolf was jealous of that. He had no reason to be, for might alone ruled the Æsir tribes, and Harolf was a bear of a man who had emerged victor from a hundred battles; yet he had ever a dark and suspicious nature that urged him often to petty cruelties.

And I, though a wolf, yet felt suddenly that I would not see Hialmar slain, who had sheltered me in his own tent—for even a wolf will fight for his own.

"There is no plot," I said, "for the Ice Woman came to me in a dream also."

"Ha!" snarled Harolf, turning his scowling, suspicious eyes in my direction. "Then you also pretend to say . . ."

"Let it be put to the test!" cried Tjarvakka. "Bring forth one of the Vanir prisoners."

Harolf hesitated but an instant, then nodded. Immediately a bound warrior was led forth from a tent next to the chief's. He was a stalwart young man with bold, fierce eyes and bright red hair— evidently a pure-blooded Vanir, unmixed with any of the blond Æsir. He stood there defiantly before the assembly.

"Give command to slay him, King Harolf," said Tjarvakka. "Then I shall read the gods' message in his entrails, and we shall see whether this tale of the Ice Woman be true or no."

Harolf gestured; and Hetlund, who was his tool, strode forth grinning, with a dagger in his hand. But the Vanir warrior cried out: "Æsir dogs! Is this how you fire your false courage? If you be truly brave men, give me a sword in my hand and let me fight, though it be against all of you."

IV. The Ice Woman's Prophecy

"Aye—let him fight!" cried Hialmar; and many other warriors cried out approvingly, their blood stirred by the brave words of the captive. Even Hetlund, hearing their outcry, glanced inquiringly at his leader; but Harolf, scowling fiercely, shook his head.

"Yapping cur," snarled Hetlund, "this will still your howls!"—and he drove his dagger into the breast of the Vanir warrior. Immediately Tjarvakka leaped up and ran forward. Ignoring the mutterings of reproach from many of the assembled warriors, he slit open the fallen man's abdomen and began to grope among the entrails. A moment later he rose, his gnarled hands smeared dark and dripping.

"False!" he screamed. "The Ice Gods give the lie to this tale we have heard. It is a coward's plot. Slay these two—aye, sacrifice them together with the Vanir captives. It is the Ice Woman's decree..!"

It was his last words that made me draw and strike, for I hated the Ice Gods, and the Ice Woman especially. Before Tjarvakka's final screech was ended, the blood was bubbling from his severed neck and his head was rolling on the sod.

A yell went up. Harolf roared and charged at me, a half dozen of his guards at his back. I parried barely in time, and the head of his axe went sailing past my ear. My backhand stroke severed the arm he had thrown up to shield himself and hacked into the junction of his neck and shoulder, plowing deep into his rib-cage to sever both spine and sternum. He gargled horribly in his dying throes, and a deluge of blood poured out on the ground. My sword was wedged fast in his body and I was forced to release its hilt, barely avoiding the spear of a charging guardsman. Then I saw a hand's-length of steel suddenly jut from the guard's breast. The man fell, spitted by the sword of an Æsir warrior.

I retrieved my sword at leisure, for I saw that the Æsir warriors were hacking down Harolf's guards, such few of them as had not thrown down their arms. Hialmar had slain Hetlund, whose brains now oozed upon the ground from his cloven skull. A great shout went up from the warriors.

"Hialmar!" they cried. "Ghor!"

Hialmar rose to the occasion; he stood atop the chair of Tjarvakka, waving his bloody sword, haranguing them with impassioned speech. Then did I wonder whether in truth the Ice Gods were with us, and not just shadows in empty dreams—for it seemed to me that what we had just accomplished must indeed be miraculous. I listened while Hialmar reminded the warriors again of the dreams sent by the Ice Woman, and of her promises of conquest. The men shouted often, clashing their blades against their shields; for Hialmar had already been popular among them, and as for Harolf, his cruelties had made him hated by many and they were glad to see him slain.

"And what of the Vanir prisoners?" I asked during a lull in the shouting.

"What would you do with them, old wolf?" Hialmar countered.

I asked that they be led forth and unbound, and Hialmar complied. A hush now settled over the tribe. My sympathy of wolf for wolf went out to these red-maned warriors, who were as out of place and endangered among the Æsir as I among the human race.

"What will you, Vanir-men?" I asked them: "fight us to your death with such weapons as we give you? Or will you join us and share in such conquests as no Nordheim tribe has yet known?"

They chose to a man to join us, and again a shout of approval went up, though not as loud as before; for Vanir and Æsir had long been blood enemies. But it was well, for those men all proved good warriors in our ranks, and eventually became the personal bodyguard of Hialmar, who was now acclaimed chief.

So became Hialmar leader of a great tribe of Æsir, and I his right-hand man. And thenceforward our eyes were turned southward, toward the civilized lands of the Hyborians, which we knew little of, but dreamed to conquer.

Chapter V
The Nemedians
Michael Moorcock

The Snow Camel was overburdened. Its two great white humps were almost wholly hidden beneath a badly stowed bundle of brocade, velvet, and silk. Five warriors in complicated armour, entirely unsuitable for the climate, surrounded the beast and they too carried bundles, under their arms and on their backs. Evidently they were survivors of some earlier disaster. Behind the first camel, its sharp hooves gripping the ice as no horse's could, came a second. This one drew a sled on which three small figures sat wrapped in a considerable wealth of pelts. My foraging party would return to our main camp with a better prize than any of us had expected, for the hunting had become poor this far South.

There were eight of us, including myself, and for all that the strangers wore heavy chain mail over which was laid plate on breast and back, arm and leg, all of ornate and, to our eyes, decadent design, we were confident.

From the cover of the frozen snow dune I drew my bow and let fly at the most distant warrior, but then, suddenly, the first camel moved its head and accepted the arrow directly in its left eye. It jerked, its legs straddled the ice, it fell to its knees and then keeled over. I cursed myself for destroying such a valuable beast. Metal clattered from within the cloth. Against the white snow gold shone: dull yellow in the murky light of the morning. The first thought of my warriors was for this treasure, but where gold was concerned I was a wolf; I ignored it. I had already nocked another arrow and taken a stranger in the throat with a red and black fletched shaft as he ran towards his fallen beast. Two others fled back to the sled as Oderic, one of our Vanir, disdaining the treacherous bow, howled and waded calf-deep through powder ice, whirling his axe and, in high, noble tones, challenging the nearest warrior to single combat. As their arrows struck his head and torso, so thickly that they almost hid his body from our eyes, Oderic gave one astonished cry and plunged, gouting red on the disturbed snow, spreadeagled.

No more of the Vanir or Æsir presented themselves as targets and, since the alien warriors had no cover, it was a simple matter for us to finish our prey rapidly and move cautiously into the open.

Guthric, nearest to me, was for rushing the sled and finishing the occupants, but I stayed him with the flat of my sword against his chest.

The three figures on the sled had not moved, save to huddle closer together. We advanced slowly, lifting our feet high as we struggled through the bloody snow: seven fur-garbed savages—a preponderance of beards, braids and bronze.

Then a figure stood up on the sled. A lad. He was fair-haired, pale-skinned, his features contrasting a little oddly with the opulence of his clothing which, to our eyes, had an eastern tinge to it. He ran towards one of the dead warriors and tried to pull the man's sword free from his grasp, but Nald, in the lead, laughed and plucked him up, holding him by the waist as he kicked. A small fist knocked Nald's horned helmet askew and this joke made Nald roar and bring the palm of his hand down hard on the boy's backside.

I got to the sled, yanking back the pelts. A younger boy and a woman. The woman was very beautiful, golden-haired, blue-eyed, about thirteen or fourteen winters.

The wolf in me had not responded at all to the sight of the gold, but the man in me responded at once to the woman. I took her by her plaited head and hauled her to her feet. She was dressed in rich reds and blues, a scarlet velvet gown trimmed in ermine and ribbon the color of sapphire. While the others gasped and exclaimed at the treasure, packing it onto the sled, I took her to one side so that I could inspect her better.

She spoke a language similar to ours, but I could not understand the words too clearly.

"Speak slower," I said.

She was breathing heavily, evidently terrified of me (my appearance, I had been told, was deemed ferocious even amongst my fellows and I had many habits associated with the wolf—a way of hunching my shoulders, glaring sideways and sniffing at anything unfamiliar).

She opened her mouth and then shook her head. She trembled and this made me utter a barking laugh, for she had no business fearing me. But she trembled the more. She was soft and weak, unlike any Æsir or Vanir woman, and this should have made me contemptuous, but instead it aroused in me a peculiar instinct I could barely recognise. Perhaps the instinct a mother wolf has toward her cub. I cuffed her, to show that she attracted me, and grinned.

She whimpered. I shrugged and placed her over my shoulder, She lay there without struggling.

Cudric and Nald were about to sword the boys when I stopped them, for no good reason save that I knew the woman would be unhappy if they died. I explained my decision, however, in terms of economics. The boys would make Æsir warriors, if trained, or else they could be sold somewhere, on our march South. Nald shrugged and shoved his captive towards me, as if to say that the responsibility was now mine. Cudric imitated Nald. I found myself with three unwilling dependents. I put nooses around the necks of the boys and led the way back to our main camp.

Hialmar was pleased with the gold and the camel, and as puzzled as the others concerning my decision to spare the lives of the two boys. I tethered them outside my tent and sent them food while I took the girl into the semi-darkness of the interior, cluttered with half-cured furs and blood-stained weapons. She began to speak rapidly again, seeming to be imploring me for some favour, gesturing either towards the boys outside or further, to the South.

I shook my head and selected a large piece of camel-meat from my bowl. "I don't understand you, woman."

She spoke more slowly, but still the accent was so unfamiliar I could detect only a word or two. Bored by this exercise, I offered her the bowl. "Meat?"

She tugged at me. She made me spill some of the contents of the bowl on my hand. I pushed her so that she fell amongst a collection of buckles and helmets, trophies of various of my fights.

I offered her the bowl again. She shook her head. She panted. I signalled for her to remove her garments, for I intended to take her as soon as I had finished eating. She shook her head again, emphatically, and crawled nearer to the tent's wall. I smiled, finished my meal, paced to where she cowered, and began to peel her.

The thin cloth came away easily. Her distinctive odour now seemed to fill the tent and again stirred me in a strange way. She began to struggle and she bit me a little, but I was amiable. I voiced the command of the dog wolf to his bitch; a low, authoritative growl. The command had the desired effect and she became docile, enabling me to finish the business quickly and efficiently. Then I wrapped her in some of my furs, lest she freeze.

I was at last in a mood to interpret her words, but she seemed reluctant to speak now. I became puzzled by her changes of mood. I grinned at her. "Speak," I encouraged her. "Slowly. I will listen."

She made a small noise in her throat.

"Speak."

A louder sound issued from her mouth.

I nodded my head, still grinning. I folded my arms on my chest and sat cross-legged in front of her, in readiness. She began to sob. I was surprised, sniffing at her face. "You hurt?"

Her whole body shook, as if she had the fever. Again this peculiar, almost paternal instinct moved me to place my arm around her little shoulders, to stroke her hair. "Speak," I said.

For a long while she sobbed, occasionally looking up into my face as if she tried to read something there. I would grin and she would sob again. But at length she began to talk—telling me her whole story.

Her name was Shanara, and the boys outside were her brothers, Tashako and Yashati. They had been prisoners of the warriors we had slain. The warriors were Hyrkanians: Shanara and the lads were the sons and daughter of a Nemedian nobleman, in line to the throne. Nemedia, it seemed, was a besieged land. The Picts encroached daily and the court, barely capable of resistance, turned upon itself. Leaders of warriors who had never seen battle boasted much of what they could do, but did no more than plot the murder of rivals. The Lord Garak, Shanara's father, had been the only one to take an army personally into the field. While he was away his children had been kidnapped, his wife and sister slain. Hyrkanians had done the work, but Shanara was certain that a Nemedian noble directed them, someone resentful of her father's heroism, of the people's respect for him, their faith in him as the only man likely to halt the Pictish advance. She hinted that she knew who the likeliest culprit was.

"What happened to you after you had been captured?" I asked.

The Hyrkanians had set off to a destination near the Eastern border. They had refused to tell the three prisoners where they were going and, as it was, they never reached the spot for, on the way, they were discovered by a large force of roving Picts. The Picts had killed most of the Hyrkanians and driven the rest, with their captives, into a deep forest where they had become lost. A series of adventures followed, on three rivers and through several countries, as the Hyrkanians attempted to make their way south again, becoming increasingly lost or diverted.

The details of her tale—the complications of the intrigues—baffled me, but the bones of it were clear enough, even familiar, and my curiosity became speculative. I went outside to where the boys shivered, their food hardly touched.

"You Nemedians have small appetites," I said. "Come inside." I pointed at the entrance with my thumb. They were slow to rise, but at last they stumbled in. When the eldest saw his sister he made a lurch at me, but the halter checked him.

"Gods! You've—you've . . ." His voice rose to a scream.

Shanara spoke. "It's all right, Tashako." Her look towards me was almost conspiratorial. I failed to understand its significance.

Tashako glared at her. "You're the Lady Shanara of Jelah—violated by a half-brute. And you say it's all right! Even the Hyrkanians dared not do what he has done. Your hopes of any sort of marriage are completely . . ."

This made her smile. "All hopes disappeared the moment the Hyrkanians seized us and slaughtered our mother and aunt. This half-brute saved our lives."

"She's married to me now," I told him, to reassure him.

Tashako glared at me. He was blue, in spite of his clothing. It occurred to me that Nemedians were more prone to the effects of cold than those bred in the snow-lands. I offered both some of my wolf-pelts and they accepted them grudgingly.

"Shanara said your land was troubled by Picts," I continued, "and only your father fights them."

"Aye," said the boy. "He and his men. Our uncle, the Lord Ushilon, hates him—for he will certainly be king when the Regent dies. The Regent is senile, but he has ruled in place of four kings who were all born with addled brains. The last died, without issue, three weeks before we were abducted—and that is why we were abducted, to force my father to renounce any claim to the throne—for the people favour my father over his brother."

"And while rivals scheme, your enemies swarm over your borders," I said.

He nodded.

The little boy, Yashati, said: "You'll help us, you and your fighters—to drive back the Picts?"

I laughed. "Why should we? The Picts are hardly our enemies."

Shanara said softly: "I had hoped—my husband—that you were sent by the gods to aid us."

Again I was moved by an unfamiliar emotion.

"You would be paid," said Tashako. "In gold."

The flap of my tent was pulled back and Hialmar stood there. He grinned at me. "Playing with children, Ghor? I'm surprised you show such softness, you who have slain so many brothers and your own mother, too. But perhaps you're playing a more complicated game, eh? Did I hear gold mentioned?"

"The gold of Nemedia," I said, "to fight the Picts."

Hialmar shrugged. He opened his hand to display a jewelled cloak-pin. "I was bringing you your share." He stared at it.

I explained who the children were and what they had told me. "We move in that direction, after all," I said. "We'd not be the first Æsir to take service with some Southern king who has forgotten how to fight."

"Nor the first to go soft in that service," said Hialmar. "We look for conquests, not employment." But he continued to stare at the gold. "This is why you saved them, eh?"

I let him believe his own explanation—I had none of my own.

"Our father would be grateful for our return," said Tashako a little over-eagerly, "and would pay."

"He has more of this?" Hialmar displayed the pin.

"That was the treasure the Hyrkanians stole from our home,"

said Shanara. She looked at the floor of the tent.

"Boxes full. Chests full," said Tashako.

"Rooms full," added Yashati. "Palaces full."

"I think you lie." Hialmar laughed casually.

"He exaggerates," said Shanara, "but not much. My father is probably the richest noble in Nemedia. It is why he is able to raise such a large army of men to fight the Picts."

"Your own people are paid to fight?" I asked in some bewilderment.

"They would not fight otherwise, most of them," said Tashako bitterly. "Men of other countries fight beside our own—but not enough, and none such warriors as yours."

"There are no warriors greater than the Æsir," said Hialmar, as a matter of fact. He hesitated, fondling the gold in his hand before, with a swift movement, passing it to me. He bent to leave the tent. "Perhaps in time," he said, "we'll take you with us to Nemedia."

The girl glanced up, staring at the pin, but not as Hialmar had done. There seemed to be sadness in her eyes.

"You recognize this?" I asked her. "It is yours?"

"My mother's. Torn from her gown as she lay dying . . ."

I put the pin into her hand. "It is of no use to me."

Tashako spoke gravely to me. "It seems, barbarian, that we are in your debt." He looked meaningfully at his sister. "But I'd remind you that you are also in ours."

These Nemedians set some material value, it seemed, on the maidenheads of their womenfolk.

The little boy said: "Tashako, do not challenge him. He could kill you so easily."

I grinned. "I've killed enough kin for one lifetime."

"Kin? We are not your kin!" Tashako was baffled.

"You are from today," I told him, "and consequently under my protection. Are you not my wife's brothers? We make a new pack within the large one. Who knows? One day we'll become a fullyfledged pack in our own right—when Shanara bears my sons and you sire your own."

This was, for me, an unwonted descent into sentimentality.

Tashako uttered some sharp remark whose significance I could not catch.

Chapter VI
Betrayal in Belverus
Charles R. Saunders

"Thus, oh Prince-Regent, my counsel is that we deport this band of barbarians from our kingdom at once!"

These loudly-spoken words brought my mind back from its wanderings. In this ornate den called a "palace", I was more the wolf than ever . . . and a trapped one at that. Even among my Æsir comrades, I had never known any shelter more substantial than a horsehide tent. Now I was standing uncomfortably in the Hall of Audiences of the Prince-Regent of Nemedia, in the city of Belverus. City . . . never before had I seen so many people in one place, crawling like a swarm of maggots over a carrion kill! Were it not for the presence of my mate Shanara, my brother-in-arms Hialmar, and the other Æsir chiefs with me in the chamber, I would long since have loped back to the forests of the North.

The man who was speaking was Lord Ushilon, uncle to Shanara and her two brothers. He was a hugely fat man, with a drooping black mustache and enough cloth on his body to make at least two Æsir travel-tents. Ushilon was speaking to an old, old man seated on a chair of stone inlaid with the sparkling green, red, and white crystals Shanara called "gems". Behind the chair was a great banner worked in the red dragon symbol of Nemedia. Flanking the sides of the chair were smaller seats for what Shanara called the "internal ambassadors" of Koth, Zingara, Argos, Ophir, Shem, Aquilonia . . . all names of importance to her, but without meaning to me.

I had laughed when Shanara had told me that the leader of the great Nemedian man-pack was a man so old that he could barely walk unaided. Yet here he sat, trembling, vacant-eyed, drooling like a cub. Wise were the ways of the wolves, who were ruled by the strong, not the senile!

"Already the land teems with fugitives from other Hyborian lands overwhelmed by the Picts," Ushilon continued. "Even the hated Aquilonians have fled here from the menace they were unable to contain. Are we now to open our gates to even more of these potential traitors? Why, these Æsir are barbarians themselves, no more advanced than the filthy Picts!"

"The estimable Lord forgets that the greatest king in our history, one who defeated you Nemedians many times, was a barbarian from Cimmeria," the Internal Ambassador from Aquilonia rejoined. "And that the cause of the rise of the Picts was the teachings of a Nemedian priest . . . "

"By Mitra, you will hold your tongue, Kaius Valkonnus! It is only by the good will of the Prince-Regent that you Aquilonian curs are permitted to live in Nemedia." Ushilon's round face was reddening.

"That and the fact that they have added three thousand swords to our army," a new voice broke in. In contrast to Ushilon, the speaker was tall, broad-shouldered, and straight as a pine. He had iron-grey hair and beard, and was clad in dented battle armour. This was Lord Garak, father of Shanara, Tashako, and Yashati, and "father" to me . . . or father-in-law. Another meaningless, puzzling custom of this "civilization."

"We need all the warriors we can find, Ushilon," Garak continued. "And these Æsir have proven their prowess by breaking through the Picts' northern lines in the old Border Kingdom to return my children to me. Mitra, old King Gorm must have lopped off heads wholesale when he heard of it! Look at us! Last of the Hyborian kingdoms not overrun with painted savages or cringing beneath the heel of the Hyrkanian. And you would turn away more armsmen? True, they demand payment for their services. But would you not prefer to spend Nemedian gold rather than Nemedian blood?"

"It is precisely Nemedian blood for which I am concerned, dear brother," Ushilon responded. "Would you have our valiant and noble race destroyed by wholesale mixing with those too weak to resist the Pict? Are we, last bastion of Hyborian civilization, to become mongrelized by the infusion of these lesser breeds? But perhaps you, dear brother, actually prefer such miscegenation . . . considering that your daughter claims to be wed to this uncouth, hairy half-brute!"

My hand shot to the hilt of the sword of Genseric. Wolf-like I snarled. "Would you try to take my mate from me, fat one? Let us meet, then, fang to fang . . . "

Amid the uproar that followed my challenge, two restraining hands were laid on mine. One was small and soft; it belonged to Shanara. The other was that of Lord Garak, who, after his initial shock and astonishment upon learning that his daughter was mine, had taken a liking to me.

"Softly, Ghor," he said. "Let me handle this."

To his brother he said, "These are changing times, Ushilon. If we do not adapt quickly, we will be crushed between the wolves of the West, and the vultures of the East. I would rather Shanara be wed to a fighting-man like Ghor than to any of these simpering scion of dead dynasties that throng our court. If his origins disturb you, I

VI. Betrayal in Belverus

will make him a duke. And speak not to me of betrayal from within. Jelah may be close to the eastern border, but the Hyrkanians who abducted my children and slew their mother and aunt must have had inside assistance of some kind . . . "

"You dare to accuse me of that heinous crime?" Ushilon roared. "Why I'll . . . "

"You'll close your flapping mouth and listen to me," the Prince-Regent cut in. The old man's vision had cleared, and his voice was firm and steady. For a moment I had a vision of the man he must have been before his declining years. "You boys have been at each others' throats since you were old enough to fight over your toys. I've had a lifetime of this squabbling over the succession to this wretched throne and I'm sick of it. Patrilineal succession, matrilineal throne-right, four witling heirs . . . By Ishtar and Mitra, perhaps this kingdom has become as decrepit as I. Let the Æsir stay, say I. Perhaps they can rid us of these bothersome menaces."

Abruptly the old man returned to his dazed state, his crown sitting askew on his wrinkled, bald head. But his word was law; Lord Garak gripped my hand firmly as he said, "It is done. We will find quarters for your people, but you and Shanara may have the palace apartments reserved for the Lords of Jelah. I always sleep in the barracks with my troops, you know."

"And I with mine," said Hialmar. "They will be pleased to learn that there will be more gold to come for fighting the Picts. Your reward to us for the return of your children was generous enough, but the sum you named as an offer to serve under your banner is sure to satisfy them."

Hialmar's blue eyes turned to me. "And you, Wolf-Brother . . . why is it that you refuse a share of the payment? By Ymir you earned it, the number of Pictish skulls your sword split in that battle!"

"What would I do with yellow metal?" I growled. "I have my mate to bear me cubs, and I have prey to kill. What more does a wolf need?"

Hialmar, who knew me well, laughed at that. But Lord Garak looked puzzled. At Shanara's insistence, her father had been but vaguely informed of my origin and early deeds. He continued to look at me strangely as Shanara led me by the hand to what was to be my first night under a roof of stone.

As we departed the Hall Of Audiences, my wolf-keen eyes noted the displeasure on the face of Lord Ushilon. Nor did I fail to observe that Tashako, the older of Shanara's brothers, was engaging his uncle in earnest conversation.

• • •

Shanara and I lay tangled in the silks and furs of a bed as big as the floor of an Æsir meeting-tent. During our lovemaking, I had forgotten the instinctive dread of confinement that had plagued me since we had first come to Belverus. What seemed like luxury to the Æsir was more like a cage for me.

During the long march from the south of Nordheim to the land of Nemedia, Shanara had overcome her fear of me, though Yashati still held me in awe, and Tashako hated me. She (Shanara) had come to understand the way a wolf loves its mate. Much to the disgust of Tashako, the proud princess returned my feelings.

These uncharacteristic feelings of mine had made me the object of some jesting among the Æsir. A few broken heads soon convinced them that I was still the Ghor who was feared even by these brawny blond giants.

Shanara had attempted to "civilize" me to an extent acceptable to her father before we reached Belverus. For her sake I had acquiesced, though her seemingly endless list of "dos" and "don'ts" made little sense to me. But she had not attempted to change my mating habits. I was her "great, hairy wolf," and she howled and yelped with the kind of pleasure only a human woman can know, never a wolf-bitch. I smiled at what the sentries posted outside our door must have been thinking as they heard her cries and my growls . . .

Shanara nestled closer to me as I caressed her soft body. In the glow of the cressets her bare skin seemed as white as that of Ythillin the Ice Woman. At the thought of that cursed name, I sat up abruptly like a startled beast.

"What troubles you, my wolf?" Shanara asked sleepily, her blond hair spilling over her small young breasts.

"Nothing," I grunted. I had never told her of Ythillin, or of the dire import of her curse and prophecy. What could a pampered child like Shanara know of the North and its harsh cold gods?

"I will miss you when you go off with my father to battle the Picts," she said, accepting my answer.

"Do not worry. The devils may be hard to kill, but we will drive them back across . . . Aquitania, is it?"

Shanara laughed, her voice like the pealing of tiny bells. "No, silly, it's Aquilonia," she corrected. "Come, let us sleep now. You must be alert for your council-of-war with Hialmar and my father in the morning."

"A wolf is always alert," I said before I drifted off into a troubled sleep.

Once again the tinkling music of the collision of millions of tiny ice crystals drifted into my ears. Once again my eyes were blinded by the boreal glow of the aura of Ythillin, goddess of the frosts. Once again she stared down at me with eyes like chips of ice in a countenance of frozen, inhuman beauty.

"So, Kinslayer, think you that there is safety within the walls of

VI. Betrayal in Belverus

Belverus? Think you that you can ignore the curse of Ythillin? Then think again, mortal! Think again, for the gods of the North have other plans for you . . ."

I wanted to spring at her throat, but unlike the last dream-vision I could neither move nor speak. The laughter of the Ice Woman echoed as she suddenly vanished. I felt a sudden frigid shock, as if her passing had drenched me in an icy waterfall. My eyes snapped open, and I realized that I was no longer in the bedchamber of the Lords of Jelah, and Shanara was no longer at my side.

I was in a large corridor of some kind, lined with rows of pillars that reminded me of a stone forest. My hands were tied behind one of these pillars, and I stood in an awkward upright position with my back scraping against the stone. Blinking drops of water from my eyes, I saw that there were others with me in this strange place.

Shanara was there. Her golden mane was disheveled and her wide blue eyes mirrored fear and confusion. Whoever it was that had provided her with a long satin robe to hide her nakedness had failed to do the same for me. But I didn't care; my thick body hair had always been protection enough.

Lord Ushilon was there. His face bore an expression of satisfaction not unlike that of a wildcat about to devour a trapped sparrow. He alternately fingered the "gems" on his hands and adjusted the sash that strained across his bulging belly.

Tashako was there. He glared at me with the total hatred only children his age can express. Mixed with this hatred was the same kind of satisfaction that marked the fat face of his uncle.

Also in the corridor were a dozen Nemedian palace guardsmen, armed with pikes and swords. Standing apart from the others was a dark-skinned stranger of a race unfamiliar to me. He wore a longsleeved robe black as midnight, and his head was shaved bald as a brown egg.

I had taken in all these people with a single glance of my wolf-sharp vision. But the main focus of my attention was the red-bearded giant standing directly in front of me. A still-dripping water bucket was gripped tightly in his huge hands. It was Tostig Bearslayer, one of the Vanir who had joined Hialmar's tribe after we Æsir had sacked the main camp of his people.

"Why have you betrayed me, Tostig?" I asked calmly.

"Betrayed?" the Vanir repeated, madness flickering in his eyes. "Betrayed? You damned beast, you do not know how long I have awaited this moment. But then how could you have ever guessed that I am the son of Hengist Ironarm, brother to your father Genseric? Ymir! That I must claim kinship to such as you! Aie, you cur, you damned mother-slaying cur!"

The crazed giant smashed a wild, open-handed blow across my

face. My head snapped back against the pillar; then I spat a mouthful of blood and saliva into his eyes. Roaring like the madman he had become, Tostig aimed a fur boot at my groin. But my foot was quicker. Tostig crumpled to the floor, groaning and clutching at his maimed manhood. I laughed at him as two of the Nemedians dragged him out of range of my feet.

"It is well that the Vanir oaf did not succeed in his purpose," the dark stranger commented.

"I disagree, Mentumenen, but it shall be as you wish," said Ushilon. "You are the last of the great Stygian sorcerers, which is why my gold helps to finance your land's war against the encroaching Black Kingdoms. Yet I cannot understand why it is so important to you to keep this half-brute alive."

"Set, the Old Serpent, so wills," Mentumenen said cryptically. "Through the power Set has given me, it was simple to have my agents slip dream-lotus into the wine these two enjoyed before . . . retiring. It will be equally simple for my agents to arrange the demise of Lord Garak, and blame it on the Æsir. And the death of the Prince-Regent . . . that will be the simplest task of all, for the old one's *ka* clings but precariously to his ancient bones."

"Excellent, my sorcerous friend, excellent," Ushilon said unctuously. Turning to me he sneered: "So, half-brute, we have met 'fang to fang', and it is clear that my fangs are superior to yours. Soon I shall be king of Nemedia, with Tashako here as my heir, as I was never fortunate enough to sire a son of my own. Then I can chart a sensible future for this country."

"What might this country's future be?" I asked. Covertly I was testing the strength of my bonds. The ropes were strong, but so was I.

"A curiosity," Ushilon mused. "An inquisitive savage. Interesting. It will be amusing to explain my plans to your ignorant ears. I will begin by ridding Nemedia of the foreign scum who choke the streets of our cities. 'Little Koth,' 'Little Argos,' 'Little Aquilonia'; all these rats' nests of fugitives will be given the choice of leaving Nemedia, or death in the streets. Your Æsir will be the first to go; Tostig will make sure of that. He has no love for his comrades.

"Then I will make peace with old Gorm. That will be simple enough. I will cede him a few unimportant western provinces to ravish. Finally, we shall make an alliance with the Hyrkanians. Together, our forces can drive the Picts back into their forests beyond the Black River. Already I have promised Shanara as bride to the Agha Junghaz of Turan to seal our secret bargain. It was there that she and her brothers were being taken before you and your fellow savages interrupted the journey."

"You cannot marry me off to some Eastern emir!" Shanara protested. "I am already wed to Ghor."

"Are you, my dear? Did a priest of Mitra say the Words of Joining over your anointed heads?"

Shanara bowed her head and bit her lip. She knew that the legal ceremony of Nemedian wedlock had never been performed for her and me. We were married only because I had said we were. And Tashako knew this as well as we.

Suddenly Shanara stamped her foot and glared defiantly at her uncle. "You are a terrible man, uncle Ushilon. You would sell your own flesh and blood to the Hyrkanians, who as everyone knows, treat their women as less than slaves. You would betray your people by conspiring with our greatest enemies in our time of peril. And you even forsake holy Mitra to enlist the services of the minions of Set! Uncle or no, you are a man no longer. You are a swine!"

Reddening furiously, Ushilon wheeled and slapped Shanara with a fat, beringed hand. With a cry of pain, the slight girl fell to the floor.

"You little strumpet! You'll not talk to me that way. Why I'll . . . "

But he got no further. For when his hand struck my mate, I reverted totally to the wolf, and Ushilon learned why the Æsir called me Ghor the Strong. The bravest man of the time of James Allison would have blanched before my feral fury.

With a snarl that froze the Nemedians in fear, I thrust the power of my thews against the ropes that bound me. They snapped loose; I was free! I thrust the guardsmen aside as though they were stuffed with feathers, and sprang at the squealing Ushilon. The Nemedian noble fumbled desperately for the dagger in his sash. By my wolfish standards, his efforts were pathetically slow. I was upon him before he had pulled the weapon more than a little way from its sheath. As my grey brothers dragged down a pregnant doe, so I bore Ushilon to the floor. He shrieked like a woman as my teeth fastened on his fleshy throat. His hands clawed desperately to my face, but I paid no more attention to his feeble blows than did a wolf-mother to the bites of its cubs.

Heeding Mentumenen's cries that he wanted me alive, the guards recovered from their shocked immobility and smashed their spear-butts into my head. Bane lanced through my skull, but I could taste Ushilon's hot, salty blood in my mouth. The last thing I heard before black oblivion finally descended was Shanara's voice screaming my name over her uncle's high-pitched cries and the low sinister laughter of Mentumenen the Stygian . . .

• • •

When I awoke again, pain was pounding like the hammer of a swordsmith against the anvil of my skull. And, though my eyes were open, I could see only utter blackness. For a moment I nearly succumbed to human panic. Had my enemies blinded me? Then the cold patience of the wolf overcame the panic, and my eyes became accustomed to a sort of dim half-light in my prison.

For it was indeed a prison in which I had awakened, and a small one at that. I was cramped in a curled-up position, and I could move my limbs but slightly before pressing against the yielding substance of the walls. Walls? It was leather, my nose told me. And the faint light had its source in three rows of stitching that stretched from the top of my prison to its bottom. By the dim light showing through the holes between the stitches, I could tell that it was still night. In short, I, Ghor the Strong, was bundled inside a giant leather bag of some sort. The indignity of my position infuriated me, and I prepared to tear my way out of my prison with a single surge of might.

Then I realized two more things about my prison which, in my flash of wolf-rage, I had overlooked. There was no ground, or floor, or other support beneath the leather bag . . . and it was moving! I could feel a rush of cold, whistling air through the stitches. And I could hear the powerful flapping of great wings overhead . . .

I felt a stab of true fear then, the kind that assails both man and beast . . . fear of the unknown. For I knew of no bird huge enough to carry a man my size through the skies as easily as an owl carries a woods-mouse. What the owner of those vast wings might be, I did not try to imagine. Instead, I forgot my discomfort at being so closely confined, and slipped into the timeless patience of the beast. Sooner or later this weird journey would end. I could only hope that it would not end by my being dropped from unguessable heights to shatter on the ground below. I wondered if I had been successful in slaying Ushilon before the spearbutts had knocked me out.

Though I could not know the exact length of time of my flight, the light showing through the stitches had brightened considerably by its end. I could tell that its end was near by the lessening of the flapping of the wings, and the diminishing of the icy wind. Abruptly I hit the ground with a bone-jarring thump.

Despite the cramps in my muscles, I struggled to tear free from my leather prison. I wanted to see what was attached to those great wings . . . as I pushed violently with my arms and legs, the stitching tore free, and the three sections of the bag fell away.

Blinking my eyes against the sudden glare of sunlight against snow, I looked up . . . and growled deep in my throat. Hovering less than a dozen feet above my head was a gigantic black sky-creature neither bat nor bird, though not without qualities of both. Its leathery wings must have spanned forty feet, and the wind from their slow beating buffeted my face and stirred up eddies of snow around me.

Did I see a glimmer of mockery in the creature's eyes before its

VI. Betrayal in Belverus 51

wings lifted it upward at an ever-increasing rate, until it was only a disappearing black dot in the sky? Did those eyes bear a disquieting resemblance to those of the Stygian sorcerer? Or was it just a trick of the snow-crystals blowing between my eyes and the bleak sun? I did not know.

Rather than waste time speculating, I stretched my aching muscles and attempted to discover just where the bat-thing had dropped me. As my sharp gaze took in the details of this new place, I quickly realized that I was to the north of Nemedia. The snows here were deeper, the woods harsher, and the wind blowing against my naked skin was as chilled as the winds of my childhood. I felt no discomfort.

I knew, then, that my path lay southward. But I did not know how great the distance to Nemedia was. I could be as distant as Asgard, or Vanaheim, or even Cimmeria . . . or as close as what was once called the Border Kingdom. But even if I were in the abode of the Frost Giants themselves, I swore, I would return to Belverus and find what had become of Shanara. If she had been harmed . . . my body shook in a frenzy of bloodlust.

Then I heard sounds coming from behind a nearby patch of woods. It was the cry of a wolf, mingled with the screech of a snow-lynx. The wolf must be alone, I thought, for no lynx would dare confront an entire pack. I hesitated . . . then loped off in the direction of the conflict. I glided through the woods with all the stealth and speed of my wild years, until I came to a clearing wherein a struggle for life and death was occurring.

Normally a lynx against a lone wolf would be an even contest. But this wolf was old, mangy and weak. My nose told me that this was a she. And there was something else about her scent. Then the claws of the lynx ripped open the wolf's belly, and its entrails spilled streaming onto the snow.

I growled a challenge and charged into the clearing. The lynx raised its tufted head and bounded away from the yelping wolf. It looked startled; probably it had never before been attacked by a naked, unarmed human. Snarling in disgust, the snow-white cat crouched on its long legs. Then it leaped in a white flash for my throat. But I was quick, even for a wolf. With a twist of my body I dodged the deadly claws and snapping teeth. While the lynx was still in midair, I grasped it by the ruff of its neck and positioned my body over its back as we both came down. Even with the cushioning of the snow, I landed so heavily upon its body that the breath was driven from its lungs. Yowling furiously, the lynx struggled to free itself. But my legs held it down while my hands slowly crushed the sides of its throat together.

The cat was sinewy and strong. It very nearly managed to roll over and disembowel me as well as the wolf before I finally broke its neck with a final surge of inhuman strength. Panting with my effort, I rose and kicked the white-furred corpse aside and went to the side of the dying wolf.

Mangy and decrepit as the beast was, its spilled guts melting the red snow, I still recognized this she-wolf as I bent over its mangled body. Her dulling eyes recognized me as well. A soft whine escaped her throat, and her tongue feebly licked my outstretched hand before she died.

This was the she-wolf whose dugs had nourished me from the time Genseric had left me to die in the snow to the time I had become strong enough to run with the pack. This wolf-bitch was my true mother, not the Vanir bitch who had condemned me to death but moments after I had been born. Yet I did not mourn this nameless she-wolf as a human would; weeping, wailing, mouthing strange ritual words for ears that could no longer hear. My tears remained frozen in my eyes as I piled a cairn of stones over her carcass.

When I was done, I sat on my haunches and uttered a single long, lingering howl. Had this been Set's answer to the Ice Gods, who meant me to conquer for their obscure purposes? Was I but a toy, to be tossed about at the whim of gods Northern and Southern?

No! I was Ghor the Strong! By whatever it was that was worshipped by a wolf I made a vow; as I had slain Raki the Swift, Sigismund the Bear, Obri the Cunning, Alwin the Silent, and Gudrun of the Shining Locks, so would I slay Lord Ushilon, Tostig Bearslayer, the boy-cub Tashako, and most especially Mentumenen the Stygian. Only black sorcery could explain why the bat-thing had dropped me at this place, at this time . . .

Also to die were every Pict and Hyrkanian I could lay hands on. They had been the source of Ushilon's ambition. Gone was the veneer of "civilization" I had acquired from Shanara. Once again I was the avenging wolf, a weapon of death and bloodlust aimed at the hearts of my hated foes!

• • •

For a week I wandered the unfamiliar wasteland, living like the wild thing I was. I ate by running down hares and digging gophers from their half-frozen burrows. Once I feasted on a badger whose skull I had split with a stone. Such chance-found stones and a club fashioned from a tree-branch were the only aspects of me still human; otherwise I was a two-legged beast of prey. I travelled in the direction I knew was south, but I did not know whether my progress was great or small.

When I heard again the baying of wolves and the cries of men, I hurried toward the source of the sound. Though I cared little for the company of men or wolves, at least men might be able to tell me

VI. Betrayal in Belverus

where I was. Or they might try to kill me . . . I must take that chance, if I was to have my vengeance.

Carrying my crude club at my side, I loped through the snow, hoping to reach the men before the wolves killed them all. In this battle, Ghor must fight against his grey brothers, not with them . . .

Finally I came to a low, snow-blanketed valley flanked by stands of fir and pine. And I saw yet another wilderness struggle, this one totally unlike the last. For the men and the wolves were not fighting against each other. They were hunting together, and had surrounded their prey: a giant elk.

In the time of Ghor these monsters were already rare. By the time of James Allison, they had been long-since extinct. But the beast pawing the snow and breathing thick plumes from its flared nostrils was as real as the blood dripping down its shaggy hide. Three spears sprouted like death-stems from its sides, but the elk seemed unweakened.

Twice the size of a stag deer, the huge elk bulked. Its massive, many-pointed antlers were wider than a man is tall. Frozen patches of crimson speckled these antlers, for the elk had taken its toll of its pursuers before being brought to bay. The trampled snow surrounding it was red with fresh-spilled blood.

The wolves were of the same gaunt grey breed I had run with in my childhood. There were five of them, and they were harassing the elk by nipping at its nose and flanks, driving it into a frenzy of frustration. Of the men, there were seven. They were lean, muscular giants as naked as I, but their steel-sinewed bodies were coated with white hair thicker than my own. Full white beards matted their brutish faces, and their pale hair grew tangled and unshorn. For weapons they carried stone-tipped spears and flint knives. Some of them bore traces of crooks in their limbs not unlike that in my own left leg. They and the wolves hunted not as master and pet, but as equals within one pack, as I had done with my grey brothers.

The hunters circled their giant prey cautiously, jabbing at it with their spears. They were waiting for the elk to weaken before driving their spears into its vitals. Three dead men and two dead wolves had taught them the danger of attacking too soon.

But caution was not the way of Ghor the Strong. I knew a way to end the hunt quickly. I crept to the hunters and their quarry so silently that neither man nor beast knew I was there until I dashed directly in front of the elk's head. With tremendous force I swung my club between the eyes of the head looming so high above my own. Then I leaped back to avoid the antlers, one blow from which could cave my ribs in like matchwood.

My club shattered at the impact of my blow; the skull of the elk did not. But the beast was momentarily stunned. And a moment was all the white-haired hunters needed to plunge their spears deep into its mighty heart. Even as it went down in its death throes, the wolves were swarming over it, tearing at its meat.

I looked at the hunters as they approached me, suspicion showing on their ice-pale, half-apish faces. As James Allison I knew that they and their tribe were the last of the ancient ape-men of the Arctic North, from whose seed the Ice Gods had seen fit to mold the ancestors of the Æsir and Vanir, and whose atavisms appeared but once every seven generations in the races of Nordheim. Many names were these half-brutes called by man. Some of these names echoed through history: Meh-teh, Yeh-ti, Mi-Go . . . ignorant anthropologists of James Allison's time would call their fossil fragments "Heidelberg Man".

They were brothers to the wolves, and had forged the first pact between man and wolfkind long ages ago. The wolves of Vanaheim had sensed my linkage to this ancient bond that day long ago on the icy wastes near the camp of Genseric the Sworder. How this pocket of the ape-men had survived so long so far south of their natural environment I did not know, either as James Allison or Ghor the Strong. Nor, as Ghor the Strong, did I care. I only laughed my barking, wolfish laugh and remembered the words of Ythillin: "Nor shall you, who are half man and half beast, ever find peace in either wolf-pack or human nation . . . "

Hell! The Ice-bitch was a liar! For I had found my people.

Chapter VII
Lord General of Nemedia
andrew j. offutt

Ythillin was right.

These were not my people, not my kind, though it took me a month to make admission of that fact to myself.

Was a month in which, amid sparkling snow and shadows of purple and indigo and a sun that glared an angry yellow-white but yielded little heat from its skyfire, I sought to be happy. Was a month in which I sought to convince myself—with steadily decreasing success—that I was home and happy. I sought, running naked amid great snow-cloaked boulders and dunes of snow like mastodonic burial-mounds and desperately life-clinging larches and mockingly green firs, to convince myself that here was life, that here was my life, that here I belonged: among men who were not men, yet beasts who were not beasts. For what else was I?

Ythillin, though, had not lied. Bitch she was, Ice-bitch who spoke for the Ice Gods themselves, but liar she was not. She knew. She knew me, far better than I knew myself.

Yet I, too, knew. I but sought to deceive myself, for such is the way of men, wherever they rise and strive and thrive, or fail and die. And aye, I am a man, raised by beasts but not of them. Deceivers of ourselves, we men are, whether individual or tribe, city or nation; we are deceivers of our women and our animals and even our get. For breathes there the father who has not sought to convince his offspring of his own infallibility, even unto godhead?

Godhead. Aye, the gods—and we seek even to deceive them, in the matter of our behaviour, our attitudes, our worthiness. Are they deceived? Who knows? What is a god?

Some say the gods are merely there, and that they care not for us who are as beetles rolling dung at their mighty feet. Others say the gods—each specific chief deity of his own tribe—created us, in their own image and for their pleasure. If such be so, they must be passing fond of cruelty, and of laughter as well!

In Belverus of Nemedia I heard a man in the street crying out to all who would give listen that it is men who created the gods, in our image. Some gave ear with interest. Some sneered, and went on about their cityish business. Others sneered, and remained to jeer and ask questions that were not questions at all but challenges. And others still were angered or offended, and they saw to it that the speaker was silenced, and that with loss of several teeth; and these were priests, servants of the gods. For whether the gods themselves are jealous or no, their servants are, and must ever seek to silence those who put forth other deities, even unto slaying them and their women and their children and beasts.

No god had created me in his own image—or if one had, I had not heard of him. Nor had I created aught of deities in my image, for there were none like me, infant into beast, beast into beast-man, man into beast, and now . . .

No. There were no gods like unto me, and no men either.

You see how my brain wallowed and moiled in the dark and the deep, amid swirling tenuous mists of wraithy never-was and might-be. I sought solution to the insoluble, during that month I spent with the Mi-Go. (For so they called themselves, though men in their arrogance named them Yeh-tih, and men have survived, so that name does.)

Or—did my mind so wallow, back then? Perhaps it is only now that I have had such intelligently questioning thoughts; now, when I am James Allison of the twentieth century—for this life. For I have been here many times before, and I will be back again and yet again, and perhaps I shall one day *remember* James Allison, as I now remember the poor lonely creature neither man nor beast that was I, who was Ghor, and his misery in that year of his growing up.

Aye, growing up. So I was. I had been a happy animal. I lived for today, for my belly, with but one thought for the morrow: Vengeance. And that I had taken. I had made myself an orphan among men thereby, and without siblings. Now a lynx had orphaned me among the beasts, and for a higher reason: its belly.

Seeking ties, some form of security—for so it is with men and with beasts—I had raped Shanara like a savage. And then decided and announced: This was my mate. Mate! Spoke I of the arrogance of humankind? My membership is assured. My mate!

And why not a she-wolf, you who are called Strong among men, and Hair-less by the wolves (though I am not), and among the Mi-Go, short-hair: Bl'dah. (They referred to that on my body, which men might well have likened to that of an animal . . .) Why not a lovely sensuous wolf-bitch, Ghor?—sleek and shining in her need; remember that one who came to you that afternoon when the snow was a field of flashing tiny suns and the sky blue as Shanara's eyes and the Needing was on her, that whining she-wolf who sought to be mounted by him who though he looked not like a wolf and smelled only partway like a wolf, was a strong animal with promise of protection and good get?

Why not a . . . "woman" of the Mi-Go?

I tried. But Shanara was not covered all over with fine white

VII. Lord General of Nemedia

hair, and had not a muzzle and a chest little different from mine, though Klu'do of the Mi-Go possessed more nipples than both of us. I tried, with Klu'do—and all I could think of was Shanara. So I closed my eyes, and went on—and all I saw behind my eyes was Shanara. And all I felt was animal.

Did that prove that I was not an animal? Neither belonging among the wolves who had been my people for so long, the kindest to me of all and the most understanding, nor among the Mi-Go with their fur like finger-long strands of silk?

No, not even that. For the Mi-Go knew sentiment, and as a rule each male clove to a single female, the first he mounted. It was not my remembering Shanara whilst I lay with Klu'do that set me apart.

As a wolf, I belonged among the Mi-Go, who were wolves of higher development, above the four-legged beasts, regardless of the wolfish nobility I would ever respect. But as a Mi-Go, I . . .

Yes. I belonged among men. And Ythillin was no liar.

Nor could I persuade the ape-men of the mountains to join me. To follow me, to make war like men, against the Picts who had conquered Zingara and Argos and Ophir and aye, most of Aquilonia, and now gnawed at Nemedia's western border.

"Picts our enemies: No," Gl'erf said, for he was chief among the Mi-Go. "Ne-me-d'—what you said—"

"Nemedians."

"Nemede'ens our enemies: No. They come this-place, they Mi-Go enemies. Mi-Go go that-place, we they enemies. Much kill. We stay this-place they stay that-place, enemies: No. Kill: No. This place our territory. That place they territory. Compete for food: No."

"Picts try steal Nemedian territory," I said.

Gl'erf looked at me. He twitched his muzzle that was not quite a nose. He scratched behind his left knee with his right foot. He dug into his full bushy mane of white-and-grey hair. He looked at me. And he shrugged.

"Others come wolf-brother place, wolf-brother territory, Mi-Go help. Others come our territory, wolf-brothers help. Picts our brother: No. Picts our kind: No. Nemedians our brother or kind: No."

"Then I must go among them, for I am their kind."

"You Mi-Go, Bl'dah. You hair only a little darker and not so rich. You welcome among Mi-Go; we brothers you. Klu'do like you— may be she bear you cub."

I thought not. I shook my head, and I sighed. And I left the Mi-Go.

I made my way down from the mountains and across the border stronghold of "King" Jarpnr with but one minor mishap. That resulted in my reaching the Nemedian border with clothing and arms: a fair cloak of deep blue woollen, a buckler with a notched rim and a grip over-tight for my big hand, and a good single-edged ax, sickle shaped. Six Nemedian soldiers on patrol stopped me, were persuaded to allow me to retain the ax, and fell in around me to ride inland. They seemed to think that they had "apprehended" me and that I was under arrest; I did not bother to disabuse them of the notion. I considered them my escort.

Only a league or so from the rising walls of Belverus, we came upon a group of richly armed and attired Nemedian horse-soldiers. With them was Hialmar. I made no comment on his fancy attire; he and others made considerable comment on the fact that I was not dead. I did learn that the ancient monarch was dead—with the Stygian's help?—and that Ushilon was kinging it in Belverus.

Soon Hialmar and I were in a sprawling black-and-red pavilion, which was that of the Lord of Jelah, who was also Captain-General of the Nemedian forces, and was also my father-in-law. As Garak's first words were "Ghor—you're not dead," I assumed that Shanara's father knew little, perhaps nothing, of the events of that night of treachery a month agone. When he advised that he had been told his elder son and I had quarreled bitterly—about Shanara—and that Tashako had slain me, I stared.

"You believed that, my lord?"

"No." Garak shrugged. "You were gone, and my daughter was sent northeast, to safety. I have no reason to love you, Vanirman. I assumed that there had indeed been more words between you and my son, and that you had been slain—most likely later. I was not minded to think on the how of it. The king's new adviser is not to my liking, as I care little for these strange, sinister men of Stygia. Yet he is a brilliant man and a mage as well, and when he confirmed what Tashako and the King said, I made no argument." He looked me very steadily in the eyes. "It was not to me a matter of great import, Ghor of Vanaheim."

"It was to me!" Hialmar heatedly interrupted.

Lord Garak nodded. "Naturally. And to those among the Æsir-Vanir force ye two brought among us. I have been instructing Lord Hialmar in the intricacies of command, and of rule and power in such a kingdom as ours, so that he better understands priorities and what is politick."

"Politick! Your daughter is my wife, by her choice and mine, Lord of Jelah! And where is she now?"

"Sent to safety in . . . a certain place. Nemedia remains leaguered about by wolves."

"Sent to Turan!" I practically shouted, and made shift to quiet my voice somewhat. "That old man who sullies the throne of your land bartered her to the Agha Junghaz of Turan! If she is fortunate, she may be one of his wives, rather than a concubine!"

VII. Lord General of Nemedia

Garak was instantly on his feet, red of face and with hand on pommel. "False! It could not . . . be . . . ." His voice trailed away like mist. His expression became more thoughtful than angry. "Once, Ushilon . . . made mention—nay, more than mere mention of such a scheme. He sought to persuade me to agree. His hope was that such an alliance with Turan might aid us in an attack against Zamora and thus divert the Hyrkanian wolves from our eastern border . . . Mitra and Ishtar! Can it be?"

"My lord, it is I who is amazed that you are yet alive! For your continued health cannot be part of the plot of the four who control Nemedia: Ushilon, Mentumenen the Stygian, a servant of Old Set and aye, a mage, and Tostig Bearslayer of the Vanir—"

"Tostig!" Hialmar interrupted, and he too pounced to his feet with hand on hilt.

"He is my cousin," I said, not wishing to go into the reasons for Tostig's hatred for me before my father-in-law. "And—I hesitate to name the fourth, Lord General, with you on your feet and pommel in fist."

Garak, staring, blinked—and sat. He showed me his empty hands, and folded them on the buckle of his belt. His attitude was that of a man composed to listen.

Then I spoke, and Garak was indeed hard put to believe, and he was much wroth that his son Tashako should conspire so with a dark mage, and that foul old man who was his uncle, and—a Vanirman! At the time, neither of us knew that without the pavilion of his Lord General another gave listen, and him a Nemedian who loved only Garak, and blamed Ushilon for the death of his wife and son, over on the Zamoran border. More wroth was he, as it fell out, even than Garak, so that the red battle-lust came even upon a man of Nemedia. (Sargan his name, and in my eyes he will ever be a hero.) Ere the sun rose on another day, Ushilon was dead by Sargan's hand, and Sargan dead too, of no less than a dozen wounds from the edges of Ushilon's tardy palace Guard.

Naturally the son of the Lord Garak, the friend and chosen of his slain uncle, proclaimed himself king over Nemedia. As naturally, the men of the palace Guard—including now Tostig slayer of the Bear—were loud in their agreement. And the crown was brought from where lay Ushilon, he who had lorded it over the land, whilst that ancient Regent outlasted four witlings. Tashako must needs pad it somewhat, for he had not yet his full growth, for all his swelled head.

News of all this reached us in our encampment before the sun was at zenith, for the spying all those people did on each other was a wonder and a disgrace, even for these who were pleased to call themselves civilized.

Even as Tashako stood at a high-arched palace window to smile royally upon the people pressing into the square below, the gates were oped to the army of Nemedia. Soon those people of Belverus were scattering, then fleeing, as iron-shod hooves rang through the streets and into the great square beneath the Window of Kings. Helmeted, mailed, well mounted and fully armed so that we were flashingly scintillant in the sunlight, the might of Nemedia clanked to a halt below the young man who stood there with the ancient crown on his head—padded somewhat.

The afternoon sun flashed then on a thousand and more uplifted blades, and Tashako—doubtless most grateful indeed to him who had slain Ushilon—began to smile, for the soldiers were lifting high their swords in a great gesture of fealty.

"Hail," we shouted out, and that chorus of warrior voices must have carried through all Belverus, "Hail, Garak, King!"

We were the army. Garak was its commander—as well as being popular. The palace guards fell away quickly before the stern-faced legions of Nemedians and Vanir-Æsir allies who came clinking into the palace. Swiftly those men of the Guard decided that they had erred; indeed Garak of Jelah was king over Nemedia, and doubtless with the blessings of Mitra and Ishtar.

And he was. King Garak entered his palace then, flanked by Hialmar and me, Ghor of the Vanir of frozen Vanaheim, leader of Æsir.

One man in the crimson-and-bronze of the Guard, a burly huge man with pale skin and a beard of scarlet, snarled and did not follow his backing comrades. His blue eyes fixed their gaze on me.

"Best flee, Tostig Bearslayer," I said, from Garak's right hand. "Else you join your father's blood-handed brother and your other cousins this day . . . cousin!"

"Bring me," Garak was bawling, "Mentumenen of Stygia!" And it was the voice of a king bent on being a king; the King.

Men moved away to obey Garak; Tostig, still glaring at me, drew steel from a well-oiled sheath. In its gemmy handsomeness, that sheath must have been a gift of his fellow plotters. And so too I drew sword, and I smiled as I stepped past Garak to meet the treacherous man of my own land. I had been provided a well-made sword by my father-in-law; Tostig, I saw, wielded that fine blade that I had latterly worn, taken from my father. *The* Sword, of Genseric the Sworder.

"This man slew my uncle, his own father!" Tostig cried, waving back those of his personal followers who would have started for his side.

"This man did treachery on the Lord Garak, Nemedia's only hope against the Picts and Hyrkanians," I shouted, the louder. "Aye,

VII. Lord General of Nemedia

and on the Lady Shanara his daughter and my wife—and on me, and thus all of us!"

With a snarl Hialmar started past me, but I stayed him and my eyes and stance showed him that to face Tostig he must first pass through me. "I have sworn an oath," I muttered, and Hialmar nodded and was still.

And we met, two barbarians of the northern snowlands. Tostig and I braced each other there amid the handsomely accoutered men of Nemedia, on the tiled floor from which soared the green marble columns of the palace of beleaguered Nemedia.

"None can face this sword and live!" Tostig snarled, and made sweep at me.

"True," I grunted, catching that terrible great blow on my new buckler and moving a pace sideward even as I launched my own overhand swing. "True, Tostig the traitor—so long as it's I who wields it!"

Now Tostig was skilled, and experienced. Too, he was nigh of a size with the bear that he had once slain, with only his sword and, at the end, a dagger. Yet I was nigh to his size though less meaty, and raised by the wolves who had imparted to me their craft and their swiftness. Skilled too was I, though perhaps less experienced than my foeman. It was the sort of man-to-man combat that might have lasted an hour or hours, for such a fight is not all swing and slash and pound as in battle among many.

Yet we were both impatient. Surely Tostig knew he was lost, but meant to exact what he thought of as vengeance and then take with him all the others he could, while they cut him down for his treachery. My impatience was of a different order. He was but one of four against whom I had sworn myself, and two others were surely in the palace. Tostig Bearslayer was in the way.

We circled, glaring at each other over our shield-rims.

I essayed a swift sideward cut, ranging upward so that he jerked up his buckler, and then sought to take his inner thigh on the backswing. But Tostig's buckler dropped swiftly to deflect that backhand slash, and his huge thick arm sent a cut that should have had my head flying far. I blocked it with buckler, twisting the shield so that the blade scraped aside and drew him slightly off-balance, and drove in. Desperately he yanked his shield back to protect himself. My sweeping chop natheless imbedded the entire width of my blade in his side—along with twisted bits of metal from his ring-mail.

I like to have died then, for my sword was wedged in mail and flesh and bone, and Tostig was fighting and heedless of the fact that he should be collapsing at my feet. He struck swiftly, even as the pain twisted his face and his blood splashed forth. I who prided myself on my swiftness moved not swiftly enough, and his edge crashed down on my helm. The sensation was that of a heavy blow; the sound was as of a clangourous metallic thunder. The sound echoed and echoed again, and I staggered, and twisted my blade from out his side and kicked him where no man can bear it. My blood-waked sword split his skull as he bent. Tostig crashed down with a force that rang loudly in the hall—-and sent pain leaping up my ankle, for he had fallen onto my foot. Blood spurted high to drench my leggings.

Only then did I become aware of the tickling at the side of my face; blood was running from beneath my helmet. I knew then that he had cloven the metal with that great fine sword, and I had moved swiftly enough at that—to save my life, if not my skin.

Legs ajerk like a wrung-neck fowl, Tostig was dead, and none opposed us among the staring members of the Guard. I pulled off my helmet and touched my head. I found but a split there, in the skin sheathing my skull. I had lost a great bit of hair, though its pale mass had taken enough of this blow so that my skull was unharmed.

Indeed, I had taken the only wound in Garak's gaining a kingdom.

Even as two men wrestled with me to keep me still whilst they pressed cloth to my head and sought to bind it there, there were shouts from a higher story of the palace, and then more shouts rose from outside. I myself held the poultice—a torn-off strip of the cloak of a king yet uncrowned—in place whilst we all whirled and rushed outside. In my hand once again was my father's sword.

We were in time to follow the direction of many men's gazes. From the palace itself, seemingly from a window though it could never have got through even one of those high-arched windows of Nemedia, flapped a huge black bird. Nay, hardly a bird, for this was as the god of all bats, with ears and claw-sprouting webbed wings. On its back rode a man—no, a boy!

Thus did Tashako and Mentumenen gain escape from a Nemedia that no longer welcomed their presence.

Aye, Garak was king, and a man to be ruler was that pine-straight Lord of Jelah and now of all Nemedia! Many years had passed since Nemedia had a king, a real ruler. Now King Garak made more strong decisions in minutes than either Ushilon or Regent had in years.

"Ye came here to fight Picts, Lord Hialmar our welcome ally— will ye take your mountain lions west then? For the Pictish savages have spread over Aquilonia like ravening locusts, and our force at the border there is sore beset."

Hialmar nodded and grinned broadly, for he felt the Picts the worse foe of the two who threatened Nemedia. And King Garak called to one of the two scribes he was keeping busy, and directed

VII. Lord General of Nemedia

him to write out that order, and promised that were it not simply and suitably worded when handed him for seal, there would be a new scribe to the king and the chief cook would have a new aide, who had been a scribe. Thus did Garak of Nemedia decide, and delegate and press, and thus men did their best for him.

"Whiles we Nemedians have barked and snapped and striven with each other in manner unworthy of our ancestors," the king said, and right loudly, "the Hyrkanians are whipping on both Zamorans and resettled Zingarans against our eastern borders, while Brythunians and their Hyrkanian masters seek to breach the mountain defenses of Jarpnr's land to the north! Hergon: do you take the Dragon and Gryphon squadrons in all haste straight along the road to our eastern border. Fortify Irilia and Ushiloa down the line, Ushiloa whence my family springs. And Hergon: if Irilia be unbesieged—do you strike east, but no more than ten leagues within Zamora. Hear me?"

"I hear, my King," the hook-nosed man with the scar-cleft eyebrow said, and he bowed. "We obey, my King."

Already Garak was looking elsewhere, thinking elsewhere. "Ganrid: see to the preparation of a proclamation. The Picts would possess our beloved Nemedia; the blood-mad Hyrkanians would ride over our fields—and now a mage of Stygia has seen fit to do battle on us in his way. He has seized the minds of my son the Lord Tashako, and King Ushilon of beloved memory, and we are saddened and much wroth. For though we have driven Mentumenen from amongst us, he has taken away our beloved son!"

That was hardly the way of it, but I remembered clever Garak's previous talk of priorities and that which was politick amid the intricacies of command. Very well then; so Ushilon was of beloved memory, and poor sweet Tashako was a captive of Mentumenen, rather than his fleeing ally!

The eagle-darting eyes of the king alit on me.

"Lord Ghor, right hand of our ally Hialmar and now of myself!"

"Aye, Lord King," I said, but I gave him a challenging look. Already I had told him, not for other ears for that would not have been *politick*, that there was but one assignment I would accept of him. Standing there with bandaged head and girt with my father's sword, I waited to hear it.

"In the absence of a priest, your marriage to my daughter is hereby proclaimed existent in the eyes of all Nemedians, and blessed by the Goddess herself!"

I smiled, and now I offered him a slight bow. He was no fool, to seek to order me to do else than that which I was bent on doing. And he accepted me as his son-in-law.

"Scribe: a letter to the Agha Junghaz of Turan, emir of that land: Garak, King of the Nemedians, has been the victim of palace treachery, and his daughter, the wife of the trusted Lord Ghor of Wolfland in Vanaheim, lord and general of Nemedia, was wrongfully sent into Turan by an evil mage of Stygia. This Mentumenen seeks thus to control both our lands. Advise him that he has not been dealing with Ushilon, King, despite the seals or documents he may hold. Garak, King of the Nemedians, thanks the Agha Junghaz for turning over to the Lord General Ghor his wife and my daughter, and for providing them with escort through Turan, Zamora-that-was, and—Corinthia. For best ye avoid Brythunia on your return, Ghor; I mean to make it ours by year's end, and we'll have no friends there!"

While the scribe scratched away on his tablet, the king my father-in-law and I gazed at each other.

"Bring her home, Ghor."

"I shall bring her home, Lord King."

And on the morrow I departed Belverus and rode eastward, with a little caravan hastily composed and consisting of twelve of my own Æsir and fifteen Nemedians. All of us were robed as merchants and drovers—and beneath those travellers' robes all of us wore mail and carried good steel.

Chapter VIII
The Oath of Agha Junghaz
Manly Wade Wellman

Necessarily, it would be a journey of days from Nemedia to Turan, and nothing as straight as the flight of an arrow. I was glad that my men were chosen from among the best warriors and wayfarers, all mounted on fine, hardy horses. My sub-chief of Æsir, grizzled, lean Skorla, could guide us by sun and stars; for he had ventured beyond Cimmeria and had commanded a ship on the western ocean, a pirate vessel as I surmised.

Pict-held Ophir and Hyrkanian-held Corinthia constantly sent out armies to fight each other; but lately they had raged to something of a standstill below Nemedia, and I hoped, optimistically, that for a time they would fall back to east and west for fear of each other. I led my party south out of Belverus, along the border between Ophir and Corinthia, toward the far desert reaches of Koth. But early on a bright morning, my outrider to the left slid in at a dead run, pointing to where a dark cloud of horsemen came galloping.

"Hyrkanians!" he cried. "Hundreds!"

"Face them, all of you!" I yelled back at the column. "Close in—now, dismount. Every fourth man hold the horses."

It was done swiftly. I marshalled my score of men on foot.

"Each of you string his bow and notch his arrow," I ordered, riding along the front of my little line. "Stand ready to shoot, all, but no man looses a shaft until I give word."

And I myself slid the loop of my bowstring into its nock on the stave and whipped an arrow from quiver as I sat my mount.

On they rode at us, those Hyrkanians, howling their medley of warcries. My men stood steady as a wall. Some of them had thrust other arrows into the earth at their feet, ready to snatch and launch in their turn. Grim as the situation was, I took time to exult in my brave, keen fighters.

The very smallness of our force made the Hyrkanians disdain ordinary good tactics. Had they spread out, their right and left elements could have curved in to crush us. But they charged in a dense body, waving swords and shields.

"Aim for their horses," I told my men, who had drawn to their very shoulders. "Now!"

For the Hyrkanians were no more than fifty long strides away as I loosed my own shot.

Our little blizzard of arrows sang in the bright air. Next moment a whole front rank of men and horses went down in a kicking mass. Others rode upon these from behind and floundered to earth in return. We heard confused orders yelled, saw an effort to regroup. My own men raised a deep-shouted cry of triumph, while they sped more arrows. These found more targets, added to the confusion. So well had our volleys gone that the Hyrkanians were falling back, to the support of more from behind. Again an exultant whoop from my archers. Had I given the word, they would have mounted and counterattacked.

But Skorla spurred to my side, pointing behind him.

"See, they come," he panted. "Picts, there at the west—"

It was true. Another great rush over the plain at our rear, shaggy men on shaggy horses, poising lances, hurrying to kill.

Instantly I made a decision, or something made it for me.

"Mount, all!" I shouted. "Away to the south. Every man with shaft on string—we'll fight our way clear of both armies—quick's the word!"

They needed no second command. Tumbling into their saddles, they rode headlong after me, away southward. At the same moment, the Picts came on from their quarter, while opposite them the rallied Hyrkanians launched a new deadly charge.

Somehow, we managed it. We rode clear of both those incoming rushes, sending a few arrows at those who at the last seemed to try to head us off on either hand. I bent over the tossing mane of my flying horse and urged him to a swifter scamper. Behind us two war parties, hating each other as they rode, rushed together.

I glanced back, just as they drove into each other, two close lines of battle. There was a smash of sound all over the land and up into the sky, like the thunder of falling timbers. I saw men and horses hurled head over heels by the impact. Those who kept their saddles rode into each other's ranks, swords flashing, lances driving.

"Faster, faster," I had wit to say, and I heard my order repeated. We sped away south, over a plain which, as I saw gratefully, was a desolate one, not a land to support great bodies of troops who must graze their horses and find water for legions of parched throats.

Our method, or our luck, had served our turn. We got away from that desperate struggle of Picts and Hyrkanians, who must forget our small handful to fight each other. Far overhead slid black specks that were birds of prey. They had seen from afar, were gathering in hopes of gorging on slain flesh.

"You are a chieftain among chieftains, Ghor," came the voice of Skorla as he rode up alongside.

"I did the only thing to do," I half-snapped. "Bid the men check

VIII. The Oath of Agha Junghaz

their pace. Now we are away, we must not ride our horses to death."

I did not speak exultantly, and Skorla grinned.

"I am like you, Ghor," he said. "Our arrows did us service, but I have always thought that even a woman can use a bow and kill safely from a distance. I read rightly your thought, it is more a man's business to get in close and strike with the sword."

"I did the only thing to do," I said again. "Let us hope for no more such pressing attentions."

Our luck held there, too. I had been right about the barrenness of the land. There was only scanty grass for our few horses, only rare water-holes for them and us. Not so much chance of a true enemy threat there, and in the days that followed we were not attacked. We saw only little parties of nomads beyond Koth's southwestern border, knots of half a dozen or so who scouted us from ridges but never dared to come close.

The thirsty land was flat for hours as we approached the boundary of Turan. Undoubtedly their patrols knew of our coming in plenty of time to gather and challenge. More than a hundred of them to our twenty-eight, half of them mounted. They wore loose gowns over their mail, with gaudy scarfs twisted around their spiked steel caps. I drew my men in close order and rode at the head of them, into Turan.

"Stand in your tracks!" bawled the biggest Turanian. Under his open gown I saw oiled links of chain mail. His blue-black beard was combed into wings, right and left. On one arm rode a round buckler, his other hand poised a great curved sword. His comrades spread into what looked like a line of battle, with ready bows and lances.

"Stand!" he whooped again, and I signalled my own party to halt. "What are you doing on Turanian ground without leave?" he challenged.

"Respect the messenger of a king," I threw back, my own hand seeking my sword beneath my cloak. "I have come with a letter for Agha Junghaz, emir of Turan, from Garak, most powerful ruler of Nemedia."

"Who is Garak, and where is Nemedia?" sneered another Turanian horseman. "We know of neither one nor the other. Our duty here is to turn back strangers whose coming is not granted by orders from the palace at Aghrapur."

"Aye, and there is no word about such as you," the wing-bearded man told me. "Back with you the way you came—no, wait. By the look of you, you are merchants. Perhaps you have something worth our taking."

I disliked him more with every word he trumpeted. "Whatever we have may be hard to take from us," I said, and motioned my own men to hold still while I spurred toward the blusterer. "You talk too much for a fighting man," I declared.

"Are you young or old?" he jeered. "Your hair is as white as a blizzard."

"And yours is as murky as mud," I returned.

"What say you, friends?" he addressed those near him. "Shall I make us some sport with this white-haired fool?"

He flourished his great sword so that it winked like lightning. He lifted his shield and rode at me, and I drove in spurs and rode at him.

It was over almost as it started. He tried to send his horse against mine to make it stumble, but I twitched bridle to come alongside him. Down swept his blade. I caught it on the edge of my buckler, pushed it up, and slid my point into his chest, through mail and bone and a hand's breadth out beyond. As he tumbled from the saddle I cleared my weapon with a swift, strong pull, then kneed my horse's flank to make him center along the front of the Turanian patrol.

"Who next, while I have my hand in?" I challenged. "If you like, fetch out as many of you as I have followers. Sport was promised you by your friend who now lies so languidly remote. Sport let it be, then. After we ride through you, I'll do my message in your town of Aghrapur."

Their ranks stirred, as though to charge.

"Wait!"

That was a deep-chested shout from behind them, and into view rode one I had not noticed. He was mounted on a sorrel horse, his sooty beard bristled. Silver mountings on his armor showed him to be an officer.

"Let us talk, stranger," he said. "If you have a written message for our ruler, give it to me."

"I will put it only into the hand of Agha Junghaz," I said.

"You are in trouble already," he warned me, coming close but not within sword-sweep. "You have already butchered a prized trooper of our emir's border guard—"

"You saw that he struck first," I reminded. "I struck last, and needed no second stroke."

"Well, it becomes more and more a matter for judgment yonder in Aghrapur. You will be escorted thither, you and your men. Here, Daula, choose out a detail to accompany them. Now, you who call yourself a messenger, put up your sword."

"Willingly, if you and your men do likewise."

He obliged. I wiped my blade on a fold of my mantle and returned it to its sheath.

The ride to Aghrapur took the rest of that day. We followed a

VIII. The Oath of Agha Junghaz

good road between green fields and tufts of orchard that contrasted with the weary desert behind us. Daula, commander of the escort, was a slim youngster with spikes of mustache, who chatted with me as cheerfully as though I had not just killed a comrade of his. He boasted of Turanian prosperity and culture, pointing out pleasant country dwellings as we trotted, and said that early Hyrkanian successes in the north of Turan had been cancelled with a strong counter-advance that caused the Hyrkanians to draw back and move through colder regions above to invade Zamora and Brythunia.

"Hyrkania is not zealous to overthrow us," he smiled.

"Perhaps they keep their zeal for attacking Nemedia," I offered. "They will prosper there no more than with you."

"Perhaps Turan and Nemedia could be allies," said Daula.

"It is of that possibility my message speaks."

At sundown we rode into Aghrapur. There were towering tawny walls with a broad double gate of brass-faced timbers. Inside, the streets were white-paved, with rows of shops rich with fabrics, housewares, fruits and vegetables. The people looked well fed and well dressed, in long gowns and headdresses wound of colored fabric. So loose were their draperies I could not judge of a man's strength or a woman's grace.

Central in Aghrapur, a low, dubious structure of coarse dark stone huddled among taller buildings. No windows in its walls, but a broad, hooded door like a gaping mouth. From blackness within drifted questing curls of smoke.

"The temple of Set, master of darkness," Daula informed me. "We worship Set in Turan. To him are made sacrifices of slaves and prisoners. All things are Set's. To speak by his name is our most binding oath."

"You love dark Set," I suggested.

"We fear him and his deep domain. Fear is stronger than love."

Mentumenen, wherever he was fled, also served Set. Reflecting on that, I wondered how baleful might be these Turanians in their own right.

We moved on past the temple, until we saw beyond the city to a tossing expanse of water, bright to the far horizon. Almost beside it rose the towering marble palace of the emir, stories and stories of it, with a domed roof and a lean spire. A sentinel at the door wanted me to turn over the message to Agha Junghaz. Again I insisted that I myself would deliver it. Sleek, imperious officers came to discuss the matter. At last our horses were led away and my followers and I were ushered into a spacious chamber with cushioned sofas and tapestry-draped walls and a crystal fountain at center. We waited there under the curious eyes of guards. At last one of the officials, a plump, curly-bearded man named Kondundu, returned.

"You alone will be admitted to our emir's great presence," he addressed me loftily. "Lay aside all weapons."

I put my sword and dagger in Skorla's keeping and followed Kondundu along a corridor, then another corridor. A curtain twitched from a narrow side doorway and for a moment a lovely, dusky woman looked out. At last we reached an arched portal with jasper facings guarded by a sentry poising lance in either hand, and I was ushered to where a man sat a great green-jewelled throne, a man with gold-circleted brows and a robe that looked to be of spun silver. Kondundu flung himself prostrate. I stood erect.

"Most mighty lord of Turan, this is the Nemedian envoy of whom your gracious ears deigned to hear me speak," jabbered Kondundu, then he went awkwardly back on all fours.

I had been studying the throne room. Its furniture was richly elegant. On all sides were curtained doorways with, I doubted not, armed men behind each curtain. In a nook rose an altar of many-hued jewels. Over it brooded the image of Set in black stone, a misshapen body with the grotesque, calculating face of a sharp-nosed beast. Then I turned to look at Agha Junghaz, and Agha Junghaz looked at me.

He was plumply well-proportioned. His smooth face had brilliant eyes and a slender nose and pursed mouth. His beard was trimmed and waxed to a tendril. It looked to be dyed with red. In one white hand he held a sceptre, a gold rod twined with a green-enamelled snake. His other hand cuddled a lizard in his lap. That lizard flickered its tongue at me.

"I am told that you bring a letter from Garak of Nemedia," said his cold voice. "We are far from there, but I thought that the rightful ruler was Ushilon." His eyes combed me. "Is it Nemedian custom not to bow before a throned emir?"

"Nemedians stand before their king, who is Garak since Ushilon died," I answered. "Here, sire, is Garak's word, by my hand from him to you."

I gave him the vellum. He read it, moving his petulant lips silently.

"You are the Lord Ghor, mentioned here," he said at last. "This will take time and thought in the answering."

"With leave, sire, it seems a simple thing to read and reply," I said, as ceremoniously as I could. "King Garak desires that I be given his beloved daughter the Lady Shanara, who is your guest, that I may fetch her back to Nemedia."

"Shanara," he breathed, his hand stroking the lizard's gleaming back. "Shanara. When I see her, my eyes are dazzled as by a heavenly spirit. She is beautiful as music."

He looked up at me. "When I saw her, I said to myself, 'Agha

VIII. The Oath of Agha Junghaz

Junghaz, emir of Turan, has a hundred wives. Why should he not have a hundred and one?' For that reason, she now undergoes teaching and preparation. By signs of the stars and moon, the proper time is at hand for me to wed her."

The blood surged within me. "I point out to you, sire, what the letter tells. She is already my wife, under Nemedian law."

He stroked the lizard. "A strange law, for she was here in Turan when the marriage was declared. Turan does not recognize that marriage."

"One ruler recognizes the word and might of another," I said, and could not keep my voice down. "I represent Garak. I am his son-in-law."

"Were I his son-in-law, he and I would be on better terms," returned Junghaz. "I need time to think. You have leave to go."

Kondundu was beside me, gesturing. Furious, I left Junghaz's presence and walked off down the corridors.

Myriads of impulses stirred in me. What if I struck down this gilded companion, whirled into the throne room again, charged upon Agha Junghaz and demanded Shanara of him? But he was surrounded by guards. I would be struck on all sides. And Shanara would be his. I must devise a plan, a sure one, not suicidal.

In the chamber where my men waited, they did not seem to have worried in my absence. Music filled the air, from a slave orchestra of harps and pipes and light drums. Fair, bare-limbed girl slaves carried tall vases of wine, filling cups for the men. There was laughter. All in that room seemed happy, save myself.

"Will not my lord drink of this wine?" murmured a soft voice behind me. "It is the emir's own choice favorite."

She was well shaped, scantily clad in gauzy fabric set with amethysts. Her head-scarf was cunningly embroidered in more colors than I knew. She offered a golden cup, brimming with drink that gave its odor at once of flowers and fruits. I gazed at her. She was no young thing, she was a full woman, but comely. She shook her head above the cup.

"Do not drink deep," she whispered.

I tasted the cup. "You are kind and fair," I said. "Forgive me if the spirit of another, fairer than you, fills my soul."

"Shanara," came her whisper, and I spilled wine on the floor.

"Do you dare name her to me?" I growled. "Who are you?"

"Speak low, for both our lives. I am Jahree, honored as the foremost of Agha Junghaz's harem. But now, mad for Shanara, he vows he will put us all aside for her. She fills his soul as she fills yours." She poured more wine for me. "Seem to be careless, cheerful—eyes are upon us. A close look would recognize me and we would both die; you as swiftly as his killers could manage, I by torture. I will help you win away from here, taking her with you."

"You make me trust you," I said. "What is to happen?"

"You and your men are to be fuddled with drink. Then you will be imprisoned, for sacrifices on the altar of Set. Agha Junghaz will return word to your ruler in Nemedia that your party has died of an unhappy accident but that he, Agha Junghaz, cements an alliance by taking Shanara for his consort. Do you wonder that I am desperate?"

"Desperation becomes you," I said, for she was lovely. "You took the risk of coming to tell me. How shall I defeat all this?"

"We can talk no longer under these watching eyes. Here, this corner is dark." She pointed a toe to draw cushions together. "Drop your cloak upon them, it will look as though you fell asleep. Pour out that magically drugged wine."

I did both of these things.

"Now, come with me."

She threw herself behind a great ornamented sofa. I did the same. A panel had opened in the floor. I followed her down upon steps as the panel closed above us.

That lower passage was dark and dubious. I heard a flutter of wings, felt a brush against my jaw, as something like a bat flew by. I barely saw Jahree's outline. Her hand took mine, to lead me.

In the dark, I gathered a sense of walls close on either side of a passage—jagged stone walls, drenched with damp. I did not know where we were going, but Jahree did. We climbed a troubling flight of steps, again we went down a winding, slippery ramp. At last she stopped me, within sight of a wash of dim radiance.

"One of his guards is there, behind a curtain," she whispered. "Settle him and go into the throne room. But swear you will not kill Agha Junghaz."

"If I did, it would but procure another tyrant on his throne," I said. "I cannot stop here to kill all tyrants."

"Let him live," she insisted. "You can be upon him before he knows. If you are the man you seem to be, you will make him swear by Set to let you go, and Shanara with you. He dare not break that oath."

"You would make me think you are kind," I said. "I know little of women, but I think all this is for your own profit."

"How wise you are. I want to be queen, not a slave of Junghaz's new queen."

She let go my hand. I tiptoed toward that wash of light.

The guard stood, sword in right hand while his left held back the curtain to peer out. So intent was he on what he saw that I was upon him without his knowing. I too could see out there. Agha Junghaz sat his throne and stroked his lizard. Before him stood

VIII. The Oath of Agha Junghaz

Shanara.

Who can speak of her sweet girl-figure, her elfin face, her eyes like brighter jewels than any in Turan or Nemedia or anywhere? She stood, silent but proud, her sun-golden hair fell in rich tumbles about her face. He talked earnestly.

I could not kill that guard without giving him a chance. I tapped his shoulder. He whirled, stared, struck with his sword. Refusing its touch against mine, I sidestepped and gave him the point in the throat, then stepped across him as he fell.

"You will be queen of Turan, Shanara," Junghaz was saying. "All things will be to your wish."

"My wish is that you send me home, my lord," she said, quietly but not timidly.

"I would never smile, never sleep, if you went. Think, Shanara..."

I crossed the floor in two great, flying leaps. I heard Shanara cry out, I did not know if in joy or terror. From the curtained recesses stepped armed and armored guards. But I leaned above that figure of royal vanity on the throne. My sword touched the waxed tendril of beard at his throat.

"Move," I dared him. "It will be your last move in this world you foul with your presence."

The drooping lids peeled from his eyes. "You are at my mercy," he stammered. "My guards—"

"If one tried to come here, you would not see it," I said. "Emir Agha Junghaz, your perfidy was noised through the air to me. You would plan to slay me and my friends by craft. Now, unsay your plans. Swear by Set that we go free, and Shanara with us."

"By Set?" he squealed, his eyes still wide with fear of me. "Men tremble to say that oath."

"Because it cannot be broken," I said. "By Set you shall swear that Shanara, my men and myself will leave your dominions safely. Swear at once, or you will know Set face to face in his dark domain. My sword yearns to slide through your neck."

He started to lift his trembling hands. I moved the sword but a finger's breadth. It pricked his soft throat. He slumped down.

"I swear," he moaned.

"Swear by Set," I commanded again. "And loudly, that all may hear."

"By Set, then," he raised his voice. "By Set I swear that all of you go free—you, Shanara, your men—beyond my borders. That I will respect you as envoys from a brother king and set you on your homeward way."

"By Set," I insisted again.

"I swear it by the name of Set, who hears me," he almost

screamed. "You are safe, by my word, to leave my domain."

I lowered my sword, but kept it ready. He clapped his hands. From the curtained nooks started his guards again.

"Hear me, all," Junghaz called to them, his voice taut with fury. "Bear witness. I have sworn that this comer from Nemedia may lead his followers home, and with him the lady Shanara." His voice almost broke upon her name. "This in the name of Set, who cannot be forsworn in Turan. Go you, and you and you, proclaim my decision and decree throughout Aghrapur."

Three of them hurried away. Junghaz, now that my sword did not menace him thirstily, seemed to compose himself.

"We feast tonight, you as an honored guest at my table," he said. "Tomorrow you will be escorted on the way you came."

At last, Shanara moved and spoke. "Ghor, you man of men," she breathed, "I had given up hope. I should have known that you would save me."

I put an arm around her softness and led her away. Junghaz probed our backs with his helplessly angry eyes.

At our chamber, I found my men more stumblingly confused than simple wine-drinking should have made them. Sternly I forbade them to drink more, and ordered the slave girls and musicians away. Then I prodded Skorla and two other under-officers into helping me. We marched the men to and fro, made them breathe air in lungfuls, until in some degree their minds cleared and they moved more surely. As we rejoiced over this, Kondundu appeared to announce in his most consequential manner that Junghaz would entertain us at a feast of honor.

That feast was spread in a mighty hall, carpeted with rich fabrics and hung with embroidered drapes. The tables were set with silver and gold dishes. Junghaz had summoned his lords and officers to sit side by side with the strangers he delighted to honor. I was placed at the high table, sitting at one end with Shanara while Junghaz and Jahree sat at the other. Various nobles ranged along the sides. There were delicate meats, savory roasted birds, sweet pastries shaped like stars, flowers, crescents. Jahree graciously came around the table, pouring wine with her own hands. Junghaz rose to propose a toast.

"To our guests here with us," he proclaimed, "and to the coming good friendship between our realm and that of Garak of Nemedia."

He spoke as if he truly meant it. The toast was drunk amid cries of approval. Jahree, refilling my goblet, took advantage of the hubbub to whisper in my ear.

"Be vigilant," she urged. "He still means to have Shanara."

"I have surmised that," I said back, smiling as though we were

VIII. The Oath of Agha Junghaz

exchanging a jest.

"His oath forces him to see you safe to the border, but—"

"Aye," I said. "Beyond there, we leave him free of his oath."

"His patrols will muster to chase you into the desert, twenty to one. Overwhelm you with spears and arrows, save only Shanara alive and bring her back to Junghaz."

"So he thinks," I said. "I have been thinking, too."

More toasts followed. I rose and drank to the health of our host and his people and to my party's safe journey away. Junghaz smiled into his cup. A slave brought me a bowl of grapes, blue and sweet.

"Skorla," I said to him at the next table, "this is better fare, I venture, than you had sailing that western sea."

"And a steadier footing than a deck," he laughed.

That made up my mind for me. There was a final round of toasts, and all had the leave of Junghaz to go.

Back in my quarters, I told my followers to belt on their weapons. Then they followed me in close order to the corridor and the entry, with Shanara in their midst. A sentinel set himself in my way.

"Not until dawn will your horses be ready," he warned us back.

"We make you a present of the horses," I snapped. "Stop us at your peril. Your emir has sworn by Set that none will harm us."

He howled for the officer of the guard as I swept him aside. We strode into the open. Overhead blazed a round, pale moon. I led at a swift stride around the corner and toward the docks. There rode several craft.

Loungers stared as we swarmed aboard the best looking of the galleys. A couple of sleepy sailors were on deck watch. We set them overside and I cut the mooring hawser with a great slash of my sword.

"Skorla," I said, "you are a captain of the sea again."

"Aye!" he shouted happily. "Fall to the oars, all of you, push us away! Ply mightily!"

The men worked the oars, unhandily but with a will, growing surer with every stroke. Skorla counted for them as he took the tiller in practiced hand and pointed us out upon the face of the Vilayet Sea, under the blazing moon and the skyful of stars. Behind us rose a jumble of dismayed cries. The servants of Junghaz had found out what we were doing, but too late.

"Where away, Ghor?" spoke Skorla from his tiller.

"Eastward," I shouted back, my arm around Shanara. "No landing on Turanian shores, for Junghaz to plan our destruction. Out and out, to what adventure may wait."

Soon the crew got up the square sail under Skorla's bellowed orders. An offshore breeze filled it. We beat forward over the moon-touched waves.

"What is beyond all this water?" Shanara asked me, holding herself close.

"More land," was all I could reply. "Unknown land. But we shall know that land, my lady Shanara, and what it holds for us."

Chapter IX
The Mouth of the Earth
Darrell Schweitzer

My Æsir and the Nemedians sang lusty battle songs as they rowed. I stood by the tiller with Skorla that first night, Shanara at my side, gazing ahead as we all did into the east. We had a good wind behind us, and we had already put many leagues between ourselves and the no doubt fuming Agha Junghaz before we witnessed our first dawn at sea. First there was a faint red glow on the water, or below it, and to me it was an omen presaging blood and slaughter, or else evidence of some vast battle fought by sea-gods beneath the waves. Then all the eastern horizon was alight, and the edge of the sun's golden shield appeared, and the waves sparkled orange and brilliant yellow and almost blinding white. The stars fled with the darkness, and the familiar constellations vanished, those of the Swordsman and the Warwain the last to go. It was a spectacular sight, and even I, Ghor the Strong, who had no particular sense of beauty and had grown up in a world of cold sunrises over glimmering glaciers, was moved by it. I had never been to sea before and this was the beginning of my first day on its breast, out of sight of land, in a strange new world. That dim, distant, and nearly forgotten thing known as James Allison was overawed by the sight, till he feared his ecstatic and weak heart would burst. He had never travelled at all in his current life, never known the basic and primal things of nature. He too had never before seen the sun, the world's first god, climb out of the belly of its mother the ocean, as fresh and newly-born as it had on the first day of creation.

Some of the others were also strangers to this environment. They stared about constantly as they toiled, gaping at watery wonders, at leaping porpoises and flying fish. Then, when Skorla called a rest, tied the tiller in place with a rope, and let the wind alone propel us, one of the Nemedians cried out, "I have such a thirst I could swallow all this!" And he waved his arm grandiosely, indicating the whole of the sea, and went to the side, leaned over, and put a handful of water to his lips.

An instant later he was sputtering and coughing.

"Horsepiss!" he spat. "It's poisoned! What magic is this?"

Skorla laughed, and the others joined in, even those who might have made the same mistake. The Nemedian put his hand to his sword-hilt, but the commander's laughter changed to a low growl, his look to an iron stare, and the man reconsidered. He went to the far front of the vessel to sulk.

"By the way," I whispered into Skorla's ear. "How much drinking water and food do we have on this thing?"

He looked shocked, as if some fell Stygian god had bewitched him.

"*By the Gods!*" he cried. "Am I the biggest fool to walk this earth since Arus the priest?"

"Peace friend. What is the matter? And lower your voice, lest your alarm cause discontent among the men."

"Brave Ghor, in our haste to seize this ship we forgot to provision her, or even check to see if she was provisioned. Of course we had little time, but so caught up were we in the boldness of our plan, and so grand a jest it seemed to beard the stupid Turanian thus, that we simply cut loose and sailed, without ever venturing below these decks."

He was genuinely ashamed. He had boasted of how fine a sea captain he had once been, and now his pride came crashing to ruin in this blunder.

"It was my plan and my order," I said. "You and the others carried it out well. There were far greater perils facing us in Turan than the prospect of an empty belly. When the wolf finds prey, he gorges himself, but when there is no meat, he is patient. Take after his example and be patient, Skorla."

"Aye! That is good advice, but will the others follow it? These city-bred women of Nemedians will turn against us if they don't get their dainties."

"Then we'll have to bash a few heads in. I am not afraid of that. Are you?"

"No, of course—"

"Then in the meantime let us go and see what we have."

The ship we had taken was sleek and shallow. It had no vast holds as Skorla said a lumbering merchantman would, just a cramped, stuffy wooden cave below the decks where cargo could be stored. It was all I could do as one used to the open of the wild to force myself to enter it.

Our inventory produced about four hundred glazed and brightly painted dishes, pots, and earthen lamps, no food at all, and one half empty, foul-smelling cask of water. Obviously, said Skorla, the vessel had just returned from a voyage the night we took her, and the owners had packed every available bit of space full of cargo, including only what stores the crew would need to survive their short trip. And it would have been a short trip too, for ships such as this one were used for light and swift trading all along the Vilayet Sea. The object of such commerce was to bring a few valued items to a

IX. The Mouth of the Earth

port quickly and sell them at high prices, before slower moving vessels could bring the same product in quantity and undercut. My friend knew all these things from his days as a pirate. He had never raided on this sea, but elsewhere things were much the same, and he knew this kind of vessel well. I had no interest in business, and looked on the pottery as useless baubles even more contemptible than gold, but I did appreciate the fact that our craft could outrun most others.

"And would it not be fleeter still," I asked, "if we were rid of this earthen garbage."

"It would."

So I ordered the men to throw it all into the sea. A couple of the Nemedians hesitated, saying that we should sell the stuff for gold, but when I gave them a choice of swimming back to Turan as merchants, dying quickly by my sword, or living to gain better loot as warriors, they obeyed me. Soon the ship's stomach was emptied, and the oars carried us even more swiftly from our foes than before, but in the act of crawling below to fetch out the cargo, all had learned the secret I could not hope to keep from them. We had no food and only a desperately low supply of filthy water. I rationed the water, as Skorla told me was done at sea, giving each man a ladle of it twice a day. There was some grumbling, and ultimately I did have to crack two or three Nemedian skulls, but there was no serious trouble. The Æsir respected and feared me, and they enforced my will merely by a glance, a touch to a sword, and simply by their towering stature and massive limbs.

Then after a day the same nature which had once charmed us fumed, like a treacherous courtier, and began to dispense slow and subtle poison.

The wind died, and becalmed we sat day after day, until the very air seemed stagnant and filled with sweat. Skorla bade the men row until they could struggle no longer, and even he and I took our place at the oars, leaving the tiller held in place by rope. When the rest period came, each took his bitter ration of water, and there was no more singing, and very little talking. All toiled miserably, like slaves, in the sullen heat, until night brought some relief. But well before then my fair-skinned Æsir were all red as boiled lobster and more foul-tempered toward the Nemedians than ever. None dared raise protest even in a glance or a gesture.

With the darkness, the conspiracy against us continued. A thin blanket of cloud covered the sky, just enough to hide the stars, but promising no rain. I could read the stars as well as any mariner. The ice-fields of the North are much like the sea, vast, hostile, and deceptively quiet, but without being able to see the sky, neither Skorla nor I had any idea of where we were or where we were going, save that when morning came the sun was well to the left ("to port", as Skorla called it) and both of us had to strain at the tiller to set the ship right again. Still we headed east, where lay the far shore of the Vilayet Sea, but nothing else was known. How far north or south were we? How far west? Had we drifted in the night back the way we had come, into the lap of Agha Junghaz?

Our situation became even more precarious as all grew weaker and the water cask approached empty. At ration time the ladles scraped the bottom through the scum, bringing up a putrid soup which some could not bear to drink. They talked of drinking piss, and licking the sweat from their bodies. Several were well-nigh delirious.

Once a Nemedian spied a great fish following by our side, and he leapt overboard, a knife in his teeth. It was a brave deed, and we cheered him on, but a foolish one, for before any could even think to aid him, the fish had eaten him, and vanished in a cloud of blood. Skorla told me that the creature was named "shark" and in it the natures of the lion, the wolf, the bear, and the vulture were joined together. It was the most fearsome thing beneath the waves, save for the great whale, which, I gathered, was like a swimming mountain with a spewing fountain on its summit.

Far away there were sea birds flying, but they seemed to shun our ship. Skorla remarked that this was contrary to his experience. Usually such fowl freely rested on a ship's sail-tree, the thing he called "mast." Still, whenever one came a little closer than the others, someone would shoot at it. Eventually I had to command the men not to waste any more arrows.

All this while Shanara lay limply in a cabin which Skorla said had been built for the ship's captain. It was in the far rear. We stood on its roof when at the tiller, and it alone was big enough for a man to stand in, and it had windows for ventilation. My mate spent most of her time resting on a silken bed. The rolling of the decks had proven too much for her land-born stomach and feet.

I would join her each night as soon as the watery sunset had faded, but after a while we both were so exhausted from the heat, the hunger and our thirst that we had to forswear even lovemaking. All I could do was curse blindly at the gods, the fates, the magic, or the stupidity which had led me to die here, slowly shrivelling away like a piece of discarded carrion.

Late on the seventh night, the Æsir who stood watch by the tiller let out a hoarse croak and stamped his foot on the planking above my head. I awoke, and went outside to see what was the matter. I found the man standing on his tiptoes, peering ahead, and Skorla was with him.

"Look," the Æsir said faintly, pointing.

IX. The Mouth of the Earth

The ship's bow was pointed into the rising sun, but that sun was not whole. Only the rim of its blinding disc was visible. The rest was a jagged blackness joined to the sea.

"Skorla, has the shark taken a bite of the sun while it is within his reach?"

My comrade only laughed in response and clapped me on the back and said, "No, north-born Ghor, no! It is an island and the sun is rising behind it." He began to shout. "Land! The gods have smiled on us after all! We're saved!"

Both of us were bellowing orders at once. Men scrambled to their benches and oars slapped the water, and the both of us shrieked with our thirst forgotten, "Row! Row till your backs break and your arms fly out of your shoulders! Row!"

They rowed, filled with hope, and singing as best they could with parched throats and cracked lips. The ship glided like a serpent over the waves. For the first time in what seemed like aeons a wind rose. The air grew cool and our sail filled, and aided us like a whole legion of fresh oarsmen. We moved so quickly that we seemed to fly from wavetop to wavetop. Then the sail was furled, and we beached the boat. As the sun rose the island grew from a black speck to a hump of thickly forested mountain rising above the waves. At the top stood bare, sheer stone cliffs. At the base was a wide, sandy shore onto which the sea drove us.

Just before we landed my lady Shanara emerged from her cabin for the first time in days. I marked once again how beautiful she seemed, her hair streaming in the wind, her face pale in the morning light. She came alive again after the long dead days in the cabin.

Unsteadily, she climbed up to where Skorla and I stood, and also looked upon the island.

"I wonder if anyone lives there," she said.

I touched the hilt of Genseric's sword.

"If anyone does, they'll give us what we want, or we'll take it with our valor." Secretly I hoped there would be fighting. After days of misery and inactivity, I longed for slaughter, as I was sure the others did.

The waves did most of our work for us, driving the craft well up onto the island. Then all save Shanara leapt into the surf and dragged the vessel well onto the dry sand. After that, by unspoken consent we went at once in search of food and water. So we marched, Shanara by my side, the ship unguarded behind us.

It was good to be in the cool shade beneath the trees. They towered above us like colossal pillars, holding up the green roof of the forest. Hundreds of feet up vines criss-crossed, forming highways for armies of chattering monkeys.

We were refreshed almost at once. Heavy dew still hung on the leaves, and all of us licked it off, and arrows were spent, but this time not wasted. We feasted on monkey meat, and quaffed monkey blood. I had mine as soon as it was slain, raw, as did the Æsir, but the Nemedians built a fire and half-cooked theirs. My lady, true to her civilised upbringing, ate with them.

A while later, in the center of the island and half way up the side of the mountain, we came upon a cold stream, gurgling out of the rock. I was still suspicious of our sudden good fortune, as if someone were torturing us with hope the way a cat lets a wounded mouse run just long enough to make escape seem possible with the next swipe of its paw even more terrible.

I called a halt, commanding all to stand behind me, and the Æsir stood calmly and the Nemedians gawked, while I got down on all fours and sniffed the water. It seemed alright. I began to lap up my fill with my tongue. Then the others rushed all around me and drank deeply, pouring the cool water over them, dunking their heads in it, and rolling and splashing like squealing children.

We rested for a time, then explored the island more thoroughly. There were no inhabitants, but once there had been some. Hidden in the underbrush not far from the spring were huge stone blocks, crumbling to the touch, moss-covered and overgrown with vines, most of them nearly buried in the earth. On them were carvings like none I had seen before. Much had been erased by time and weather, but still many discernible figures remained, and few of them were human. There were a few manlike shapes, but these were small, and more often than not around the edges or in other unimportant positions. Monsters dominated the reliefs. Perhaps they were intended to be gods of some sort, huge squid-faced things with tentacles, claws and wings. They were colossi, depicted as being taller than mountains, if the curved and jagged lines behind them were supposed to be mountains.

There was also writing of some sort on the blocks, which I asked Shanara to read, but she couldn't. The script was strange to her, but it was very ancient, she said, similar to things scholars puzzled over in her country, dating back to the times of ancient kingdoms with names which to me were only noises: Valusia, Atlantis, Lemuria, and others. Perhaps they meant more to James Allison, and perhaps he more than Ghor the Strong was impressed by the final and most spectacular discovery of the day.

We found a huge stone face all but buried in the jungle floor. It had cracked long ago under tremendous forces, perhaps the rising of this isle from the sea during the great cataclysm (so speculated Allison; Ghor knew nothing of such things). The visage was that of a bird, but it was wider and flatter. It had high cheekbones like a man, and close human eyes. But it also had once possessed a beak,

IX. The Mouth of the Earth

which now had long since broken off and crumbled into dust. Still the rough stump of it was almost as high as a man is tall, and three times that wide. Perhaps to Allison this meant or suggested something, but to me, Ghor, and the others present, it was just a curiosity.

Night was rapidly approaching. I ordered a camp to be made by the spring.

"Should we not go back to the beach and guard the ship?" one of the Æsir suggested.

"No," said I. "There is no one on this isle to attack us, and if an enemy should come from the sea, it is best that he not find us in the open on the beach. We'll spy him first and have the advantage. So we camp here."

I had sentries posted, four Nemedians a good hundred paces from the camp, one in each direction, and four Æsir much closer. Thus if anyone or anything approached, the outer sentries would raise the alarm and the inner sentries would echo it, and the camp would be awake and ready to meet the danger. Besides, I did not care to sleep with only Nemedians awake to guard me. Some of them might still bear me grudges for sore heads gained on the ship.

The sunset was long and deeply red, foretelling much blood, but that I assumed was for the future, once we left this place. Shanara and I slept apart from the others that night on an outspread cloak, and for the first time in many days we had each other as wolf and mate. When sleep finally came I had no dreams.

The sentries were to be relieved every three hours. I came halfway to wakefulness once as the guards were changed and a few words were spoken. If this happened again, I slept through it. Thus, it was either in the second or third watch that I leapt to my feet to the sounds of shouting and tumult.

The moon was up and full. The bare cliffs above glowed, and the clearing by the spring where we were camped was brilliantly lit, and by moonlight I beheld something which filled me with amazement and rage. There was strife in the jungle. I could hear shouts and the clangor of steel, and others just awaking heard it also and ran to join in. But running towards me in abject terror were five Nemedians, fleeing the battle.

"*Cowards! Dogs!*" I screamed. "Will you desert Ghor and the Æsir? By all your gods you will not!"

They scattered when I raised Genseric's sword on high, and shrieked like women when I came at them in my blind rage. One tried to put a shield between himself and my anger, and I cut him a low blow beneath it, through his mailshirt and his belly and his spine, chopping his body entirely in two before his face could register anything but helpless surprise. He went down gurgling and spewing blood.

I who could run down the swiftest game had no trouble catching another of the cowards by the neck. I did not slay him at once, but yanked him to his knees, my left hand still on his throat. He stared up at me with wide eyes and whimpered, while I roared to him.

"Craven thing! What has so unmanned you?"

He stumbled, and found words. "Lord—lord—run! Run for your life and your sanity. Blackest sorcery—none can stand against—!"

I tightened my grip, all but breaking his neck.

"What foe? Speak, snivelling cur!"

"Lord, hear me and believe," he pleaded. "Legions of bronze warriors attacked the watch, men with beaked masks and plumes on their helmets, and metal wings on their backs so they seemed like furious birds as they swooped down on us out of the treetops, tearing guts with claws and swords, shooting fire with their spears!"

"And you leave the rest to fight while you escape? If you cannot live like a man, you cannot die like one." And in the strength of my fury I crushed his neck entirely with my one hand, then yanked till his head came free. I threw it at one of the fleeing figures and felled him. In all this, only seconds had passed. I would not be held from the fight myself. Whirling Genseric's huge blade over my head, and with shield raised on high, I charged into the jungle, screaming the warcry of the northern berserker.

But the battle reached me before I came to it. The Nemedian had spoken truly, and hundreds, nay, thousands of winged men were descending from the starry sky, flapping stiffly through the branches with flaming spears and silver swords in their hands, and shields of beaten gold. Were they men at all, covered from head to foot with armor, or mechanical things? I could not know as I fought them, and my mad blood-fury abolished all thoughts. I fought with speed, with strength and with agility a man of James Allison's time could never have comprehended, and I smashed metal bodies, hewing off heads and limbs. But they did not die. Some of them lay still, while others grotesquely crawled and hopped after I had maimed them. And they shed no blood, as living things would. Still I fought on, hopelessly, eternally, while more and more of them came, crowding upon one another, blotting the moon from the sky. Their wings, their masks, their shields were everywhere, a sea of metal. Around me others still fought. Sometimes between the waves of bronze and the sheets of fire I saw an Æsir, or aye, even a brave Nemedian, battling desperately, and sometimes I saw them go down. Once Skorla was beside me for an instant. Then he was gone. Then a headless, limbless trunk dropped out of the sky in front of me, sending a foe tumbling with its weight. Even in death my brave friend fought for me.

The very earth came into the fray against us. The mountain

IX. The Mouth of the Earth

trembled and roared, sending avalanches of boulders and earth down over man and harpy alike. The trees cast down their limbs, then fell, and huge vines cut the sky like whips wielded by titans.

It was more than my senses could bear. Suddenly I seemed to be alone, tumbling upward in a black cloud, then in a wave of stone and men and earth, and all I could see was the mountain peak, supreme and haughty beneath the moon. *And the face of the mountain opened up*, revealing two gigantic, red-flaming eyes, and opened again an endless cavern of a mouth, out of which came a tongue, swift as a toad's, but as powerful as a waterfall. It seized me and bore me up, and the earth was rent apart to swallow me, and all from then on was sheerest madness. First I was falling in darkness and in thunder. Still Genseric's sword was in my hand, and still I swung wildly with it, but connected with nothing. I could not even conceive of the forces at work around me. I was an ant in a raging torrent, a mere speck on a vast sea of blood and broken stone . . . Somewhere I glimpsed a huge bat-thing, and whatever primitive terror I might have had of the unknown vanished with the recognition. *Mentumenen!* He was part of this! But who else? *What else?* Even the greatest of the Stygian sorcerers could not command such forces. Even he could not make the earth move, make the mountain open its mouth. He had allies. This was the doing of gods, and things greater than gods.

Falling through utter darkness . . .

I came to . . .

Rest on a featureless ebon plain.

Before me stood a great mass of folk, and in the forefront of them were my four brothers, Raki the Swift, Sigismund the Bear, Obri the Cunning, and Alwin the Silent, plus my father Genseric, Gudrun of the Shining Locks, my mother, plus all the others I had slain, all of them with looks of venomous hatred on their faces. With them also were Agha Junghaz, the black Mentumenen, and the brat Tashako. They spoke as if with one voice:

"Hail, unnatural thing! Hail Ghor kin-slayer! All nature, all the earth and all the things beyond the earth revile thee. The most basic of all commandments hast thou violated. Does the whelp turn upon the wolf-bitch? *No!* But Ghor turned. Think not to escape thy doom, thou abomination lower than the beast! Behold! All things cry for vengeance. *Behold thy nemesis!* We are all joined together to oppose thee!"

I cannot say entirely what followed after this. There was a flash of light, then an explosion of thunder so great my whole body seemed crushed to pieces, and then, when the bedazzlement had left my eyes, I saw before me, not a crowd of foes, but a single enemy, a bronze giant vast enough that he could have held the world between his outstretched legs. His face was a featureless mask, half shrouded in dark smoke. Around his ears lightning flickered.

His sword descended slowly, inevitably, unstoppably, like the onrush of time, ready to split the earth.

And in a red dream more vivid, more fury-filled than life, I raised my own sword, not Genseric's any longer, but *my sword*, and shouted *"Ghor defies all things! Ghor exacts his own just vengeance. I will not deny what I have done. I-I shall fight all mankind, all gods, all demons. I shall flatten the earth with my sword. I shall crash down the planets. I shall uncreate all, raze all to slag and LAUGHING leap as it falls into the primal screaming chaos whence it came! Again I slay Genseric and his folk! Again, and again, and again!"*

Then the giant and I contended. Either he shrank to the stature of a man, or I grew to be a giant. I cannot say, but I think it was the latter. Nothing was clear to me, as I raged with a bloodlust even the most crazed berserker never dreamed possible. I seem to recall the earth shaken, mountains tumbled as we fought. When our blades met white sparks flew, and the heavens roared. I fought on and on, awash in faces and blood and foes the blank mask suspended before me. It was as if my whole body were crushed and crushed and crushed, beyond pain, beyond death, into a new state entirely where the senses could not follow. The only reality was hatred, the only color that of blood, the only sounds screams, grunts, and the smashing of metal upon metal.

Gradually the combat slackened. I was not aware of seeing, or of feeling anything by that point, save a slow batement of my own fury. The tide of gore receded from me. The giant was gone. I still held the sword of Genseric. And pain returned.

I found myself staggering in a daze, beneath the bright morning sun, on the beach near where our ship had landed. All around me lay the mutilated corpses of my comrades, hacked to pieces by foes of unnatural fury. The trunk of Skorla was as it had fallen, and the headless man, and the Nemedian cut in half were as I remembered.

What—how had this happened? Had those all been carried down the mountain and out of the jungle? I looked up at the bare-faced summit, and it was still, eyeless as it had always been. Birds and monkeys screeched in the trees.

I saw to my added horror and incomprehension that there were no foemen lying there, only my fellows, the Æsir and the Nemedians. And my sword alone was completely red. I could not comprehend—

I was weak, in the greatest agony I had ever known. The pain localised, to one side, then one limb. My whole body was covered with wounds, my right thigh slashed deeply, the knee laid bare to

IX. The Mouth of the Earth

the bone, but it was on my left where the greatest hurt was. I stared dumbly and saw that my arm had been hewed off just below the elbow.

Like an automaton I knelt in the bloody sand, took a belt from a dead man, and bound the wound. My mind was not functioning at all, but my survival instincts made me do this. With the effort and the added pain, I fainted, but even then I found no peace, for a thought came which forced me back into consciousness. I stumbled to my feet and ran from one end of the beach to the other, looking among the lifeless bodies, kicking them here and there. The one I sought was not among them. "Shanara! *Shanara!*"

Just before I fainted again, I chanced to look to the unknown east and see, far out over the water, scarcely more than specks, two wide-winged things I knew were not birds, carrying between them a limp burden.

Chapter X
The Gods Defied
A. E. Van Vogt

The gods had struck so murderously that, after all these years of accepting the world as it was, I was shaken. My left arm severed at the elbow, I stood on the sandy shore beside a restless sea, all the while suppressing groans of pain. Stood there with my feet sunk in the wet sand, and strove with my eagle vision to pierce the misty distances where I had last seen two flying beings carrying my beautiful lost Shanara to an unknown fate. In vain I gazed.

Yet already I could feel an inward bracing for what must surely be: the pursuit. So, tensing my muscles, grinding my teeth, I spun around. And walked again through the fallen, slaughtered dead. A stiff breeze was blowing. It stirred the trees through which I, Ghor, who had once been the Strong, moved with an outward appearance of determination.

Yet, as I trod that bloodied ground, at a deep of my being there was a strange, terrible thought . . . that the gods had finally rendered a long-considered basic decision.

Against me.

Nay, more; worse. The decision was against what I *was*. What I stood for. An awesome feeling I had, that the world of life was unfinished. And that they had been watching all these years which way the turn should go.

As the meaning and the threat of that realization grew more into my consciousness the wolf that I was in spirit, the beast in me, drew back slitted lips. I walked, then, grimly, showing hard, white teeth. And several times I spat at the emptiness and desertedness around me. It was defiance, yay.

What galled the savagery inside me was a conviction that the choice had been made too quickly. I was accidentally a product of the Croat Wild. Though pooooooed of a human brain, I belonged to the mult-millenia parade of Nature, unsullied. We beasts represented a great purity. We were in pulsing unity with the beat of the vast universe around us.

The direction of that untamed life reflected the changing climate of the immense earth on which we all dwelt. And yet, now, abruptly, from above, a fateful decision had been made to change that direction by force.

Much too soon. I could even guess, now, that the gods had de-

X. The Gods Defied 89

liberately introduced civilization. Perhaps, it was their child. And that what was to me a pallid alternative to the forests, the animals, and the primeval sea was to them an object of pride and self-congratulation. Perhaps, an exact facet of civilization appealed to them especially. What could it be? If I could decide *that*, then I would make my attack exactly at the point of their peak admiration.

With that grim thought, I ceased my tense striding. Came to a full stop. Raised my head, and glared upward. Standing there, I lifted the shining sword of Genseric until it pointed at the grey heavens above. And I roared: "Ythillin, come!" I screamed. "Mad hating woman of the Ice Gods, I would have words with thee! Ythillin!"

Can a human being dare to demand attention of the gods? He could—he can—if there is a great decision being rendered by those self-same gods. And if he—accidentally—is the only aware entity of the innumerable victims of that decision. So strong was my conviction of being the spokesman for the wilderness, I actually felt that the transformation could not really happen unless I agreed to it, or was overwhelmed.

"*Ythillin!*" I bellowed, "you cunning creature, using me to help create a civilization whereby the gods could then be fortified in destroying my kind. Despicable schemer, reveal yourself!"

I had other dark words quivering at the tip of my tongue. But they remained unuttered as a mist took form in front of me.

Sword clutched warily, I poised, waiting. Not sure of what I would do with the witch woman when she materialized.

I admit there was a taste of steely triumph as I savored the fact that my angry demand was being answered.

The feeling of a partial victory achieved . . . faded abruptly. The form had solidified, and it was not Ythillin.

With a response of horror, I recognized the creature-being in the mist: Mentumenen!

So this was the answer of the gods. Not Ythillin, she of the Ice Gods, but the demon magician who played the game of even more powerful beings.

Those sly eyes smiled with enigmatic, satiric intent into mine. The voice, strangely harsh, as if accustomed to a more rasping language, said in my Æsir dialect:

"You have no doubt wondered why in our past association you were merely rendered unconscious and not slaughtered. It was the will of the gods of the south that they observe your wildness yet a little longer. In their fairness they granted the possibility that perhaps there was an additional lesson for them to learn about your kind, and your life direction. That lesson, they believe, they have now learned. And the overwhelming decision is against what you stand for. So—"

The voice sound of the magician continued to violate the otherwise silent air of the uninhabited island where I had already lost so much. But as the meaning came to that deadly stage, I ceased to hear the words he uttered. My mind had not during any of those minutes entirely ceased considering ways of escape from the super-being. But now, suddenly, escape or attack—or what?—was all that my attention could encompass.

In fleeting moments of memory, I recalled my past experiences with Mentumenen. I found no encouragement in anything I recalled. In fact what I remembered established beyond all question that he was at least of demon level, perhaps even half a god. And what I had seen of him proved that his powers transcended all human limitations. Limitations which, even when I was in full possession of my physical strength, I had always accepted and adjusted to.

Edging carefully off to one side toward firmer ground, I summoned up one basic defensive thought: Demon Mentumenen, beware a wounded wolf!

I may have been dangerous before. But as an undamaged being, at some deep inside me there was always a survival instinct. There was a constant hot calculation of chances, and even a willingness to retreat in the face of obvious danger.

A wounded wolf has a different hot mixture in his feverish brain. Suddenly, the impossible has happened. The earlier, timeless sense of invulnerability was forcibly penetrated. Negated all too visibly— for there dangles what is left of bleeding flesh. And every torn nerve end screams a fearful message of desperation.

Yes, beware a wounded wolf!

As James Allison, of course, I know that isn't as true as it sounds. Having—as Allison—read history in my search for what followed the time of Ghor, I realize that men of equally grim determination as anything ancient humans ever experienced, used mutilation as a method of controlling dangerous individuals.

After Caesar's victory over the forces of Vercingetorix, every captured male of the opposing army had his right hand cut off, and the wrist immediately bound by tight thongs—even as I had, myself, tied my severed arm. My purpose, now, and the Roman purpose was to ensure that the mutilation did not cause death by bleeding. It was Roman justice, Roman mercy, an extremely high level of civilization, which did not kill the defeated, did not even in such instances enslave; simply rendered incapable of ever again waging warfare against Rome.

So, even as I snarled my intent at vengeance and opposition to the gods as only Ghor could, that deep inner part of me cringed as Vercingetorix must have, also.

X. The Gods Defied

It was the other way for me to go. The way of withdrawal. The way of accepting limitations. How many limbs do you have to remove from a wild beast before it will finally lie down and die? Or—as in the case of a man—before he will admit to himself: I am now, at last, no better than the farmer who was tilling the soil two journeys ago, back there. And we left him unharmed because we recognized that somebody must do that kind of labor. Somebody—not us, not men of spirit—but somebody.

As I stood there—even as I raged there—I could feel all these possibilities already moving through that part of my brain that calculates the truth of things from moment to moment. And there was a feeling of, perhaps, now, finally, I should do what, in her womanly way, Shanara had already intimated—not in direct words—but by a few well-shed tears, and by other signals that were not lost on me, but which I dismissed as being beneath the notice of Ghor, the warrior.

All this emotion and diminished thinking could have led to some large self-restriction—had I been given time to let the darkness inside me continue its silent, deadly argument. But, as often happens, a warrior is not allowed time to think. In this case, my enemy saw that I was sorely wounded and handicapped. And so he moved rapidly in for the kill.

Beware attacking a wounded wolf! He has nothing to lose. He will fight to the death. And he is extra dangerous. Because now he does not really care whether, indeed, he lives or dies.

And, possibly, being wounded, he is forced to be cunning rather than aggressive.

A direct attack on a god or a demon is, of course, as impossible as an assault by a pack of wolves against a water buffalo. I had watched headstrong young wolves learn this bitter lesson the hard way, with the death of half their companions, and everyone that was still alive limping off wounded or maimed.

A wise pack worries a dangerous prey. A few make false lunges toward the head. Whereupon, the distracted victim-to-be turns to face an array of sharp, strong teeth. And as he does so, other attackers rush in against his rear legs. One, two, three quick, slashing nips—and then away. It takes time, this method, and many fierce bites. But presently the massive creature's hind legs can no longer support him ... Brave, powerful buffalo, your hour for being a tasty meal for a hungry pack has arrived—

My first sword stroke was aimed cunningly at Mentumenen's robe. As he did a twisting thrust with his stave, seeking to jab with it at a control point in my body—I had heard of these demon devices, and twisted away—his cloak flailed through the air. I neatly ripped one end with razor sharp Genseric.

Demons are evidently not any smarter than humans, for he laughed in glee, and taunted: "Missed! But then, you will discover that you will always miss."

It was a battle, there on the sandy island, with my one cunning strategy against his ever more irritable attacks. Each time he stabbed angrily at me with his rod, my task was to evade the thrust by a hair's breadth, so that he would be encouraged to believe that victory was near, and each time my great sword cut one more shred from his flowing magician's robe.

The protective robe became a tattered thing. And there came an unwary moment when he stepped back into one of the tatters—and stumbled.

In that instant of marvelous opportunity, what other fighters would have attempted, I cannot predict. My sword flicked down deliberately and cut at the tassel at the rear of the slipper he wore on his right foot. It was as small an advantage as anyone could possibly take of an enemy being momentarily at his mercy.

By the time that apparently futile thrust was made, Mentumenen had freed his other foot from its entanglement. Visibly exultant at his escape, he probed again, almost contemptuous.

Twelve thrusts later he was treading with bare feet the rough ground in the brush towards which I had led him as I retreated. Both his slippers were gone. A portion of his left pantaloon was sliced open. One sleeve of his black goat's-wool coat was ripped from wrist to elbow. And a tiny streak of blood trickled from the little finger of his left hand—the result of my first intentional cut at living flesh.

He did not seem concerned. The lean, dark countenance was serious, yes, but the eyes were narrowed, and unworried. Was he stupid? I believe that his inner situation was much worse for him than that. He was an agent of the gods, with special personal powers. So he literally could not conceive of any mortal being dangerous to him. After all, he need but touch certain key spots in my body with his rod—two at minimum, three at most—and I would instantly be stricken.

Yet even for a naive Great Power there is finally a moment of realization. For Mentumenen that moment did not dawn until he was stark naked except for a dangling piece of coat that spanned across his left shoulder and hung by a thread over his right hip.

At that instant—a thought. A startled blink. At that instant he fumed and ran. It was so sudden that I, who had been wary, was—I admit it—caught by surprise. Naturally, almost at once I raced after; but even while doing so I recollected who this was. So I loped; I did not charge recklessly.

And so, as I rounded an outjut of rock, there above me, his na-

X. The Gods Defied

ked body awkwardly straddling his rod, was my vicious enemy. Seeing him do that magical escape by air, where I could not follow, I shouted after him: "And tell your masters that I and my wild beasts defy them all, and will defeat their false decision, and never, never agree to it."

He was higher, floating up on a strong wind, as I heard his voice come back at me. The words that came down from that wind-blown height were: "Remember your Ice Gods' warning. Success up to a certain time you could have. And then a turning point. Evidently, this island is not your place of doom, but soon—soon!—you will taste the bitter disaster of a male who has lost his woman, not to death, but to another. A woman who has finally grown old enough to realize that a great stinking brute used and abused her by force."

The island was, indeed, not my time of doom. That very day, late in the afternoon hope arrived as I was inspecting the emptiness of the vessel that had brought my ill-fated army to its night of total slaughter—inspecting it with the thought that, perhaps, I would, myself, set it on course. My hope was that fair winds would drive the vessel eastward. It was there, in that direction, I had last seen Shanara being transported by two of the flying metal men whom the gods had sent to destroy me. And to there, of course, I must go with all haste.

In spite of Mentumenen's shattering prediction about her future negative attitude toward me, now, still, she needed me. My hope had to be that I could rescue her before she suffered some desperately ill fate.

As for that vile prediction, itself, I spat on it. Literally spat over the railing into the water. It was an expression of my contempt and my dismissal of the foul creature's claim that Shanara would reject me and my love for her. It was well known, I told myself grimly, that demons were sly creatures, given to cheating and lying for their masters in the sky.

I say, I was considering such a lone voyage when a distant sail appeared. Soon, a large craft lay to, off shore. And, presently, I was being rowed to it. By morning I had made an agreement with its master, whereby a skeleton crew from his vessel would ferry me to the unknown east lands. In exchange for this desperately needed opportunity to follow Shanara, I presented him with the ship.

Intending never again to possess any mark or stigma of advanced civilization.

Chapter XI
Swordsmith and Sorcerer
Brian Lumley

Alone.

Alone of all the men I had recently known, of that brave warrior band I had led to snatch Shanara from lecherous, treacherous Agha Junghaz—aye, that band I had led yet again, out onto the deep bosom of the Sea of Vilayet—only to leave them at the last, dead to a man, on a gore-spattered isle of madness and mayhem.

A man alone: a lone wolf.

A crippled wolf.

Ghor the Cripple, who was once Ghor the Strong.

Ah, I was still Ghor, but more and more the old Ghor was slipping away from me, shrivelling and dwindling in time and distance. Like my left forearm that rotted now with the bodies of my former colleagues on an unnamed isle. For while a three-legged wolf must soon die, the loss of a limb need not necessarily doom a clever man, and so the man in me must now rise to the surface of my being. The Man-facet and not that of the wolf. Neither wolf nor Mi-go facet but Man. Homo-sapiens, or as close as I might ever get to Homo-sapiens . . .

For I could no longer afford to remain a missing link, a half-brute more creature than man and as much wolfling as creature. No, for now I must think and plan above the momentary and immediate hungers of the pack, beyond the strong and willing flesh of a Mi-go bitch in heat. If I was to survive I must think more fully like a man, putting aside all animal lusts and passions until . . . until what?

As the ship—which had been mine but now belonged to my rescuer, a Turanian sailor, some of whose men now sailed me through dangerous Zaporoskan waters—as this ship approached land I made a break from my brooding to think back on what had gone . . .

When the Turanian had found me on the bloody shore of that island of nightmare, his first thought had plainly been to set his men upon me and murder me there and then. But those that landed in the small boat with him numbered only two—three of them all told—and they were sailors, not warriors.

Instead the Turanian struck a bargain with me: my ship for safe conduct to the eastern coast. And why not? Of what use a ship to me, half-crippled and alone? But our bargain came near to being broken almost as soon as it was struck when I saw what the sea

XI. Swordsmith and Sorcerer

captain's colleagues were doing to the bodies of my dead comrades.

Ghouls!—They were slicing off corpse fingers for rings of gold and silver, hacking at stiffened limbs for bangles and bracelets, tearing jewels from those that wore them in their ears and breaking the golden teeth from the gaping jaws of my dead warriors! As a wolf grown up among wolves I had often eaten the flesh of men freshly dead, but out of hunger and the will to live and for no other reason. These men were like snow-vultures at the bright jewel eyes of men nobly dead; aye, and they sickened me worse than the pain in my stump of an arm.

Seeing that even in my weakened state I was close to going into a berserk rage, the Turanian captain hurriedly told me that this was loot to ensure the safety of my passage. His crew did not care for Northmen and the trinkets would be offered as bribes to those who would volunteer to sail me into Zaporoskan territory. As soon as he said this the two ghouls who were still at their bloody work at once cried out that they would volunteer for the duty.

Ah, brave volunteers, Kaphra Thall and Zorass Jhadra!—robbers of the dead!—so, I had your word to give me safe conduct and sail me to the eastern shore, did I? And after that, what then? Who would guarantee your safety?

Genseric's sword, slightly tarnished now and dull, trembled in my good right hand. And all the muscles tensed in that hand and arm as if, with a mind of their own, they strained against my own will to lift the great blade and kill, kill, *kill!*

Later, I had promised myself, later.

And now it *was* later, and the germ of a plan had formed in my mind . . .

Thus as the ship drew nigh a rocky shore backed by dense jungles and low, lush hills, I stood up from where I crouched on the deck of the ship and went to the man at the tiller. It was Zorass Jhadra, whose nervous eyes scanned the early morning ocean for sign of any strange ship. I knew why, for I had overheard my escort talking during the late hours of the previous night. These were waters immemorially infamous for their pirates.

The night conversation of my—companions?—whispered where the four had gathered around the tiller in the light of an oil lamp, their faces ruddy in its glow—had told me much. And because my plan put on flesh by the moment I had been eager for local knowledge, to know how best I might discover the whereabouts of my Shanara and follow her wherever she had gone. These are some of the things I learned:

The morning would find us some few leagues south of where the mouth of the Zaporoska emptied into the Vilayet, and between our ship and the river would stand a city of peculiarly mongrel lineage. Four hundred years ago the Turanians had built a massive fort there on the sea, manning it with warships from Aghrapur and other cities of the western shores. The task of these ships had been simple: to put an end to the activities of the pirate hordes whose vessels and settlements were like flies all along the flanks of the Zaporoskan river.

But within a few short decades the pirates themselves had taken control of the fortress, had subverted the masters of the war vessels permanently stationed there, and inevitably a pirate Armada had set about the sack of Aghrapur itself. In the ensuing sea battle of Aghrapur both sides had lost more than half their men-o'-war, and the surviving vessels had limped back to their respective berths to lick wounds and tend to the ravages of war. Then for more than two hundred years an uneasy peace had fallen over the waters of the Vilayet. The Turanians had their own problems, the Zaporoskans, too, to a lesser extent, and history would wait for neither one.

Thus the fortress on the eastern coast became Zaporakh—-a small, high-walled inner city surrounded by a vastly mushrooming maze of streets and shops without—into which was drawn as unlikely a mixture of humanity as could be imagined. For now that they were grown used to the comforts of a civilized, more or less static existence, many of the pirates became shopkeepers and merchants in their own rights, aye, and their sons after them.

Trading all around the coasts of the Vilayet, they fumed against the true, nomad pirates of the river and almost wiped them out. Trade links were forged: by sea with the western coastal towns and cities, overland all along the eastern seaboard, and as far east as Khitai of the jade cupolas and opium houses.

The freshly opened sea- and land-routes flourished, drawing into the maw of Zaporakh all the mongrels and traders and thieves of a world in turmoil. Slant-eyed silk merchants from Khitai rubbed shoulders with bearded Hyrkanian swordsmiths and wandering Cimmerian adventurers and mercenaries; exiled Turanian lords built houses and palaces above streets where black Zamboulan cannibals had learned to eat the meat of less sentient creatures; men from Iranistan and Brythunia drank together in wharfside taverns and diced for the doubtful favours of Zamoran whores . . .

And out of these polyglot hordes emerged the strangest of all emblems and insignia of civilization in those troubled times, and the name of Zaporakh became synonymous with (of all things) hospitality!

Then the pirates returned . . .

The hawks of the sea were back, plundering afresh in seas which had all but forgotten they ever existed. Their numbers were smaller now, true, but by the same token the pickings were all the richer.

XI. Swordsmith and Sorcerer

Their bases were the old places up the river, where they could hide for months on end if need be before venturing out across the Vilayet once more, and it was reckoned that only a very few years could pass before they would constitute just such a threat as that great plague of pirates of old.

And it was pirates that Zorass Jhadra and the other three Turanians feared right now, the pirates that stood out to sea and watched the approach routes to Zaporakh for easy pickings. Merchantmen from the city usually went out under paid guard of warships, but occasionally a captain would be unable or unwilling to pay for such protection. Such as these were especially prone to attacks.

Of course, our little ship could offer nothing of riches. No, but it would make fine sport for pirates spoiling for fun and games!

Now we were headed south along the coast for Zaporakh. An hour's sailing should bring us safely into port—or would if we went unmolested. It was because I felt we would not go unmolested that I approached Zorass Jhadra at the tiller. He could not smell danger as I could, nor were his eyes those of a wolf. The sails of the hawk closing with us from the sea had been blowing on the horizon for at least three minutes when I brought them to his attention:

"Sails, Zorass Jhadra—pirate sails. She'll run us down long before we make Zaporakh . . . "

"Sails? Pirates?" the other spun round, searching the open sea. Then he saw the half-crescent sails, one large and one small, that seemed to grow out of the horizon. Immediately his face twisted into a fear-filled visage.

"Kaphra Thall!" he shouted. "Jorim, Heram Philoss—up on deck, quick—pirates!"

"Pirates?" shouted Kaphra Thall, his booted feet clattering on the planking as he sprang from below, wide awake where a second before he had slept. "Where?"

Behind him, tumbling out from the cool shade below decks, the other men came with cries of alarm on their lips.

"There she is—there!" cried Zorass Jhadra, pointing a trembling hand. "And a fast one by the cut of her sails. She'll have us before we round the headland."

Heram Philoss, a more experienced sailor, held a spittle-damp finger into the breeze. "Not necessarily. There's a good wind off the land and ours is a light craft. If we run full with the wind she'll have trouble catching us."

"Hold," I said, putting my back to the rail. "You are paid to take me to Zaporakh." For a moment they looked at me in blank astonishment, as if they saw me for the first time. Then, ignoring me, Heram Philoss snatched the tiller from Zorass Jhadra while the other two sprang to attend to the sails and rigging.

"No," I growled low, warningly in my throat, "we do not head for the open sea." I struck Heram Philoss with my shoulder, knocking him from the tiller to crash to the deck.

As he cursed and sprang to his feet, yanking a long knife from his belt, it was as if Genseric's great sword struck of its own will. At the last moment he went wide-eyed and tried to lean backwards. Too late. The sword's tip whistled between his grimacing teeth, cutting loose his lower jaw and slicing into his windpipe. Down he went and was dead in a moment.

Now the other three threw themselves upon me, and the ship was left to wallow side-on to the wind. Zorass Jhadra's wild lunge took his curved blade high over my shoulder as I bent at the knee, driving Genseric's sword up into his groin and ripping him to his navel. "You are a mongrel cur and a ghoul," I told his corpse as it toppled, "and I am a wolf."

"*I am a wolf!*" I fumed on the other two who gazed at me now wide-eyed and horror-stricken. With one good arm, towering in my rage, evil of eye and splashed with blood I faced them . . . and with a whining snarl rising in my throat I flew at them. Kaphra Thall put up his blade before my single down-flashing blow, only to watch his sword shiver into fragments in the moment before my own split him through head, neck and breast.

This left Jorim the Slow, who had circled round behind me with his axe. With my wolf's ears I heard the hiss of his heavy weapon as it sliced air, and falling to my knees I spun with Genseric's sword outstretched and dark with blood. The flat of Jorim's axe slid over my skull, barely bruising my flesh, but my blade opened up his belly and got fast in the bag of it as his entrails sprang out on the deck to drench me in their sticky welter. I ripped the sword free and drove its point to his heart before his legs could buckle. He fell to the deck and died with blood bursting from his lips.

I looked for more men to kill but there were none, only pirates looming closer. I grabbed the tiller and turned the ship toward the tip of the headland. On the other side of those wave-splashed rocks I should be in sight of Zaporakh, barely a league and a half away.

By the time I had the ship level with the point the hawk was nearly on me. Hard eyes leered from scarred, tanned faces as the pirate drew alongside. It could only be a matter of moments before they locked the two vessels together with grappling irons. They would find little of value aboard, barely enough to cover their time and trouble, and then they would kill me and sink the ship for sport.

I took a small water cask and emptied it, throwing it on the deck within easy reach. Then I took back the belongings of my old comrades, the booty stolen by the ghouls Kaphra Thall and Zorass

XI. Swordsmith and Sorcerer

Jhadra. I took it as quickly as I could, as they had taken it, folding it in cloth. I stuffed the bundle in the water cask—fingers, ear-lobes and all. Then I made fast Genseric's sword to my body.

Now the pirate was very close and I could see the twirl of grappling irons in the air. Throwing oil on the sails of my ship, I set them afire—then threw the tiller over until the sharp prow of my vessel came round and the wind off the land filled the gouting sails. Too late the pirates saw their doom. I rammed them and my blazing sails collapsed onto their deck. I, too, was thrown down, and when I regained my feet I saw that both ships were broken open and doomed to a weedy grave.

I snatched up the cask and as I did so saw a flying shadow on the deck. One of the pirates had boarded my ship, doubtless bent on revenge. Wild with fury he pounced, his sword flashing down. I threw up the cask before me and his blade stuck in the rim. Before he could tug it loose I kicked him in the groin and as he doubled over swung the cask against his head. Blood and brains flew—-but I was off balance.

My feet slipped in gore and I fell, toppling over the low deck-rail. As I went my head struck the rail a terrific blow, then—

• • •

—She swam up out of green deeps, supremely beautiful, awesome in her beauty, yet cold as the limitless deeps from which she seemed to rise. Green she was, as seen through ocean spume and eyes clouding in death. Drowning eyes—wolf eyes—my eyes!

But when she spoke to me I knew she was no siren, no creature of the sea. She was in my mind, not in the waves that surrounded me; for unconsciousness is much like a dream, and as all of her kind she could bend dreams to her own purpose. For she was a Goddess, the Goddess Ythillin, the Ice Woman, first daughter of those Gods of Ice whose children the Frost Giants were.

"So, Ghor, it is come to this," she said, her voice the wind that drives snow flurries whining over the glaciers. "You would flee the world of men without fulfilling the prophecy of the Ice Gods, would you?"

"Let me drown," I snarled, "but only leave me be."

"Ah, no!" she denied me. "For there's work for you yet, mother-slayer."

"Oh? And shall I still save a civilization from destruction and give it to the Æsir?" I scorned her, seeing the bubbles of my harsh laughter rising before my face as water filled me. "Let me drown, I say—or save me if you can. One way or the other, ice-bitch, but I'll not suffer your prattle and witch-wife's prophecies. And since I know you'll not save me—then drown with me!"

With that I would have reached for her throat—except that I

discovered my one good hand caught in the ropes that were wound tight about the water cask. "My hand!" I cried in outrage. "Give me back my hand for a boon, ice-bitch, and I'd choke out your life with it!"

And she laughed like a pattering of hailstones. "There's sulphur in you, Ghor—strife in your soul and hell in your eyes—aye, and life in your veins for all that you'd forsake it without a word of complaint. So it is with all your kind. But no, you'll not die here. Would you die, and have done with life—and Shanara?"

"Speak not her name, witch of the white waste!" I was moved to answer. "My pleasures were few, but Shanara was one of them. Now she is lost to me—as is my arm—and many good friends also. Why not my life, too?"

Now her eyes were serious and close and it seemed I felt her frozen breath on my cheek. "You may not yet die, Ghor. I once said that it was your lot to save a civilization. Now I say you shall save *all* of Earthly civilizations, all of sanity and order. *Mentumenen has pitted himself against all the gods—against the Gods of the South as well as those of the North—and to aid him he has called up powers he cannot control.* They are powers which would destroy us all!

"For the time being Mentumenen is mortal, human despite his sorceries, but more and more the man in him is driven out and the alien darkness in him grows. Soon he will not be Mentumenen at all but a true avatar of one of those he serves, a demon clothed in man's form. And who can say what monstrous magicks they may work through him then? For the present: he has Shanara and would use her to control you, to pit you against his enemies, against your own Ice Gods themselves . . . "

"As you would pit me against him?" I sneered. "And what, pray, are you Ice Gods to me?"

If a Goddess can shrug, Ythillin shrugged. "Despite your irreverence, your arrogance, you would save your Shanara—if you could. Our desire is to save an entire universe. The means and motives of gods are infinitely greater than those of mortals." She paused for a moment, then continued:

"I have cursed you and my curse is inviolable, but in spite of that I may yet grant you a boon. You asked for your hand back that you might choke me. You shall have an arm, of sorts. And since magick has taken your Shanara from you, magick shall aid you in finding her. Now I will say something to you. Forget what you will of all this but do not forget my next words:

"There will be a swordsmith and a sorcerer. The former works in blue steel and you will know him when you see him; the other deals in white magick. Seek them out. Disobey if you dare, mother-slayer, but if you do, not only is Shanara doomed but all of

XI. Swordsmith and Sorcerer

the many future worlds of man . . . "

And with that she was gone.

Strong arms were pulling me out of the sea onto the deck of a man-o'-war. "Only one of the black-hearted dogs survived, eh?" a voice came to me through my retching of salt water, bringing me back to my senses. "Only one pirate, with his great sword strapped to him yet, and all the brave lads of the little trader gone to the bottom with their ship. Well, we know how to deal with this dog!"

"Hold!" I cried. Finding my feet set upon a deck once more, I struggled free of the arms that restrained me. The water cask was still fastened to my good arm. "I was the master of that trader," I snarled, "not a pirate. What use a pirate with only one arm? Now then, I've lost a ship and many friends—so where's all of this Zaporakh hospitality I've heard so much of? You are a ship out of Zaporakh, are you not?"

"That we are," the speaker agreed. "But can you prove who you are?"

"No," I glared at the speaker, who was obviously the captain of the warship, "but I can crack the skulls of any who name me liar!" And I swung my water-cask menacingly.

The captain—a short-bearded man whose rank showed in his bearing and the fact that he wore a red sash and turban fastened with a clasp of office—frowned at me and slitted his eyes a little, then made up his mind. He grinned and said: "Well, pirate or none you're the only survivor; and if it was you rammed that scabby sea-hawk—"

"It was."

"Then you've a right to the hospitality of Zaporakh. We can't have honest traders suffering at the hands of—"

"Have you a cabin I can use?" I cut him off. "I would like to be alone for a little while—to take stock of things and say a few words of thanks that I am spared." It was a subterfuge and totally out of character for me, for I never had need of lying. Neither had I prayed to gods nor offered thanks for anything—certainly not for something which was all my own doing. I simply did not want anyone to see the small bundle I had placed in the water cask. It would be difficult to explain the bits of gristle that accompanied the various baubles. Without a doubt I should be branded a pirate if they were seen.

And so I was shown to a cabin with a window above decks, from which I disposed of the unwanted bits of flesh into the sea before the ship berthed in Zaporakh. Before leaving the vessel I asked the captain:

"Perhaps you can help me yet again. I need firstly . . . a swordsmith?" And he directed me to the hot-reeking wharfside shop of a weaponcaster.

From the doorway I watched the man at work in the smoky glow of his forge, and from the first I knew he was the one. He was working on a hook fastened to a steel cup. Occasionally he would pause to try the cup on the wrist-stump of an old sailor who had lost his hand. Finally the wicked-looking hook was satisfactory and they strapped it on. The gnarled mariner waved it about in the air a little, grinned gummily, paid his due and turned to leave the shop. That was when they saw me. I brushed past the old man and approached the smith, holding out my ruined left arm.

"Something special," I told him. "A long knife, a crossbow, a hook. A weapon. You can do it?"

Slowly he nodded. "Yes, I can do it." He looked into my eyes and shuddered. Strong man as he was, with mighty shoulders and hands strong as the metals with which they worked, he gazed into my eyes and trembled—then cursed low in his throat, saying:

"I . . . I knew you . . . were coming."

"Oh?"

"Last night, in a dream, I was visited."

I nodded. "By a woman, a goddess of ice. I know."

"She called herself—"

"Ythillin," I finished it for him, my voice sour. "Listen, I have some baubles, gems, some gold and silver. It is yours if—"

"No, no," he quickly held up his hands. "I want nothing. And I can start work at once. I drew the plans this morning . . ."

• • •

From then until my new "arm" was finished I stayed with Dar'ah Humarl at his shop. Above the actual workshop on a platform half-open to the sky, I lay awake at nights listening to the deep snoring from the shadowy bulk of Dar'ah upon his corner cot. The "arm"—an awesome weapon, indeed an arsenal—took all of thirteen days to complete, and Dar'ah worked a good fourteen hours every day. During that time all other would-be customers were turned away while the smith's attention was centered solely upon the completion of this one task.

We spoke very little; he worked and sweated while I watched, though I helped wherever I could; and gradually a silent kinship, a mutual admiration built up between us. I liked both Dar'ah's strength and his silence; and his awe of me, inspired no doubt by Ythillin during her dream-visit, turned slowly to a friendly, hesitant curiosity. It made me wonder what the ice-bitch had told him of me, which I determined to inquire of him before we parted company.

I had, too, finally persuaded him to accept those trinkets which once belonged to my comrades slain on the isle of madness. Since so-called "civilized" men put such store by these inedible baubles,

XI. Swordsmith and Sorcerer

doubtless the gift would make Dar'ah Humarl a fairly rich man. I could not have foreseen it, but it would also make him a dead man.

Late on the thirteenth night my new limb was finished and lacquered black and gleaming, then hung up to dry, and Dar'ah promised me that on the morrow I would once more be a whole man—or as nearly so as his art could make me. From the things I had given him he took a massive golden ring set with a red gem and went out, returning presently with an armful of bread and meats and weighted down with skins of wine slung over his massive shoulders. Also, in his pouch he now carried a good many of the thin triangular coins of Zaporakh, enough to furnish him a fine living for a third part of a year.

I drank much wine and unaccustomed to the sweet stuff quickly grew drowsy. Dar'ah laughed without malice as I swayed and almost fell from the rough ladder that led to my bed of boards in the room above. When I awoke I knew something was wrong. Above me, seen through the open roof, a moon nearing its full glared down through fleet clouds like some bloodshot eye of evil. There was a blood smell.

What had awakened me?

A cry? A scuffle down below? Dar'ah's form no longer seemed to fill its customary corner. Quickly, my head reeling, I went to his pallet to make sure. He was not there, nor were the gold and silver trinkets to be found beneath his blanket! I hurried down into the shop.

My metal arm hung in its dim niche in the wall, hidden from all but the keenest eye, but of Dar'ah there was no sign. The blood smell was thicker here, and a moment later I almost fell over his body . . . Dar'ah's head lay elsewhere. I found his pouch and it was empty.

My head was clearer now and my nose picked out three distinct man-odours in the air. They must have seen Dar'ah in the city when he went bartering. Yes, there had been three of them, I knew it. They had followed him back here and waited. When all was quiet they had entered and one of them had crept upstairs. He had taken the trinkets but had disturbed Dar'ah in his sleeping. Dar'ah had followed the thief down into the shop where the other two had hidden in shadows. Swiftly, silently they had cut him down.

Black villainy!—and civilization the villain . . .

• • •

I found them in a tavern not far from the sea, one of the several places in Zaporakh that stayed open all through the night to cater for fishermen, travellers and traders getting late into port. This was one of the lower dives, however, and my three stood at the bar, a wineskin between them and dice rolling as they gamed for their spoils. They looked like outcast Hyrkanians, hardened killers. I watched one gemmed bangle change hands and knew it for a trinket that had once encircled the upper arm of one of my men.

Approaching the men at the bar, I stepped between the noisy, drunken and gambling customers of this den. Coming up to the three, I leaned close to one of them, whispering:

"Do you know Dar'ah?"

"What . . . ?" He turned, reaching for his knife. I threw back the cloak that covered my new arm and twisted the metal wrist with my true hand. A slender, razor-honed blade flashed into view, sliding easily into the man's side. Feeling little resistance I turned my body, almost cutting my goggle eyed victim in half. Lifting my arm I sliced at the second Hyrkanian and his face opened up redly from ear to ear.

As his comrades toppled the third man backed away, turned and ran. I twisted my metal wrist again as he reached the open door. The red blade flashed from sight into the metal case and I held up the arm to point it at the door which framed the back of the last robber. Then, before he could vanish from sight, I pressed a stud set in the metal arm. There came the sound of a powerful spring released and I felt a slight recoil. A metal bolt struck my prey in the spine, flinging him out into the street.

Leaving the tavern I stooped to wrench my bolt from the dead man's back, and glancing behind me I saw through the open doorway a sea of frozen, stupefied faces. Then I was away at a lope up the night street, a dark shadow that quickly melted into the greater darkness.

Up above me the moon looked down and smiled grimly at some secret only he knew. A moon nearing its full. I stared at the yellow face in the sky and snarled, then wondered at the fire that flowed in my veins. Something strange was happening, which had never happened before.

A swordsmith and a sorcerer, the ice-bitch had told me. Well, I had found my swordsmith and now must seek out the sorcerer, a white magician. Yet even without him I felt that the seeds of magic were already sown within me. Again I glanced at the moon, and instinctively fell into the crouch of the wolf. Then I threw back my head and howled, howled long and wild in the streets of Zaporakh. And in their beds I knew many citizens shuddered in strangeling dreams this night . . .

Chapter XII
The Gift of Lycanthropy
Frank Belknap Long

I knew not what guided me through the maze of unfamiliar streets, past dimly lit wineshops, with the raucous shouts of drunken revelers drifting out into the night.

Never before had I felt quite so much like a wolf as my breath came and went, as if its intake was slowed by the fierce clashing of my teeth. Never once could I remember stopping to stand erect like a man, for some deep-seated instinct prevented me from drawing myself up to my full height.

I made half-growling sounds deep in my throat which seemed as natural to me as breathing, as natural as they would have been if I had been the leader of a wolf pack bent on slaying and dismembering the self-deceiving creature called "Man."

What wolves did men did also, but with more cunning and guile, pretending always to possess, deep in their minds, another self they could summon forth in battle attire at will, to fight for what they liked to call justice and mercy. In some strange way, it made the slaying of their own kind less troublesome to them. But always the slaying went on and on, just as it did with wolves. Was it not better then to *be* a wolf, totally untroubled by guilt?

There is nothing strange or unnatural about what wolves do when they slay and whenever I felt I was becoming more like a man I was assailed by rage and self-reproach and I made haste to put all such thoughts from my mind.

The narrow streets twisted and turned and some ended in blind alleys as they had in the border kingdoms of Nemedia, particularly in the city of Belverus, which seemed as remote to me now as was Argos and Shem and the tropical rain forests of Keshan, forcing me to circle back to escape from the sea-bordering maze that was Zaporakh. I have said that I knew not what was guiding me. But that would not have been strictly true if I could have given more thought to everything that I knew or suspected.

I never for a moment doubted that I was still under the spell of the Ice Bitch, however remote she may have been from me in space at that particular time, and that her powers remained so great that I would soon be loping inland, straight as an arrow, toward the habitation of the White Magician. I knew as well that she was implanting in my mind images, however nebulous, that would unfailingly guide me when I left Zaporakh, and passed into the surrounding countryside, if a desert waste without flowering shrubs or animal life of any kind could be thought of as a countryside.

I even knew that the habitation I sought would be of stone, a tower perhaps on an almost featureless plain, or some rock-walled chamber deep underground.

I was sure that Ythillin's guidance would not fail me. Had she not come to me out of the sea, swimming up out of the depths, awesome in her beauty, when I had come close to perishing, saying things that had made me think of her, once again, as both bitch, and the goddess she had proclaimed herself to be? So sure was I that if she had chosen to preserve me then, when my eyes had been clouding in death, her purpose in guiding me now would remain steadfast.

Exactly what that purpose was I did not know—only that meeting and talking with the White Magician was as important to her as it had now become to me.

And that was why I endured with patience retracing my course a dozen times within the boundaries of Zaporakh, knowing I would soon be on its outskirts and loping onward until its white towers, silvered by moonlight, became a receding blur in the distance.

But that, too, proved no more than a mind's gaze image, for when once Zaporakh was actually behind me and the desert waste stretched out before me with only a few scattered boulders arising, as far as my eyes could see, in a monotonous expanse of sand, my urge to make haste was so great that I did not turn to glance back until the city had vanished from view.

The horizon ahead seemed to blend with the plain in a featureless glimmering, but a vast cliff wall soon appeared in the distance as I continued on. When I drew near to it I saw that the rock had been hollowed out to create a tunnel-like cave in direct line with my approach. It appeared to be lighted from deep within by a dull, reddish glow that seeped out upon the plain, forming a luminous, blood-red figure of a configuration I had never seen before.

Its half-triangular, half-circular shape made me feel for an instant it might be a sorcerer's talisman in luminous form which it would be dangerous for me to cross. But nothing happened as I passed through it and entered the cave.

It was a very large cave and for a moment my wolfish eyes saw only a number of vague shadow-shapes that seemed to be leaping up and down.

Then the light seemed to grow a little brighter and I saw—

I had split the skulls of many enemies. I had sliced off their arms and legs and plunged my sword deep into their vitals. I had eviscerated them by slicing downward from their chests to their groins sending them crashing with a wolf's merciless howl.

XII. The Gift of Lycanthropy

But the skeletons that dangled from the walls impaled on iron hooks had endured mutilations that would have made anyone less capable than I was of surmounting all fear back away quickly and go fleeing from the cave, for what had happened to intruders in the past could happen again, and seemed infinitely more akin to black sorcery than white.

For an instant the skeletons seemed clothed once more in human flesh as they swayed back and forth with the light playing over them. In the red gleaming it was as if they were still being ripped and torn asunder in a hundred hideous ways, for enough flesh still adhered to the bones to make it clear that what had been done to them had seldom been duplicated. No, not even by the dwarfed human ghouls, cannibals all, that crowded around campfires in far Keshan, and muttered and mumbled low, as they tossed into campfires, one by one, every sliced-off part of what had once been a man.

He came toward me out of the shadows, the hairiest creature on two legs I had ever seen, with the features and carriage of a man. His chest, which was barrel-shaped, was covered with hair so thick it seemed almost furlike, and his huge, muscular arms would have made an ape feel an instant kinship, despite the slight difference between human hair, however thick, and the body covering of an ape.

"Don't let my small trophy collection alarm you," he said, without preamble and in a surprisingly soft-spoken voice. "Those were Ythillin's enemies—and mine. It is necessary to be harsh in dealing with men whose every instinct is hostile. It serves as a warning; it keeps rumors flying in all directions over land and sea, and in every crevice there are deadly vipers who must be discouraged from venturing forth."

He paused an instant, then went on quickly. "Ythillin has assured me you seek my aid as a friend. And although I am entirely human I have only the warmest of friendly feelings toward wolves and their kith and kin."

He nodded and his lips split in a toothless grin. "You have no doubt heard that I am myself part beast and often turn into one and run savagely through the night. But that is wholly untrue. I am a magician and a magician can transform himself in outward appearance in any way that suits his fancy. But that outward appearance is an illusion which exists solely in the eyes of the beholder. It would not mean that I would cease to be as I am now, even if I seemed to transform myself into a crocodile, which I could easily accomplish at this moment, right before your eyes."

I spoke then for the first time, but I hardly recognized the half-wolf sounds that came from my lips until, with a supreme effort, I found myself forming words that I felt would be comprehensible to him. Or was I mistaken? He seemed to understand what I was trying to say before I regained my mastery of the human tongue.

"I do not need to transform myself in any way," I said. "In your eyes or the eyes of others. I am far more of a wolf than a man and the men and women who know me find that out quickly enough, with no need of magic to create meaningless illusion."

"You have always thought of yourself as a wolf," he said. "And that is understandable. You were raised by wolves, and it was as a wolf you watched your own mother being torn apart by wolves. But that is an illusion in your mind. I think it comes and goes. I am sure you know at times that I speak only the truth, painful as it may be for you to confess your human kinship, even to yourself."

I said nothing, for his words were as salt on a wound that bled.

"What if I made you a true wolf?" he said. "In every fiber of your being, whenever you wished to become one? Then you would become what no man could ever be, whenever the need arose for you to join forces with and secure the aid of all of the great powers that are far older than Man, and can only communicate with those who share their primal impulses, both on earth and in the gulfs between the stars. In the vastness of those cosmic gulfs there is a sharing and a kinship. Yes, even with wolves who run savagely through the night in the full of the moon."

"You could make me—"

"A true wolf," he reiterated, before I could go on. "It is within my power to bestow upon you the priceless gift of Lycanthropy. There are only a few words that you must say. They would be dangerous ones for me, but not for you. Ythillin will protect me when I utter them, as I must, and I will not be changed in any way. But at any other time—

"No matter. My safety is assured, and for you the transformation will take only a moment or two and will last as long as you wish it to endure. Then, whenever you so desire, you may regain your human form, simply by repeating the words in reverse. You need finger no talisman. You need take no magic brew. I will see to all of that, with Ythillin's aid."

"Is that her wish?" I asked. "That cold and merciless—"

"No, no, you do her an injustice," he said. "In the depths of her mind she is attracted to you. But all amorousness she puts aside when she has some great purpose in mind that even I have not fully fathomed."

"There may be truth in what you say," I told him. "Very well. Tell me the words that I must speak—"

"It is not as simple as that," he said. "I must go into a trance first and summon all of my inner strength to make the words truly magical. And I must summon as well Ythillin's now distant presence to

XII. The Gift of Lycanthropy

aid me."

"Distant?" I asked. "It was almost as if I heard her voice guiding me to you."

"Her guiding presence was no more than an aura to which she had given instructions," he replied. "It was implanted in your mind that last time you saw her. I will still need more of her assistance."

He was staring at me very steadily, and his way of moving his arms when he spoke was, I suddenly realized, no more abrupt than the quick responses which came from his lips when he saw I was troubled by some still unspoken thoughts.

"You are telling yourself that no one would bestow a priceless gift and expect nothing in return," he said. "You would regard with mistrust anyone whose generosity exceeded all bounds in that respect, and your mistrust would be justified. But the favor I shall ask of you is a small one, as favors go. Have you ever heard of Lamaril?"

I shook my head, puzzled.

"Lamaril the Invincible," he said. "He is coming down from the North to lay waste to the coastal plains and bind into slavery everyone lucky enough to survive his barbarous onslaught. Or perhaps I should say, unlucky enough. But he will destroy me through nights and days of slow torture, because we were in conflict once and he bears me an undying enmity."

He paused an instant, still staring at me steadily. "He leads a mighty army of thousands of heavily armed men," he went on slowly. "But he always rides ahead of his legions, a full league ahead to establish his recklessness and courage, in the eyes of all men everywhere. He is like a savage child in his self-love, but not like a child otherwise. Destroy him and his legions will scatter in panic and despair, since they worship him as a god."

"Although I have never heard of him," I said, "he must be brave beyond most men to take so great a risk. To ride alone when men of every breed—pirates and human flesh eaters who would just as soon kill as look at you, merchants who would kill as readily to protect their wares from the rapacity of an invading army, tavern roisterers with long, sharp knives who will go out into the desert at night by twos and threes to waylay any stranger to gain the price of one more drink—"

"You have never before seen such a man," the White Magician said before I could finish. "He is huge of girth and well over seven feet in height, protected both by the magic spells known to his people, and armor forged by the most skillful of weapon makers. He bears me, as I have said, an enmity that would make him take delight in seeing me impaled above the ramparts of Zaporakh, dangling from an iron spike."

"Whether the favor be a large or small one," I said, "I promise you that I will hold it a small enough recompense for the gift of Lycanthropy."

He looked pleased. "That is all that I could ask."

If his motions had seemed abrupt before, they were more so now, for without saying another word he sat down upon the floor of the cave and folded his legs in front of him.

I watched him closely as he sat cross-legged on the floor, no longer staring at me, the fur cape that hung from his shoulders—it was fastened in the middle of his chest by a jeweled clasp of intricate design—seeming almost to blend with the hairiness of his unclothed arms and legs and the bulging expanse of wrinkled grey flesh in the region of his navel. Not once did he lower his eyes in contemplation to where he had been cut at birth from his mother, as did the shaven-headed priests of Nemedia, but stared straight ahead into vacancy.

It was not the first time I had seen a man pass into a deep trance through his own willing. It has been said that such states can be dangerous and that a journey undertaken in the dark of the mind may turn the body corpselike and stop its breathing.

I have never seen anyone, man or woman go mad or die in convulsions on awakening from such a trance. But occurrences of that nature have been reported too often to be thought of as fabrications.

But it was not that so much as what he had told me about the power that could be gained from such an inward journey that I chose to dwell on now, since no other possible outcome was of such vital and immediate concern to me.

I had no great knowledge of magic. But that a few spoken words or a simple hexagram traced in the sand after the undertaking of such a journey could shatter the swords of a thousand advancing warriors and send them into the wildest kind of battle disarray I had once confirmed with my own eyes, though the magician who had wrought that spell had been unknown to me.

As the memory of what had happened on that never-to-be-forgotten day came sweeping back into my mind I did something I was later to regret. I detached Genseric's sword and my new weapon arm with its screw-onable hook, fumed about and set both down a short distance from me.

I had remembered something else that it might have been better not to have recalled, or to have blotted from my mind with a deliberate effort of will. When an act of magic is about to be performed, whether for good or ill, it was thought wise not to tempt fate by arming one's self with a deadly weapon.

Sorcery I had never feared, as men do, or allowed it to stay my hand in battle, even though I had seen with my own eyes a thousand swords shattered and the weapon wielders destroyed, but I had been told, many times, by men familiar with the darkest secrets

XII. The Gift of Lycanthropy

of sorcery, that a flashing sword in a human hand invites destruction. Genseric's deadly blade and my new arm were both more a part of me than any ordinary weapon, though I could detach them at will. Wisdom and fearlessness in battle are things apart, and I saw no reason to abandon all caution in the presence of a White Magician who practiced black magic as well, as the skeletons that dangled on the cave wall had made abundantly clear.

I knew that I could regain my weapon arm quickly enough should the need arise. Was I matching my wolf cunning against a man who had promised me a gift it seemed well within his power to bestow? I did not know, could not be sure. A wolf as well as a man does things at times that are foolish and unwise, but to abandon all caution is a greater risk.

There was more to it than that. If any transformation was to take place in me, if the gift of Lycanthropy was a reality, it might well have been better if I had experienced the change nude. But an artificial limb that served as a weapon might prove a handicap indeed. How could I make use of it as a true wolf? And would it not delay and handicap such a change?

It was almost as if the seated figure facing me, in the depths of his trance, knew the strange conflict that was taking place in my mind and wanted me to put my new weapon arm aside. I was firmly convinced it would have been a mistake to trust him completely as far as the promise he had made and I had made to him in return. But not to have trusted him at all seemed unwise also, for Lycanthropy was a gift which he alone, with Ythillin's aid, could bestow. It was a gift to be prized, for once I possessed it I might even find a way to rescue Shanara, my lost love, and restore her to my arms, after I had fulfilled my promise to him.

I was still watching the White Magician closely and suddenly his expression became less vacant. His nostrils quivered, as if like an animal excited by a strange and unfamiliar scent, his inward journey had aroused in him an emotion which, even in his trancelike state, was mirrored in his features.

I, too, had known such excitement when my wolfish instincts had taken complete possession of me, and even so small a thing as a faint odor had made me sniff the air and grind my teeth in a frenzy of anticipation.

Just between sleeping and waking I have traveled great distances, across grey wastes and frozen tundras, for dreams and the state into which he had passed were alike in many ways and I had no way of knowing how long his trance would last.

I only knew I experienced no surprise when it was over, in as short a time as it would have taken me to cross to the opposite wall of the cave and return again to where he was sitting.

He got to his feet slowly, drawing his fur cape more firmly around him, and looked at me with no trace of agitation in his gaze. I knew at once that he had not failed to complete the task he had set himself before sinking into a trance, for there can be no mistaking the difference—in calmness and assurance—between a man who has succeeded in a difficult task and one who has failed.

I thought for a moment he was going to speak the words then and there, but he took a slow step backwards, and continued to look at me, very thoughtfully now.

"We must both be careful to avoid mistakes," he said. "There are spells that are not easy to cast, simple as they may seem in superficial ways. The slightest mistake in what must be done can have dangerous, even fatal consequences. Do you understand?"

I nodded, impatient for him to go on but knowing that I must not let my attention stray for an instant from what he felt he must tell me.

He did not speak again for a full minute, as if he wanted me to know that he was aware of my impatience, and was relieved that I had made no attempt to interrupt him by asking questions.

"The words are quite simple ones," he said, finally. "They are in a tongue unknown to you, but that is of no importance. They are harsh, short words without sibilants, and if you can say, 'Tit tat,' you can say them also. It does not matter if you cannot speak them exactly as I am about to do. They are so laden with magic now that even if you spoke them crudely and stammeringly the Lycanthropic transformation would start instantly.

"As I have said before, Ythillin has made certain that I will be protected when I utter them. If she had not done so, I, too, would become a wolf."

"You would have me speak them now?"

He shook his head. "That is the last thing that I or Ythillin would want you to do," he said. "You must leave this cave as you are now, if you are to keep the promise you made me, and what she may later ask of you, for she has earned your gratitude. You will know when the right time comes. It will be when you see Lamaril riding alone in the desert . . . "

"But if I do not speak the words after you—"

"You must memorize them," he said cutting me short. "Simply listen attentively. Four words, no more—all of one and two syllables. I will speak them slowly."

"My memory—"

Again he cut me short. "They will be deeply engraved on your memory the instant you hear them. You will never forget them. That, too, is part of the magic."

He waited, but when I said nothing went on quickly: "You must

XII. The Gift of Lycanthropy

banish from your thoughts the widely held but mistaken belief that Lycanthropy must await the rising of the moon or a change in its phases as it passes from crescent to round. You may repeat the words at any time, whenever you wish the transformation to occur. And when you repeat them in reverse, the last word first, you will regain your human form as swiftly as you fell to all fours. Just listen now. I ask no more."

He drew himself up to his full height and what I had thought might be incredible words seemed as commonplace as the gibberish of some drunken reveler struggling homeward in the night.

I memorized the words the instant he fell silent, repeating them three or four times in my mind and taking care to guard against so much as moving my lips. The faintest of murmurs might have escaped me, and tight-lipped silence was, I felt, the only absolute safeguard.

I had lowered my eyes for an instant to avoid the slightest distraction and was only aware that a sudden shuffling sound had replaced the White Magician's harsh breathing.

I thought he had simply taken a few more steps backward, as a man will often do when he has been standing close to someone with an exacting task completed. Alert as I am to small sounds ordinarily I gave it no heed until the harsh breathing began again with something chillingly different about it. It seemed more like a panting.

I looked up abruptly then, and saw that there was no longer a human figure facing me. A huge furry shape with pointed ears, bared teeth and savagely gleaming eyes was backing slowly away from me, saliva dripping from its black-rimmed jaws.

It was backing away, I knew instantly, only far enough to enable it to hurl itself straight at me in a flying leap and bear me to the floor of the cave with the rapacious howling of a hunger-maddened wolf. A gigantic wolf, the largest I have ever seen or gone loping with through forests of the night feeling myself to be more than the equal in strength of the breed that had nurtured me and claimed me as their own. But never before had I set eyes on a wolf such as this.

In two or three more seconds, at most, I was sure that the monstrous beast would be at my throat. Not only was it between me and the weapon arm I had made the mistake of detaching but it was certain to leap the instant I moved in that direction, or in any direction. If I had been cursed with human stupidity at its worst, I might have been foolish enough to believe otherwise. But I was not so cursed.

There was a long pikestaff hanging on the wall within reach of my hand, with shreds of blackened flesh still clinging to its pointed iron head, which was two-thirds unsheathed.

I ripped the weapon down just as the great beast leapt and struck out at him as he came hurtling toward me. I struck out with all my strength and the point of the terrible blade pierced him in the eye and passed deep into his skull with a bone-splintering crunch.

He rose on his hind limbs, clawing at the air and I tugged at the weapon till it came loose, leapt backwards and stabbed him twice, the second thrust carrying the blade so deep into his vitals that the entire weapon was torn from my clasp and carried with him as he thudded to the floor of the cave.

Shaken a little by the suddenness of his leap, but otherwise as calm as I always remained when a killing went smoothly and without injury to myself and the pure joy of slaying was kept within bounds by circumstances of an unusual nature, I watched the great beast become a man again.

The White Magician's body was twisted in a half-loop and became continuously more twisted as he thrashed up and down, tearing frenziedly at his chest in a futile effort to dislodge the iron shaft that had impaled him. The grey wolf tail had shriveled and vanished and his animal hairiness had taken only a moment longer to become once more a human hairiness, so encrimsoned where it was most dense that his chest seemed covered with tiny, threadlike blood worms from a tidal pool as the dark wetness swelled and spread.

Suddenly a convulsive trembling seized him, and he arched himself twice, the long wolf snout, already greatly shortened, turning slowly into a human nose and a spreading flatness that was quickly transformed into the other lineaments.

For the barest instant, just before he flattened out on the cave floor and lay still, with a thin trickle of blood running from his mouth, he trained on me a look which made me remember the times when a killing rage had overcome me and I had felt myself to be driven by forces over which I had no control. At such times I had felt myself to be wholly a wolf and yet, when the madness passed, a strange, almost tormenting doubt had taken hold of me, although I could still have killed in a totally remorseless way, unshaken by the gushing forth of an adversary's blood or the dismemberment of his limbs.

But not to be completely sure of anything, to be torn by uncertainty as to what the totally unexpected might mean was like being caught in a raging flood at the brink of a precipice, with no rocks or overhanging boughs to cling to as the torrent rushed on.

I had spoken the transforming words only in my mind. My lips had not moved. It was the White Wizard who had spoken them aloud, after assuring me, more than once, that his instructional utterance would be of no danger to himself. If he had wanted to destroy me from the first could he not have done so without deceiving me in so contrived and complicated a way? A single blow while my back was turned would have felled me, or a sword-thrust the instant I was inside the cave.

Had the Ice Bitch deceived and betrayed him with a false promise? Had she wanted him to become a wolf, knowing that no counter spell she could cast in advance would stop the Lycanthropic change when once he had spoken the words?

Had she wanted him to leap upon me and tear out my throat? Or to slay himself, knowing that if I attacked him with a pikestaff it would be the same as if he had chosen to die by impaling himself upon it? Perhaps she had been certain, with her precognitive powers, that I would do exactly that, since in an act of folly I had detached my new arm and set it down a short distance from me.

The blade of a pikestaff could grind and tear and rend as a sword could not, rupturing and mangling the vital organs in an even more savage way. It is thought that a stake, driven through the heart of a vampire, can put an end to his nightly wanderings forever. Might not the mangling inflicted by a pikestaff destroy the magical powers of a sorcerer in much the same way, denying him the slightest chance of defeating death? Had he earned the Ice Bitch's undying hatred in some way unknown to me, and brought that kind of retribution upon himself? Might it not be possible that such a retribution could only be accomplished through Lycanthropy? A werewolf, like a vampire, was an unnatural creature and if slain in his transformed state might well remain forever dead. It would matter not at all if he regained his human form again before all the breath left his body. He would crumble into dust and never rise again.

They were wild thoughts, perhaps wholly untrue, and I put them from me. I was only sure of one thing. I was in the deadliest kind of danger as long as I remained in the cave. I walked quickly to where my new weapon arm was lying, picked it up and re-attached it. Upon sheathing Genseric's sword, I passed out into the night.

The desert which stretched out before me was still silvery with moonlight. Miles upon miles of nothing but sand, with only a few scattered boulders to break its monotony from the cave to an horizon so distant that it seemed to blend with a wilderness of stars.

I began to walk, swaying a little, still assailed by doubts, but determined not to falter or turn back toward the coast. If the slumped, lifeless figure I had left lying in the red-lit cave had spoken the truth I now had the gift of Lycanthropy and was following some course that was too predetermined to alter in any way. Knowing that I could become a wolf in outward form was more important to me than anything else, and there was no weapon, however miraculous, I would have traded for a gift so priceless. I was now walking erect like a man, but for the moment walking seemed, for some strange reason, easier than loping. Perhaps it was because I was more contemptuous of men than ever before, and could adopt their ways for purposes of convenience without any loss of my wolf pridefulness.

For a long time I continued on over the grey waste, feeling a need simply to keep walking, in search of a figure I felt I would eventually encounter if I did not abandon all thought of pursuing a course I no more than obscurely understood. I only knew that the Ice Bitch was still guiding me, and her guidance was not lacking in purpose. Even if that purpose was cold and remorseless and linked with acts of betrayal, I could not believe she actually sought my destruction. The prophecy she had made to me on our first meeting had angered me, almost beyond endurance, for she had told me that danger and strife would be mine for all the years of my life, and I would never find peace and my years would be few in number.

But she had also made it plain that she had no wish to side with my enemies and that it would be my destiny to save a civilization, in fact all civilization, in some crucial future conflict. Hence I had no choice but to follow her guidance cautiously, for I was in a new land, a strange land, and a wolf without allies in such a land would be certain to find his survival endangered.

I lost track of time as I continued on over the desert. I only know that the minutes lengthened into hours and that the present darkness was replaced by the brightness of another sunrise and then by the coming of another night, with the moonlight flooding down.

He came into view at first as no more than a jogging dot on the far horizon. But swiftly the dot grew larger and became a mounted human figure, crossing the plain in my direction, the moonlight glimmering on his breastshield and helmet.

His mount alone was astonishing, for he rode a creature I had never set eyes on before, striped like a zebra, and with the general aspect of a horse. But its head was reptilian and flattened, and kept bobbing to the right and left as it carried him swiftly across the plain. I had heard of such creatures, mythical beasts of legend from far northern lands, but such accounts I had never taken seriously. Magic can work strange miracles, and I was almost sure that the head of the beast was illusionary, created by some sorcerer's spell, the better to strike terror in the eyes of a beholder when Lamaril the Invincible rode coastward ahead of his legions and entirely alone, as the White Magician had informed me was his wont.

As he drew nearer everything the White Magician had told me about him was fully confirmed. He was the hugest man I had ever seen, apart from actual giants, who are ill-proportioned and ungainly of aspect. He had the look of a proud warrior whose every sinew had been strengthened by battle, and he bore himself like some legendary prince whose right to command had not been questioned from birth, even when he had been no more than an infant mewing and plucking in his nurse's arms.

XII. The Gift of Lycanthropy 117

His helmet and breastshield were of intricate design, but the sword he carried was without ornamentation of any kind, a naked blade, long and sharp, which he held aloft in his hand as he rode, as if his decimations had already begun. Or perhaps as a warning to any desert ghoul mad enough to leap from behind a boulder in a wild attempt to bring him down.

His sudden appearance on the desert rim had taken me by surprise and a decision I might have made earlier I was forced to make at once. How binding was the promise I had made to the White Magician now that he was dead, and the slaying of Lamaril could mean nothing to him?

How binding when I knew so little as to why he had perished and the part the Ice Bitch might have played in his destruction? The answer came quick and certain. Even if the Ice Bitch had betrayed us both for purposes of her own, the pledge would still have to be kept. Otherwise I would know nothing. The gift of Lycanthropy was in some way linked to my destiny, and some instinct told me that, for good or ill, I must now pursue that destiny to the utmost. It would have been dangerous to do otherwise, for the thread of one's destiny can seldom be cut and I lacked all positive knowledge as to the wisdom of attempting it.

I removed my new arm for the second time, and set it down along with Genseric's blade on the sand. I stood very straight for a moment, precisely as the White Wizard had done before pronouncing the four words that had brought destruction upon him. I pronounced them slowly and clearly.

For a moment nothing happened. Then, when I looked down over myself, I saw that my body had begun to lengthen and change shape, becoming much narrower from my chest to my hips.

Coarse white hair had started to appear on my torso and thighs, and it spread so quickly that even before I dropped to all fours I knew that my clothes had disappeared as my new arm might possibly have done if I had not taken it off. I gave it hardly a thought, for it was well in accord with what has been said about the Lycanthropic change. Garments vanish in some strange way, and regain their substance when the need for them returns. I only knew as I bounded forward across the plain that the howl that came from my throat was more savage than it had ever been before, and my jaws had become so completely the jaws of a wolf that the clash of my teeth jerked my head to right and left and streaked the sand with a whitish froth.

Lamaril's mount was less than eighty feet distant from me now, but he had seemingly not seen me. He was staring straight ahead with a preoccupied air, as if meditating on his coming conquests.

Without waiting for him to come any nearer I loped out across the sand directly in his path, so swiftly that when his vision centered on me it was too late for him to do anything but rein in his mount and raise his great sword in self-defense. He had need for such defense, for in another moment I had left the ground and was leaping straight for his throat.

It was a sudden flash of moonlight on his sword that saved him. It was too late for him to have run me through but the flash so distorted his aim that the sword struck me flatside on the right flank, hurling me to the sand.

He dismounted instantly, with a bellow of rage so loud that it echoed back from some distant crag or cave, and let his mount gallop on. He faced me again with his sword upraised, advancing upon me with a string of oaths in a language unknown to me. I knew they were oaths by the fierce look in his eyes and the rigid set of his jaw.

His hugeness alone would have cowered most men, formidably armed as he was, but hugeness in a figure as vulnerable as a man means nothing to a wolf.

It was only his reputed skill at swordplay, which the White Wizard had extolled, which made me cautious for an instant and kept me from leaping straight at him again.

I circled about him instead, so swiftly that twice he lunged at me and missed. My chance came at last, when he turned for the barest instant to determine the source of what was probably no more than an imagined sound at his back or one made by the wind ruffling the sand.

I leapt at his right leg, sank my teeth into it, and tore and ripped at the flesh until he began to scream, his sword falling to the sand. It was a pitiful thing to hear such a scream coming from a man of fabled and heroic mold. But I showed him no mercy and I am sure he expected none.

I did not stop with his leg and went on and on with the slaughter, until the sand about him was darkly sodden and glistening, and his throat torn out.

I turned abruptly, rejoicing in what I saw and not in any way sickened by it, as a man might well have been. I turned because regaining my human form had suddenly become of vital concern to me. I had to know if the Lycanthropic transformation could be reversed at will, as the White Magician had said. If not, if he had lied to me, the new land at which I had arrived might prove hostile and dangerous to such an extent that I could not hope to survive for long with my belly hugging the ground and wolf cries coming from my throat.

A stout warrior in human form may be hated and feared, but a wolf running through the night is looked upon as ferocity incarnate, and becomes an instant target for hurled javelins and

XII. The Gift of Lycanthropy

poison-tipped arrows.

I went loping back across the sand to where I had left my weapons and in my haste to get arm and sword securely in my clasp again I spoke the words in reverse the instant I came in sight of them.

More swiftly than I could have anticipated I found myself arising to an almost upright position. I had no doubt that I remained for a moment longer almost entirely a wolf in bodily form, still half-crouching on my haunches. But the change that was making me rise was accompanied by a lessening of the fur on my back and thighs. I could distinctly feel the loss of its heaviness, and there was a faint rustling sound as the skin beneath became enveloped in the slight tightness of a returning garment. It was as if the substance of my clothing had dissolved and been held in suspension by magic, hovering over me all the while like an aura. It puzzled me less when I remembered how ice could turn into moist air, and then become ice again.

The instant I had arisen to full human height my new arm seemed almost to leap into my hand. I had no clear recollection of even bending and picking it up, but I must have done so. As I stared down at it swaying a little, a voice spoke to me in the wind-swept, moon-brightened waste. Whence it came I did not know, only that it was clear and bell-like, as if the Ice Bitch had broken through all barriers of space and time to bring me a message that was straining her powers to the utmost. A tinkling accompanied the syllables of her speech, as if millions of tiny ice crystals were swirling around and around inside a jar of glass as large as the earth, dissolving, reforming and beating against the glass until it became resonant with the faintest of musical sounds.

"You have done well," the voice said. "It is only with your human form cast off, only with the great gift of Lycanthropy yours to summon at will . . . that you can be sure of triumph in the struggles which must still be waged, against enemies more fearsome than any you have yet met. Blood must flow freely, for the danger is great that all life will otherwise vanish from the earth.

"You have slain many times before without pity and without remorse. But just thinking of yourself as a wolf in human form was not enough. What is true of wolves is just as true of a lion or a bear or some small furry creature of the wild that must slay to survive. They alone can draw strength from the great Old Ones, who sway in the timeless winds that blow cold upon us from the depths of space. The Old Ones have not yet awakened and still lie dreaming, and they sway in a way that men would think mindless, for Man can possess no knowledge of what that kind of mindlessness can mean. They are far more ancient, stronger, wiser than the Ice Gods, whose first daughter I am, in ways that would be incomprehensible to Man. Only when you run savagely through the night as a true wolf will their still half-somnolent strength flow into you, for men cannot communicate with them except in fugitive dreams, vague and terrifying, which they blot from their minds on awakening, in dread of going mad.

"A day will come when the Old Ones will awaken and earth will quake with their unchained rage, for they were cast into outer darkness by an accident of Time. But that day is far in the future and it would be unwise to dwell upon it now, for there is no certainty that the earth will someday be destroyed. It is enough to know that Yog-Sothoth and ocean-dreaming Cthulhu can strengthen you now as you run through the night as a true wolf, and that if you strain your ears you can hear the far-off baying of the Hounds of Tindalos."

In all of my wanderings I had never heard anyone speak of such gods. But it was well in accord with what she had said. There were gods so fearsome that men blotted all knowledge of them from their minds, lest madness overtake them.

Strangely enough, it was a matter less awesome but of more immediate importance to me that made me raise my own voice in sudden anger and fierce protest.

"Why did you betray the White Magician?" I asked. "Was it necessary for him to be transformed into a true wolf and be slain by me? Did he lie when he told me that he could speak the transforming words without endangering himself in any way? Did you not promise him he would be protected by the powerful magic you helped him summon to his aid in the deep trance into which he passed? Did you secretly hate him and wish him to be destroyed?"

"How can you hate a miserable worm?" she replied. "And what are promises given to a worm? He was a wretched, deceitful creature, willing to aid me only to gain my favor, in the hope of draining away some of my magical powers to his own advantage. His destruction was of no importance. It was all part of the testing I wished you to undergo, to make sure the gift of Lycanthropy would be worthily bestowed.

"In human form you slew a monstrous beast, instantly alert to the peril you were in, quick to seize a weapon that served you well. Then, as a true wolf, you slew again, and there was no more formidable warrior chieftain in all of this new land than Lamaril the Invincible. You did well to follow my guidance and in your slaying you did well also.

"Together we will do better still. Our destinies are now joined and I will henceforth never be wholly absent when you slay again. But your strength will come from the Old Ones as well."

"But there is much that I do not understand," I said. "If the Old Ones you speak of are utterly malignant and hostile, not only to

XII. The Gift of Lycanthropy

man, but to the guardians of Earth's civilization—yes, even to the Ice Gods—how can they defend and protect us in the struggle that must still be waged? Are they not both your enemies and mine? And has it not been predicted that I am destined to save Nemedia?"

"Save Nemedia you will," she said, "for now, when you run as a true wolf through the night, the inscrutable powers of the Old Ones will strengthen you in more than one way. Those powers will become so much a part of you that you will now be able to *bend them to our purpose*."

"To our purpose?" I persisted. "I still do not quite understand. Are you saying the Old Ones can be made to either defend, or destroy us?"

"I may seem to speak in riddles, but it is not really so," Ythillin said. "The Old Ones themselves cannot be swayed by man or wolf. Neither can they be swayed by the Ice Gods. They are beyond and above all such swaying. But their powers can be drawn into every fiber of your being whenever you become a true wolf—inscrutable powers, which even then you will not completely understand, but which can be bent to defend and protect you, and aid you in the destruction of Nemedia's enemies."

Ythillin paused, then went on swiftly, her voice becoming even more persuasive because of its increasing earnestness. "As I have said, even the lowliest of animals, the small furry creatures of the forest, can become more formidable and dangerous through their instinctive use of those powers. In a very primitive way even they can bend such powers to their use in a struggle for survival."

"But man, too, is an animal," I said. "Why does he not share with a wolf—"

Before I could say more she answered my incomplete question with a persuasiveness that carried total conviction. Knowing man as I did, there was no need for me to question her further.

"Man's vaunted reason—a pitiful thing, really, a cloak for ignorance—prevents him from bending to his purpose the powers which he does, to some extent, possess. Every living creature can draw strength from the Old Ones in moments of deadly peril.

"A few men, perhaps because of their rapaciousness and barbaric near-madness may go far in making use of such powers, but never as successfully as can a wolf or a tiger. Mentumenen, for instance, has deluded himself into believing that the powers of the Old Ones can be bent to serve the enemies of Nemedia. In his near-madness he even thinks that it is the Old Ones themselves he has summoned to his aid. In the first surmise he is not entirely mistaken. He can bend the powers to some extent but you can defeat him by bending them more strongly in defense. In the second surmise he is entirely mistaken. In both he is now courting defeat and disaster."

Chapter XIII
The War Among the Gods
Adrian Cole

Ythillin's last words to me out in that cold desert fortified my purpose. "You must find Shanara. She is closer than you think. Follow Lamaril's beast north." The revelations the Ice Bitch had made had filled my head with strange images, confusing as much as enlightening me. I spat a curse for her but loped northward, following the clear spoor of the reptilian horse that had been Lamaril's. As I crossed the rolling dunes, I was deeply aware of the beast within me now, scarcely beneath my crust, and the urge to take upon me the shape of the wolf grew more urgent with each mile. In that feral state I had been closer than ever to the pulsing wilds.

Topping another of the endless dunes, I saw before me in a natural hollow an oasis, or what I took to be one. The thought of water spurred me downwards to those still shadows, but something else about the place instinctively cautioned me. A wolf smells sorcery even more readily than a man. That animal in me sniffed at the brooding atmosphere, for something undefined lurked in that place. But I must have water. I bared my teeth in a snarl and clutching my sword moved stealthily into the first of the trees.

The hair from my neck to the base of my spine stiffened; I had known the aura of the supernatural times enough, but here something awesome seemed to stir. I thought of the grim island in the Vilayet Sea. But this place was dissimilar. These trees, though, were not of the desert. Their trunks were too gnarled to be palms, their leaves were like sprawling canopies. As I moved through them to the pool at the heart of the oasis, it was as though the trees whispered to themselves and then pressed in like great sheaves of grass. I growled like a predator at its kill watching for jealous rivals. I dipped my face to the water. It was like heady wine and I took my fill.

As I rose from the water, I stared up at the night sky. Here in the desert it is ablaze with a million stars, scattered like jewels over a velvet cloak—and yet now I saw none! Above me all was black, as though a colossal shadow had shut me into that place of mystery. Something rustled the trees, as if they breathed and would bend down to enfold me.

"Ghor!" hissed a voice. "Child of the earth!"

Both Genseric's sword and the blade in Dar'ah Humarl's

weapon flashed. The killing mood was on me—I needed but a lead. Something moved among those thick leaves

"We are your brothers. Be guided by us." As they spoke, three figures dropped to the sand and stood before me openly. They were unarmed and too diminutive to offer a real threat. Their skin was the texture of tree bark, their grotesque arms like slender branches. As they faced me, I heard the gentle creaking of their bodies.

"Who are you?" I growled.

"Elementals," they breathed as one. "Our purpose is to serve you, though we serve one greater. We must take you to her." They approached me and still I was cautious, distrustful. They made a circle around me. I readied my blades, but when the movement came it was from an unexpected quarter. The ground beneath me rippled. Then it moved distinctly and began to subside. I had heard of such phenomena in the desert, but this was no natural thing, I was certain. It was too late to attack the elementals, or indeed move, for I was being swallowed up by the earth.

"Beshrew your fears, Ghor," whispered the elementals, peering down at me. "Your enemies are far away. Take what blessings you shall find below and be strengthened."

To my horror the sand began to fall in on me. I was being buried alive! Too late I screamed out a stream of abuse at the gods and whatever things had trapped me, for the soft, reassuring voices of the elementals did nothing to calm me. The sky blotted out; sand crushed me to my knees. It squeezed in on me from all sides, pressing me down, down, into the cold earth below. It filled my eyes, my ears, my mouth. Everything—all my fire, my trapped bestiality— all shut off as though I had died.

What followed was more like a dream than reality. I knew that I had been entombed, deep down in the earth. There was nothing around me for vast distances but solid earth and sand—somehow I knew that. And yet I did not writhe in mental anguish. Warmth suffused me, and then peace, and last a feeling of unique awareness. I was one with the earth, the womb that had bred me.

Her voice drifted into my dream of peace like a soft tide, so calm and still that even the raw violence of the beast was subdued for a time. I knew it was the very earth that spoke to me, just as I sensed her every fibre stretching away from me in a vast circle that embraced all her creations, animate and inanimate.

"You are a child of the earth, Ghor. Draw strength from me."

I wanted to speak, to question, but I could not. My mind was like a vessel into which she would pour the dizzy wine of truth. I tasted the earth, smelled it, heard it whisper around me.

"I have drawn you far into me that the gods hear nothing of what I must tell you. The gods—how they use my poor children!"

she said. "How they are using you, Ghor, in this endless war. And they have told you so little—hinted at pieces of a broken mirage, no more. Fed you images that draw you on to the destiny they have already woven for you. And yet you have the power to carve your own path, even if it should lead to the goals they have chosen for you.

"Long has this war among gods racked me, who am forced to fight against them! Gods of Order and Gods of Chaos! Forever they will strive, embroiling not one universe but all! How I despise them, for they tear me and my true children like wolves at a carcass. The Gods of Order—they such as the Ice Gods whom Ythillin serves—seek to build civilization up to great heights, for they believe that men and the gods can only co-exist if man climbs up from barbarism. They seek to bind together all the internecine nations of your world, Ghor—bind them together under a new empire that will be greater than any other that has gone before. Nemedia!

"But as ever, the Chaos Lords oppose them, as they oppose all life. Once before they embroiled themselves in a cosmic war that destroyed the very fabric of the world. I almost died and became no more than a sterile rock, but I found the strength to go on. I grew strong again, as you can see; I gave my children new power. Yet those vile Chaos Lords still seek to disrupt and destroy the works of Order and of me and completely rework the fabric of life to their own debased cause, perverting and disjointing this world and all others—even those of the future.

"Thus they clash eternally. Many are the deities that strive and countless their pantheons, Innumerable are the demigods and demons, the spirits and the beings in the dark places that contend, for this dreadful celestial war sucks into its voracious maw all things living.

"I despise them for it! Gods of Order and Gods of Chaos! I was never a part of them, for they have abused me and molded my children to their ends, not mine! I will oppose them, for I must if my body is to survive. I will cast them out, god by god, demon by demon,

"There are others here, too. Aeons ago there were monstrous beings that swam amongst the stars of the many universes. They served not the Chaos Lords, but their own heinous whims, no less terrible. They, too, took of my life force and made from it offspring of their own. For this blasphemy they were enchained by other gods and forced into eternal banishment. Now they slumber, immortal but incarcerated. Many of them are embedded deep in me. I hold these Old Ones and keep them stilled in their fretful dreaming. Ythillin has spoken to you of them. Beware of using their powers! There will be a price if you do.

XIII. The War Among the Gods

"You, Ghor, are not as other men. You have sensed this from your very birth—just as Gudrun, your mother, sensed it. When she had you left for the wolves, it was not your crippled leg that prompted her; she knew you were a child of the earth. More beast than man, whom nature would look after. Have I not done so? Did you ever marvel at your wild life, your ability to survive where other men would have perished?

"There are men and men, Ghor—my true children, and those that the gods have warped to their schemes. It was the elemental in you that singled you out in the eyes of the Ice Gods. To establish Nemedia as all-powerful, fountain of civilization, they have to wreak violence and havoc, for only then can they subjugate all others. They need a man who is more than a man (and they have used such men before, as they did with the pink-eyed albino sorcerer and the Cimmerian colossus). This time you are that man. No one is closer to the rawness of nature than Ghor the Strong! You are destined to save their civilization and build its foundations in blood! Yet civilization is against your nature, so you defy them.

"But what of my desires, Ghor? I say again—I oppose them all, who would rape me and taint me with their spawn! I oppose these Gods of Order for they seek to enforce an unnatural order on my randomness that will lead to total destruction. I oppose the Chaos Lords, who seek to change all things and create new universes that have no place for sanity, only pain.

"Thus I say to you, earth child, go forth and establish this Nemedian empire as has been prophesied. Subjugate the other ravening nations. I will bend this to my own scheme of things, for know this—I will bring it down. Not through fire and flood and earthquake and storm, but through these very chattels of the Ice Gods! I will drive them south: Cimmerian, Vanir, Æsir—drive them shivering before the wall of *ice*. The very gods that they seem to worship will seem to have turned against them. There will be wars and more wars, but the Ice Gods will pass away! Oh, they will be replaced, for the Gods of Order are as imperishable as those of Chaos, and I will oppose them once more.

"So follow your destiny, Ghor! Establish Nemedia, even if it is not for yourself. If you fail in this, it will be to the benefit of the Chaos Lords. If they change the future we have seen for one of their making, we are all lost. You have been given weapons and powers to aid you—Chaos took away your arm and Ythillin has given you a new one, as she has given you, through the White Magician, the gift of Lycanthropy. Use that gift with care, for it will bring you closer to me. You have another weapon, the powers of which I have masked from the Ice Gods since first it came into the world. Genseric's sword. It was forged by fire elementals deep within my bosom when I was young. If you call upon the dreaming powers of the Old Ones, the sword will protect you from the consequences, for without it you would sink into the depths of their will, as men have done ere now and will again.

"Above all, beware of Mentumenen! That demigod seeks power and sovereignty over the world and that before all else. Yet he is the tool of Set and the Chaos Lords, though he does not realize how they use him! He schemes to put Tashako on Nemedia's throne, for he has corrupted the youth and stolen his wits. He will use Shanara against you, too, Ghor. How heartless the gods are! They have used her as bait to ensnare you from the first, goading you on with her loveliness. But they will never let you win her. Did the Ice Bitch not tell you you would die without seed? Have you not wondered that Shanara's belly remains fallow after so long with you? Aye, seedless you will be, for you are to have no future claim to the kingship of Nemedia. The Ice Gods will use the elemental in you to win a throne for them, but ultimately they seek to destroy that part of man and make man their own. I will be a mother without children when they have done. No, earth child, Hialmar is to be king of Nemedia. Mentumenen plays on that, too, for he knows that if Shanara and Hialmar become lovers, there will be much hate between you and your friend. This rift will split Nemedia in twain and leave her powerless to rise to glory.

"You must not let Mentumenen destroy the empire before it is born! Chaos and its future must be thwarted! Accept that Shanara is not for you. Accept Hialmar's destiny, his glory; it is he that will slay the Pictish sovereign, Gorm. Do not oppose Hialmar, for in so doing you serve Chaos. And Chaos has already sought to trick you into serving it and abandoning me. On the island in the Vilayet you awoke from a dream of winged, bronze monsters and found your men slain—for a time you thought it was by your bloody hand they had died. I heard you shout out that you would fight all mankind, all gods and all demons. And that you would flatten the earth with your sword. In your vision, the shades of the dead—your family and all you had slain—taunted you. *All nature, all the earth and things beyond the earth revile thee*, they laughed. Such are the twisted lies of Chaos! Beware, for Chaos would use you. Turn not against the elemental in you, Ghor, for all nature and all the earth are your real hope. We are your allies. Grasp firmly your convictions that you speak for the wilderness, for it is so! You are my voice, my sword, my champion!"

My mind was a cauldron, seething with visions, bubbling with the numerous images I had been shown in this dream. The whole of the cosmic tapestry was at last before me, as though, until now, I had been staring at mere sections of it. Ythillin had not lied to me,

XIII. The War Among the Gods

no! Yet she had cheated me. I had been right to mistrust her. She had shown me and told me just enough to make me go on. Teasing me, using Shanara to goad me. Shanara! Was it true what the earth oracle had told me? That I could never win her? I had no time to think on that, for the voice came to me anew.

"Chaos has become violently active since Mentumenen unwittingly drew upon those absolute, destructive forces he cannot control. His dealings with Set and other blasphemous Southern entities has presaged a number of irruptions of evil, like pestilences upon the earth. Lamaril and his army was one such plague. He was a Chaos minion. The White Magician who served Ythillin, Telordric, tried to destroy Lamaril and what followed him, but failed. Telordric fled here from the north, with Lamaril sworn to destroying him. In his battle, Telordric had been corrupted by Chaos and so earned the wrath of Ythillin, whom he served. It was because of that wrath that he died—through you, Ghor. Ythillin could easily have destroyed Telordric herself, but she left it to you and did not tell you the real reason why. The elemental in you purified Telordric as he died, and his soul went not to Chaos, but into the earth womb. Had Ythillin destroyed him, she would have sent him to Chaos, and she would never send so much as a mote of dust to her hated enemies! So once more you were deceived.

"Telordric told you that Lamaril's legions would scatter in panic and despair if you killed Lamaril. They should have. But Mentumenen has reorganized them. Even now, with Tashako and the captive Shanara, the black sorcerer is preparing to take the army across the Vilayet Sea. He will unleash it wherever it suits him. I cannot say where. I cannot read what is in Mentumenen's heart, for it is so corrupted by Chaos that what small part of him was once of the earth is dead within him.

"You, Ghor, must go north. Find the army and a way to destroy it! Aye, and the sorcerer, too, if you can. Take Shanara back to Belverus if you triumph, in spite of what I have said of her destiny. But destroy Lamaril's army. If you do not, Chaos will grow bolder and will likely spawn even greater horrors. The fabric between dimensions is so thin! Know, Ghor, that a titanic struggle is imminent, not only here on your world, but across the cosmos. There have been upheavals and cataclysms before, but the outcome of this conflict will decide the fate, not only of me, but of all universes and all times. The conflict between you and Mentumenen is the fulcrum on which the Cosmic Balance rests."

A great sigh followed this, as though the earth had tired herself. Silence surrounded me and from it I drew new strength: the earth nourished me as I had never been nourished before. The earth had said all she would say to her child. She had unlocked the mysteries that had puzzled me. Now I must choose a path.

Mentumenen and Shanara were near. I must find them. I would bring whatever powers I could down on the sorcerer's head. He was the vent through which Chaos would spill out onto the earth.

I shook my head and found myself standing once more beside the pool. The elementals had gone and the trees were no longer the strange growths they had been, but palms. Beside me I found raw meat, freshly killed, and I wasted no time asking myself how it had got there. I sank my teeth into it and tore chunks from it, chewing like a ravenous beast. Such would I be. If I was to win anything, I now knew, I must reject the last remnants of civilized man that clung to me. I was an earth child, a beast of the wild, and only through my untamed spirit could I take what was mine and the earth mother's.

The sky was clear again, shot with stars, and an immense full moon rode the heavens. I threw back my head and bayed at it, the sounds that came from my throat purely those of a wolf. I sucked in the night air, scenting out the spoor of Lamaril's beast. I looked north. Somewhere there, at the edge of the Vilayet, they would be. Finishing my feast, I loped on across the dunes.

For two days and nights I tracked the Chaos beast, pausing only to hunt for food, a predator of the desert more deadly than the jackals. I tore my kills apart and drank the hot blood from their jugulars, delighting in the beast blood singing in my veins. James Allison was never further from me, for I had truly reverted to my primeval self. All modern man's complexes and phobias were gone. I was a child of the earth, my heart, my veins, pulsing with the same raw energy that sang in the vitals of the planet beneath me. Telordric's strange gift had opened up my mind to the earth mother as he could never have realized.

At last I reached a place, high on a scarp of broken rocks, where I could look down at a valley. There, a few miles from the moonlit waters of the Vilayet, I saw the host of Lamaril. Darkness obscured those minions at this distance, but I knew they were not of this dimension. Spawn of some deep abyss they must be, for they were ranked like men risen from graves, and were as silent as the mummies I had seen beneath the ruins of northern cities. Above them flapped creatures whose form I could not see, even by the glare of that immense moon, but I guessed that they were Chaos-born, too. Set there by Mentumenen, ever watchful.

There were tents in the distance—tents where perhaps Shanara would be, and the brat, Tashako. I would claw him to earth and tear out his throat before the night was out. The earth mother had told me I must destroy this horde. Yet how was I to do that? Become a werewolf and run amok? But there were thousands of beast beings below me, arranged like statues. If I attacked, would they become animate?

No, I must attack Mentumenen directly. He could not know I was here, so close. I would become a wolf, though, and slink about the perimeters of the camp. I was loathe to hide Genseric's sword, now that I knew its true purpose, but decided to bury it with my false arm. I marked the spot in my mind, then uttered Telordric's mystic words. At once my transformation began. I was a white wolf, silvered by moonlight, prowling through the dunes at the edge of the vast encampment. I made for the tents.

There were hound-like beasts tethered outside—three-headed horrors that were not spawned on this world. Their scarlet eyes flashed out at the night as they got my scent. As one they leapt up and began snarling, rattling their chains. I loped back into shadow. Men came to the tent flaps and my hackles rose, for Tashako was with them. They held high their torches, searching the night landscape, but saw me not. Yet the hound-beasts snarled on. Let the men unleash them! I would rip them to shreds and toss their carcasses back into the camp! But the men quelled them.

If Mentumenen was here, I would not be able to get to him without being detected. I could not risk a direct attack, even though I could bring utter havoc on the camp. Sheer numbers weighed against me. I thought hard on the words of Ythillin—and of the earth mother. The powers of the Old Ones were not of Chaos, but they were within my reach. Telordric had spoken grim names—Yog-Sothoth, Cthulhu, and the Hounds of Tindalos. Hounds! Somewhere in the back of my wolf-mind I could hear their baying, as if from some point far out among the stars—or *behind* them. Would the Hounds not aid a werewolf? I would see.

Searching deep inside myself, I found the hidden keys that would bring the Hounds to me. The earth mother had told me that she kept the Old Ones imprisoned; now I sensed that she was draining off something of their powers to aid me, for I knew what I must do. I found a place of flat sand and with my claws scratched out two squares, one inside the other. I then urinated at the four points of the inner square and stood within it. I raised my head to the moon and the waiting stars. The Hounds of Tindalos would come to me through the angles of the outer square. I began to bay, and it seemed as though the very earth shook.

At once the camp exploded with life. A terrible wailing broke out amongst the zombie-like beings of the army. The hound creatures shrieked in madness. It was as though Chaos strained at its own leash, sensing that some terrible force was arriving.

The ground at my feet was slick with saliva as I bayed. The stars seemed to me to ripple and blur as if seen through a disturbed pool. I heard a deep, soul-shaking growl and turned. Behind me, within the first square, stood a lean, shaggy monster, tall at the shoulder as a man. It had eyes that would turn a sane man mad, and teeth that flashed like knives; from them dripped sizzling saliva, more deadly than any poison for I knew that one drop spelled utter corruption. Creatures of the first evil of creation, they pressed forward in a pack, a dozen of the horrors, sniffling and snarling at my urine. The sound of their dreadful breathing blew over me like a wave from the depths of any cosmic hell, but they kept off me. These were the Hounds of Tindalos, and terrible was their hunger.

With an insane shriek of joy, I leapt from my inner square and burst through the Hounds, charging down upon the camp where bedlam now reigned. At once the Hounds behind me set up such a baying and slavering as no mortal ears have heard. As a unified pack, we burst into the camp, tearing and slashing at all living things in our way. How I controlled the hellish pack I cannot say, but the Hounds of Tindalos did my killing as well as their own. They set upon Lamaril's army, gorging themselves ferociously, ripping apart all those that stood before them. No beast of earthly realms ever knew such hunger.

Now I saw the hell-spawn that made up this Chaos army. Awful beings, parodies of humanity and bestiality, some more reptile than man, shrieked and hissed before us. Some were clawed, some flicked curling tentacles; some crawled, some hopped. Here was proof enough that Chaos had ripped its way into this dimension. I would feel no remorse in shredding this vile gathering. Such things that flapped in the air, multi-headed and with razor claws, screamed as they swooped upon us. I caught one leathery beast and sank my teeth into its wing, pulling it down on top of me. I was a whirlwind, a volcano of savagery. It was as though some dark, preternatural force had filled me and blotted out everything but the killing mania. Slick with blood, I tore off the head of the Chaos being, tossing the body far from me. I ripped out the throats of other monsters, thinking that I would raise the very Old Ones themselves if I had to!

Time was suspended while that madness vented itself. Then the first of the tents was before me. I barely controlled my frenzy enough to rip its hangings aside. Therein, Tashako stood behind his human guards. With a feral roar, I rushed upon them. They cut at me with their blades, but I moved like quicksilver. I was too fast for them and knocked them to the sand, tearing out their throats in a welter of blood. I was up before Tashako could bolt and smashed him to the ground. I placed a claw upon his throat. He was screaming. Now I could see how Chaos had corrupted him, for he was more tainted by Chaos than humanity; his skin had changed, as if the very fabric of his body had been remoulded into something repellent to this world.

XIII. The War Among the Gods

I could not speak, beast that I was, but I growled out the words that again made me Ghor, the half-man. Tashako fell deathly silent, studying my terrible visage.

"Ghor?" he croaked. "Can it be you? Has Chaos corrupted you also?"

I felt no pity for one who had betrayed me and who had sought my death. With my one bare hand I gripped his thin neck and twisted it like the dried stem of a plant. It was a merciful death. I wiped away the thick blood from my face and went outside. The Hounds had unleashed chaos on Chaos. As far as the eye could see there was an ocean of bloodshed. The noise was frightful.

I rushed to the other tents, ripping them down, but they were empty, save for the mangled corpses of Mentumenen's human acolytes. But where was the sorcerer?

From overhead came the sound of thick wings, beating at the night sky frenetically. A Hound leapt up and barely missed those rising claws. It was the huge flying creature I had seen before—the last time upon the island in the sea.

"Ghor!" shrilled a voice. High-pitched, full of terror, it was that of Shanara. I stood helplessly as the bird monster (which I knew to be the metamorphosed Mentumenen) rose upwards towards the moon. Again he had escaped me. But I thought not of him, only Shanara. My longing for her gushed back like the hot blood I had spilled. She had shouted but one word, my name, but in that shouting had been a world of meaning. Love? Aye, it was there. Whatever the gods had decreed—whatever the earth mother had confirmed—I knew Shanara loved me. That one thought kept me from insanity.

I stifled my bestial rage. I must organize my pursuit. I looked at the pandemonium before me. It must stop. I would not destroy the Chaos spawn of Lamaril. I would *use* it!

I bayed at the moon, calling off the Hounds of Tindalos. As before, they obeyed me. They dropped to their bellies in the sand, thick black tongues lolling, licking the blood and ordure of the dead from their lean bodies. They waited. The army was like a wounded beast, groaning with terror and pain. I would use it. If I must win Nemedia, I would need allies. I had used the dark horrors of the Hounds—I would use these. Aye, and any that would aid me. I would be the instrument of destruction, just as Mentumenen sought to be. To the abyss with all gods! Once I had used this grim army, I would destroy it, just as the earth mother had insisted.

Quickly I went up into the dunes to find the sword of Genseric and my mechanical arm. I moved more like a wolf now than ever, by pure instinct. Was there a dividing line between man-wolf and werewolf? If so, it grew thinner by the hour. I took up the sword and bayed again at the heavens. Let all the gods hear me! I was their toy no longer. Let them clash and bring about the downfall of man, I would survive! I and my brothers of the wild—we would survive and we would seed the earth anew.

I called off the Hounds. They slinked off into the desert, and though they were out of sight, the sound of their rasping breathing still reached me like a hot desert wind. Tomorrow I would begin the long march that would eventually bring me upon the rear of the Hyrkanians. The Hounds of Tindalos would patrol the flanks of my unearthly army, and those that broke ranks they would devour, Fear would be my whip. I would smash aside any who stood in my way.

Let the gods meet, let the earth shake, let the stars tremble. The children of the earth scorned them.

Chapter XIV
The Ways of Chaos
Ramsey Campbell

At dawn the army reached the steppes. Hard earth the colour of baked dung, interrupted only by tussocks of grass like spiky yellow scalps, spread monotonously to the horizon. The sky was more bare than the land; not a cloud relieved its glaring. Already the horizon was blurred by heat and roving dust. I scanned it constantly, alert for patrols. Though my sight was keen as any wolf's, I had to strain to penetrate the haze—yet I was glad of that, for it helped me not to dwell on the troops I presumed to command.

All of the humans save one had died in the attack. Perhaps some of the things which marched before me had once been human. Their unnaturally regular tread, monotonous as the stamping of a gigantic mechanical hammer, veiled them in clouds of dust, but I had only to glance about me to glimpse horrors.

Here was a swollen lip that dangled lower than the chin, here a head which kept rising from a moist pit between shoulders, there a giant figure on whose left jowl, quivering and blinking as he marched, simpered a rudimentary face. A shape which trudged on the left of my mount might almost have been a shaggy warrior, except that his eyes, whenever the dust stung them, withdrew like snail's horns into his flesh. Often I was near to falling on these creatures, to rend them to death in revulsion, in clean animal rage. But I must not, for they were leading me to my prey.

Mentumenen had erred. Remembering, I grinned savagely. Last night, as he had escaped bearing Shanara, the heads of his army had turned to watch him. When the worst of his creatures had begun to struggle in the direction he had taken, I was ready to slaughter them until I saw how they would aid me. In their mindless way, the troops of Chaos were still loyal to Mentumenen, and would follow him as best they could. Since their compulsion was leading them also toward the Hyrkranians, I was doubly right to follow.

The one human who had survived the attack, I had spared. The smell of his fear had led me to the dune behind which he had been cowering. His dark skin and his shaven crown showed him to be one of Mentumenen's acolytes, though it was weedy with stubble now. About to tear out his gulping throat, I had reconsidered: what might he tell me of his master's plans? I had bound his hands—a distasteful task, for his left arm was corrupted by Chaos, the fingertips bloated and gelatinous—and now he rode beside me.

His gratitude disgusted me. I thought of a beaten mongrel, snuffling and licking his master's feet. More intolerably, he seemed to think I had spared him because he was human, as though we were brothers. Nor did he seem likely to prove useful; something—his alliance with Chaos, or Mentumenen's power—had robbed him of the memory of his own name. When we made camp, I was determined that I would pry his secrets from him by whatever means were necessary.

By noon I could bear him no longer: neither his fawning gaze nor his silence. Now the steppes were a featureless sea of parched grass, the colour of senile skin, which rustled harshly beneath the marchers. A pall of brownish clouds seemed to weigh down the air. Infrequent breezes raised shapeless ghosts of dust that hissed through the grass. At the edge of the army, where long angular shapes formed in the grass, the hiss had a slobbering quality, and I knew the Hounds of Tindalos were vigilant. Yet I felt alone with the suffocated landscape, the horizon which appeared to be receding, the clouds of flies which rose from stagnant gullies to feed on the horde. I was growing desperate for action. When several wild horses thundered by on the horizon, it was minutes before I could be sure they were not a patrol.

My gaze was drawn to a marcher ahead of me, his fattened head swollen almost to the breadth of his shoulders. A swarm of flies was feasting there. As I watched, a dozen moist holes gaped in the hairless head and swallowed the flies. I could bear no more; I must act or run amok. Drawing Genseric's sword, I pricked the throat of the bound acolyte. "Tell me of Mentumenen," I snarled. "Enlighten me, or rot here, feeding the flies."

The Stygian's face crumpled; he looked ready to blubber. "The Master," he whispered fearfully. "Mustn't sleep. He is waiting for me in my dreams. He wants to—" He fell silent, shuddering.

Did the wretch fear more than nightmares? I remembered how Mentumenen had appeared to me on the island of the massacre. Seizing the rein of his mount, I drew blood from the Stygian's throat with my sword. "Speak, or there will be no wakening."

"Set is waiting," he babbled. Perhaps the threat of death had reminded him. "Once I saw his snout. He stands always at the Master's shoulder, listening..."

I was tired of his ravings, and barely able to prevent my sword from thrusting deep. Perhaps he sensed this, for all at once he grew perfectly calm, as though he knew he was doomed whatever he might say. "I know what the Master intends," he whispered.

"Tell me quickly," my sword-point said for me.

He glared about, fearing perhaps that the deformed horde might

XIV. The Ways of Chaos

fall on him to silence him. "The chiefs of the Hyrkranians and of the Picts will dream of him. He will persuade them to unite against Nemedia—he has ways to persuade them even of that. He will offer them allies beside which this army is as naught. But when they have conquered Nemedia, the chiefs will be his puppets and he will be emperor."

His calm was brief. His eyes began jerking wildly, his bloated fingertips pinched shut his lips. If he had known that Mentumenen was himself a puppet of Chaos, how much worse his fear of the horde might have been! But my sour grin tightened, dragging savagely at my teeth. If Mentumenen was a puppet, what was I?

I glared across the endless fields of scorched grass. Nothing seemed to move out there but dust, groping feebly into the yellowish air then sinking back. I was alone with my brooding, for I felt estranged from both humanity and gods. The Ice Gods would rob me of a throne, the earth goddess who claimed to have borne me would steal my mate. Only Chaos had aided me, leading me unwittingly toward my goal.

How I craved the taste of blood, the cries of battle, the moans of the wounded and vanquished—anything rather than the dust that coated my tongue, the ceaseless thirsty rustling of the grass! How I yearned to cut down Shanara's captors, to bear her away—but for whom?

The Stygian acolyte flinched, but I was not snarling at him. By all the gods—if any were to be trusted enough to be so invoked—I would not give up Shanara again. The Lord Garak had stolen her to present to the oily emir; now Hialmar sought to win her. Would he fight for her tooth and claw, as I already had? No, he would seduce her with soft words; he was too weak to gain her otherwise from me—too human.

Perhaps my mind was parched and suffocated, that I thought these things of my friend; yet who could say that they were not true? Could I truly call any man friend? Was not the dead landscape proof that the earth goddess had deserted me until she had a use for me once more? Balked of a victim, my lust to savage could only turn inward.

Then I glimpsed a blur on the horizon which neither drifted nor changed, only stood and grew more solid. It was a small forest, the first I had seen all day. My surge of gratitude soured at once, for it was the horde of Chaos, not the earth goddess, that had led me here. Nevertheless I knew that the infrequent forests of the steppes were to be found on the banks of lakes or rivers. My thirst was a harsh ache in my throat as I followed the horde.

The foremost of the creatures had almost reached the lake when a small mounted troop of Hyrkranians came into view beyond the trees. They had been making for the water. Now, no doubt aghast at the size and nature of the army, they turned and fled. The chorus of abominable sounds with which the army set off in pursuit was no more savage than my own roar of glee; at last I had adversaries. Unsheathing Genseric's sword, I spurred my mount onward.

Red rage filled me. I bore down on the Hyrkranians' left flank. I disdained to use the artificial arm—not only was it difficult to operate while I held the sword, but it was a product of civilization, hence loathsome—yet it saved me from an arrow which my shield failed to deflect, as the Hyrkranians took a desperate stand. Then I was on them, and they must have seen their deaths glaring out of my eyes.

The first of them was distracted by the things that followed me. My sword plunged through his guts and out beyond them, thrust there as much by the force of my ride as by my instincts; I felt the blade scrape his spine. As I wrenched the blade free he toppled, limp as his spilling entrails.

A warrior taller than I chopped down my shield with a blow that should have lopped my arm—but that arm was metal, and his blade recoiled, ringing. Its edge cut into my upper arm. Maddened, I smashed his shield away, and my sword cleaved deep into his side, which opened like a dyke full of blood.

Somewhere within the hot crimson mist I thought that I was serving the earth goddess, after all; the thirsty ground was drinking deep of blood, the parched grass was wet now, crimson. I hurled down a warrior with a blow of my shield, which was still clamped fast by my metal arm. As he fell, my sword split his skull and almost scalped him.

A fourth warrior was trying to flee two creatures which resembled men, except that their arms were long as their bodies. These arms they had wrapped about the hindquarters of his mount, which they were struggling to topple. Something besides rage made me cut him down; though he must die, at least he deserved a warrior's death. My blow almost scythed his head from his shoulders. The two creatures still clung to the screaming horse, one of whose legs they had now bitten off. Sickened, I killed the beast.

The Hyrkranians were vanquished. My rage was fading, sated, and I was able to survey the battlefield. At once I began to tremble with a new rage; bile rose to my throat. This had not been a battle, for the things I had thought to command fought neither like men nor like animals. Their savagery was perverted, distorted, the antithesis of life.

Some of the Hyrkranians still lived. One creature was reaching a tentacle down the throat of a victim to disembowel him. Two leathery men were dismembering and eating a dying warrior. A screaming naked Hyrkranian was being dragged through razor-sharp grass. Everywhere I looked the inhuman army was satisfying its unnatural lusts on the wounded, the dying, and even the dead.

And this was the army I had thought to wield! My revulsion against them was no more violent than my disgust with my own stupidity. Had Mentumenen hoped that I would choose not to destroy the army, and that the forces of Chaos would corrupt me as they had Tashako? Might he have foreseen that I would delude myself that I could control the army, whereas I could only follow? Had my growing hatred of all life been the first symptom of my corruption?

Mentumenen had not reckoned with my new powers. My face a grim mask, I rode away from the carnage, toward the lake. The Stygian acolyte was cowering behind the trees. At least he had taken no part in the carnage, and for the moment I was loath to kill him. When I had made certain that his bonds were secure, I rode to the far side of the lake. Once my mount had drunk its fill I tethered it, then I hid my sword and my metal arm among the exposed roots of trees.

Merely to loose the Hounds of Tindalos on the army would not be enough. I had participated in their atrocities against the Hyrkranians, however inadvertently; now I must lead the pack against them, to clean myself of their corruption. I spoke the words of changing, and at once my pelt was hot and thick, my fangs and claws were sharp, eager to tear. I could barely restrain my animal rage long enough to perform the ritual of the squares.

The Hounds came loping through the lattices of trees and shadows. Why did they seem more scrawny, more angular? Was I growing able to see them clearly? In a dreadful way their slavering faces seemed almost human, as humanity might have looked if it had evolved from something unimaginably alien, toward an intelligence dark and distant as the rim of the universe. But I had no time for such reflections now. Howling, I led the pack to the abominable horde.

Some of the creatures were too intent on their perversions even to glimpse their oncoming doom. Those which fled were outrun effortlessly by the pack. I ran down horror after horror, ripping their throats with my teeth, spitting out the gelatinous flesh. Its taste and texture maddened me with disgust, with a fury that could not bear to leave one of the monsters alive. Their cries—squeals, moist gobbling, thick jellied roars—drove me to greater frenzy.

When the last of them was destroyed I lay panting, licking my wounds. Around me in the grass, beyond the wide patch that glistened with blood and inhuman liquids, lay the pack, yet this reminiscence of my childhood among the wolves less heartened than dismayed me: the angular limbs of the Hounds at rest reminded me of the bunched legs of spiders, ready to seize prey. Nevertheless I was too exhausted by the slaughter to move away.

All at once my mind, purged of thought and attuned to the pack by the shared slaughter, seemed to glimpse the dreaming of the Hounds. They were one mind, and their thoughts were the dreams of their masters, the Old Ones. I glimpsed eyes large as a man's head, opening far beneath sea and stone. Something shapeless and black as liquescence bubbled amid limitless darkness; the bubbles seemed to dance to the rhythms of an atrocious piping, or to become misshapen objects which crawled about the pitchy surface with a kind of life before sinking back into the depths. A great dark shape—leathery wings, or webbed claws, or something beyond words—loomed toward the world.

I jerked into full consciousness. The eyes of the Hounds—which I could call eyes only because they were located where those organs should be—watched me unreadably. What forces had I wakened by calling on the pack? How could I be sure of withstanding those utterly alien powers? I had no words nor ritual to dismiss the Hounds, but I must beware of calling on them often, for what else might I unleash?

And so I had nothing: neither an army nor the Hounds. I could only trust that Genseric's sword would arm me against Mentumenen. I must follow the route that the horde had been pursuing, and trust that would lead me to him. Muttering the words of change, I made for the lake.

Once more I found my human aspect difficult to regain. My skin felt stubbled, and I had to make a conscious effort to rise from all fours. Had the change affected my vision? For a moment I scanned the gloom beneath the trees. Shadows slithered over trunks, dimness swayed beneath them; I felt I was trying to peer deep into mud. Then I ran forward, roaring. My horse had gone.

Even before I reached the tree I knew that Genseric's sword had been stolen. The Hounds had not alerted me; why should they, when it served to protect me from their masters? The metal arm still lay beneath the roots; the double burden must have proved too heavy for the thief.

As I seized the arm and thrust my stump viciously into the socket, I saw him. The Stygian acolyte, his hands unbound now, was fleeing toward the horizon in the direction the horde had been following. He was crouched low over his horse, as if praying to remain unseen. The sword of Genseric gleamed dully in his arms, the left of which looked boneless. Chaos had helped him struggle free.

XIV. The Ways of Chaos

I was about to call the Hounds, whatever the consequences, when I saw my horse. He stood at the far edge of the forest, and I had taken him for a shaking mass of branches and foliage. Had he snapped his reins for fear of the Hounds? At least the thief had been unable to catch him.

I paced toward him through the tangle of roots and sparse undergrowth, and struggled to suppress my blood-lust, lest it panic him. Though I had ridden him only since the battle by the Vilayet, he seemed to have sensed the animal in me, and to know that it meant him no harm. Though he tossed his head and backed away, snorting, he suffered me to stroke him while I murmured sounds I knew instinctively rather than understood, and eventually to mount him.

Still murmuring, I coaxed him out of the forest; then my rage would be contained no longer. With an inarticulate shout that was more of wolf than of man, I spurred the horse in pursuit of the Stygian, who had almost reached the horizon. Already the horse was foaming, its flanks were beginning to sweat—but I would ride it until its heart burst, so long as I retrieved the sword.

The sky had darkened, and was rumbling. A shower of rain dashed into my face, both refreshing and frustrating me; I was thirsty now not for water but for the Stygian's blood. Already I was gaining on him. When the bald head turned and saw me, he began to kick wildly at his horse's flanks.

The shower was over, having scarcely relieved the oppression. Feeble gleams of lightning tried to part the clouds. The sky was a slate cliff tilted close to the browned landscape, and about to topple. There was nothing but the miniature horse and rider ahead, apparently suspended between the changeless landscape and sky but in fact growing nearer. I gripped the metal wrist. Soon my prey would be in range.

The landscape was not quite changeless. Another small forest sprang into view on the horizon, and seemed to be the acolyte's goal. Before long my wolfish gaze spied the reason. A figure was perched in one of the foremost trees. Above the bat-wings that cloaked its body its face was vaguely human, insofar as it resembled anything even faintly wholesome. It was Mentumenen.

Why had he not flown to meet his acolyte? Perhaps it amused the sorcerer to play us both. Though I could not be sure that the acolyte was yet in range, I could wait no longer. Gripping my steed with both legs, I steadied my aim as best I could with my remaining hand before I loosed the metal bolt.

At first it seemed that the bolt would fly over the acolyte's head. Then it curved down, too low, too far, losing impetus. My gasp was as loud as my victim's when it struck him at the base of his spine.

Though it failed to penetrate, it knocked him from his horse. Genseric's sword was hurled from his arms, to impale the ground several yards away.

When I heard the unfurling of leathery wings I grinned viciously, for I was sure that I would be first to reach the sword. The acolyte lay stunned, face gaping at the sky. As I spurred my mount into a final effort, I realised that the bat-winged crature had not even taken flight. Let him venture within my reach once I had Genseric's sword!

Moments later I saw why he was biding his time. From behind the trees, a dozen Hyrkranians rode out at me.

By the gods, I would battle them too. I was nearer the sword than they were, and my horse seemed as frenzied as I. Let me only grasp the sword, and whatever the outcome, more of their blood than of mine would be spilled on this field. But I was nowhere near the sword when the first arrow ploughed into my thigh.

Though it felt as though a red-hot poker had been plunged into my flesh, I might still have reached the sword had not a second arrow pierced my steed's eye. When I crashed to the ground, which was hard as stone, the beast fell on top of me, pinning my metal arm. Now I was weaponless, and unable to struggle free, for my arm was caught almost up to the shoulder.

My death was riding at me, two Hyrkranian horsemen with swords raised to chop me like meat. But their commander shouted behind them "Take him alive!"

In the moments before they reached me, as I dragged wildly at my trapped stump and tried vainly to heave the corpse away with my free arm, I saw the bat-winged creature rise flapping from the trees. It swooped down on the acolyte, and its claws ripped out a handful of his upturned throat. His usefulness, or his ability to amuse, was finished.

When the Hyrkranians dismounted I kicked out wildly, snarling like a trapped beast. I had kicked aside one sword when the hilt of the other struck me a blow that would have caved in a lesser man's skull. I thought my skull had broken too, for darkness flooded in. Just before it blinded me I saw the thing that was Mentumenen sailing triumphantly toward the zenith, Genseric's sword in its claws.

Chapter XV
The Caves of Stygia
H. Warner Munn

It was as though a sooty cloud descended across my vision. Shot with fiery sparks it was, circling, spiraling down; tenebrous but growing ever more dense. I heard the Hyrkanian metal jingling around me; I heard laughter and sneers.

I think it was that which roused me from descending stupor. My sight cleared. I glared up at the Hyrkanians through a sea of crimson.

"Ythillin!" I sent out a soundless call, as I had done before. "If you bear any affection for me, beautiful Sea-Bitch; Girl-Guide through many dangers; Mentor, protector and Tormentor. I need your help!

"Earth-Mother, Gaea, who say I am your son, come to my aid!

"And, Sword—Sword, of Genseric," I apostrophized aloud, although my voice seemed no more than a muted whisper to my own ears. "Mighty Sword, with which my destiny is intertwined, leave those windy realms and return to Earth whence you were forged and thus to my hand!"

The crimson paled. Within it, stood the Ice-Daughter of the Gods, her lovely body hued like a pearl dipped in blood. She smiled down upon me, for once not in scorn. Never had I seen her more fair, more desirable—more dangerous, but not this time to me.

No! She turned upon my would-be captors. Her arm swung in a circle around me, pointing at them with a forefinger sculptured as by an artist of the snows. She breathed. A little cloud of vapor rolled along that perfect arm. It whirled and grew and streamed as the finger directed. Snowflakes sprang forth in a spraying shower. Under them, the bodies of the Hyrkanians turned white; fern fronds of frost decorated their armor; eyes glazed to balls of ice and the silence of outer space came down upon all. They stood, immobile statues, mouths half-open, swords half-drawn, scornful grins still on their faces.

Now Ythillin turned her gaze on me. Ice blue were her eyes. Chill was her smile. Cold as death, the aura about her. I scarcely felt it. No stranger I, to gelid winds.

Over her shoulder, I saw the bat-winged creature circling high and higher, a mote in the iron-gray sky. Suddenly, the clouds separated and lit as by magic. I knew the intent of Mentumenen as though

I was brother to his mind.

He meant to come down with the stoop of an eagle, slashing with Sword, gripping with claws, diving with iron beak open to tear. First Ythillin, vulnerable now in the body she had assumed, no longer phantom or creature of a dream; then me, pinned as I was beneath the dead horse.

I tried to speak, but my voice was only a croaking caw. The wings retracted against the huge body, diminished by height to the size of a wasp. The sorcerer came plunging toward earth, his speed outdistancing the whistle of his pinions.

I raised my free arm and pointed. Ythillin must have thought I gestured at her.

Now she no longer smiled. Her voice was crystal. "You asked my help. Was that not enough? Why did you call also upon Gaea? If she means more to you, then let her help you now!"

Her body became transparent, a film of iridescence, a wisp and vanished. I was left lorn and alone.

Thought is faster than the speed of demons; faster, even than light itself as James Allison could have told me, as Ghor, could communing have given such knowledge in that dread onrushing moment.

Ythillin had not deserted me permanently, I was sure. I smiled wryly, even in my moment of danger. Her enmity still existed, but here was jealousy.

Shanara, my love, rankled in that cold heart of Ythillin still and now another cause for hate of me had arisen. Whatever was to befall me, I felt that I had unwittingly struck back. I wondered how her emotions might have ruled her, if I had called upon her alone, instead of including the Earth-Mother.

Men are complex of nature. So—certainly—was she. She had shown me that she could be truly woman, if only for an instant . . .

The sweet face of Shanara rose before me then. No! I was not— would not be—drawn thus to the Ice-Bitch! It would take more than this to prove her even friend.

She had come to my call. She had saved me—but for her own purpose. Now, she had left me to my own devices for escape. Somewhere she was watching. Doubtlessly laughing at my dilemma. My help must come from within. I cursed her again, as so many times before.

My thoughts had raced. The diving shape above had scarcely enlarged. Lying thus, on the warm breast of the Earth-Mother, like Antaeus, I drew strength from her.

I strained and twisted at my imprisoned arm. I dared not speak the Words of Power while thus attached and pinned, otherwise, if time had permitted I might with fangs have ripped loose the ham-

XV. The Caves of Stygia

pering horse flesh.

As wolf and wolf only, I felt that I could meet the bat-winged creature on partially even terms. I pulled mightily. I felt something click and knew that the knife had shot forth. I swung my metal fingers, now lengthened by a foot of razor sharp steel, and slashed and stabbed.

Blood of horse and slippery fat coated my arm. I tugged and cursed. I pulled loose. Huge as Eagle, Condor, Roc, my enemy came down—Sword gleaming in the sun ready to impale me, eviscerate me! Damnation to you, Ythillin! My curse upon the aloof Ice Gods! Oh, Mother Gaea! Is this the end of Ghor?

Then I saw that the gleam was brightening, reddening, far beyond the flashing reflection of the sun. The sheen was that of incandescence!

I, James Allison, had seen the stoop of Stukas; their leveling off; their bombs falling. Ghor, looking up, saw all this. Here were the sable wings, now wide-spread, buffeting the air lest the sorcerer in this shape go plunging to earth; here was the whistling shriek of the dive-bomber's passage prophesied by Mentumenen's horrible scream of pain in that far distant age, for, falling out of the sky as the bat-creature leveled off, was the last item to render the analogy perfect!

An incendiary needling down! I, as Ghor, had never seen or imagined such a thing. I did not need to do so, for I recognized it. Sword, red-hot, white-hot, hilt smoking from the charred talon which had held it—falling, plunging straight at the circle of frozen warriors of which I was at the center. And, as though Earth-Mother had spoken to me, her beloved son, I knew what she would have said. "You said, 'Sword, return whence you were forged!' It is doing so, and if you would have it to your hand, you must go hence and recover it."

It struck, plunged deep into the ground and disappeared. The sorcerer, screaming in agony, rose into the sky, followed by a trailing stream of smoke and vanished into a cloud. From it, rain began to fall.

Now, I knew that without Sword, I was vulnerable to the corrupting influence of the winged, star-headed Old Ones. I was under a disadvantage here. Without Sword, it was too dangerous to call upon their dubious help. How long it might be before their attention was drawn to me, I could no more than guess. I looked at the hole where Sword had sunk into the ground. A little spiral of steam came up from it. Were I mole or mouse, I might have entered that straight and perpendicular shaft. As man I could not. As wolf? I thought I knew a way to come where Sword should be, but if so, the entrance to the home of the Fire-Elementals was far and my time might be shorter than I had any way of knowing.

The Stygian acolyte had told me much. Perhaps he had other knowledge which would be of value to me. I strode toward his body. In the hot sun, the frozen men and horses were thawing. They collapsed or bent, or fell. One sat, mouth open, with sword across his lap, with such a ludicrous expression that I favored him with a tight grin as I passed. He did not notice me, because he was dead.

But the acolyte did! He lay in a puddle of blood, his body almost drained white from the horrid wound in his throat. He could make no sound, except that I heard air bubbling within his chest, as he sought to form words.

He gestured at the blade which was still thrust out from between my steel fingers, making a motion that his head should be completely severed from his body. I squatted beside him.

"You dared not sleep because of Set. Now you dare not die, is that true?"

He nodded. His fingers scrabbled at the ground, making marks like runes. They were frantic in their haste.

"Free me by fire. Then I can sleep. Even Set cannot reassemble ash! Ghor—by the love you bore your mother—free me!"

"I slew my mother. I do not love you. If you serve me, I will free you, but you must serve me first. Then you can sleep."

His nails clawed the ground. I read "To sleep—yes! To sleep forever—yes! I will serve. I will serve well."

"Then lead me to the entrance of the Stygian Caves, where I can be led to the home of the Fire Elementals. But first—"

I retrieved the bolt, placed it into its socket, thus compressing the spring. A touch of the button and the dagger was drawn back. I removed the belt of one of the dead Hyrkanians, fastened it tight about the metal wrist and removed the mechanical arm. I buckled the strap around the acolyte's waist. The arm dangled now at his side.

"Rise!" I snarled. "You are dead and I cannot kill you again, but while you move and retain your soul within your rotting body, you can feel pain."

The writhing of his features, the trembling of his hands, the quivering of his muscles all told me that my guess had struck home.

"I know many ways to bring you pain," I gritted and my strong fingers showed him one of them. He bubbled and whined. His eyes were frantic and beseeching. I released him then.

"Remember. Teeth can do worse." I said the Words of Power and together, were-wolf and dead man, we started upon our way.

Northwest I had meant to go. Westward, I must. First to the Caves of Stygia, situated well within the powers of Set. Then, deeply as I must, we would lope and run into those unholy confines, seek-

XV. The Caves of Stygia

ing Sword. Sword I must have. My heart reached out to Shanara. My mind outraced my body. Ythillin, beware! Taunt me not again!

One thing I knew and one thing only. Before I died, as all men must, I would see Mentumenen's foul blood on Sword, corrosive and cursed though it might well be.

As I, James Allison, look upon what I have written, I sometimes marvel that I, Ghor, remember so clearly some things that have happened and yet fail to recall in detail others that seem to me—weak man in a lesser world than his—equally important.

Possibly it is because that to a man of action, incidents of action were impressed indelibly upon Ghor's memory and hence upon mine and interludes of no account to him were erased from the subconscious filing system that psychiatrists claim we possess.

However that may be, the journey to Stygia I felt—as Ghor—to be a weary one and long, but devoid of incident. I remember—

• • •

The sun was a ball of fire in a brassy sky. The sand I loped upon was like the lid of a furnace. The acolyte beside me, running tirelessly, was a withered stick of a man, bloodless now, desiccated, his joints rasping, creaking from loss of fluid, yet alive, tortured by heat, longing for death in the body and oblivion for his soul. For a long time I was less than man. The power drawn from the Old Ones corrupted me more and more.

Sometimes I ran ahead; sometimes, for sheer pleasure, I trotted behind him, nipping at his heels—my fangs clashing, but careful not to nick his sliding tendons, for even in my red thoughts which daily became more of the beast and less of the human, I knew that I needed him as guide. Even so, my deteriorating sense of humanity would have led me soon to feed as a wolf should. My hunger became ravenous. I felt that it would soon become impossible to resist it. My regret at being obliged to draw upon the dangerous power almost disappeared. I enjoyed being a wolf!

I remember—there was no smell of decay about him. I thought this strange at the time. Now, I do not, for I have seen another body mummified by heat and aridity in the Arizona dry lands and one desert varies little from another. No smell—but vultures crossed the sun disc, circling patiently high above, waiting for the meal they were sure would be theirs. They knew a dead man when they saw one!

So I, Ghor, and my grisly companion, came together across the desert which separates Turan from the dark land of Stygia and entered the domain of Set. A line of hazy cloud, hovering above the River Styx, told us that the border lay ahead. As we came nearer, tortured desiccated trees lifted their dry leafless arms toward us as though mutely beseeching for the water—or perhaps to warn us back from the Dark Land.

If so, the warning was unnecessary for now. I had no desire to cross that stream as yet.

Only the vultures saw us come to the mighty hole where the River Styx plunged in thunder to become lost in the Stygian Caves.

When we came out—if we ever did—it would be on the other side and we would be in Stygia.

Our last sight of the vultures was their circling swoop, shrieking with anger and disappointment, around the lip of the abyss where we set foot to descend stairs hewed from the living rock during eons so long past that only King Kull might have known that those chisels were held by human hands or the writhing fingers of the Serpent Men he fought in Valusia.

All that I know is that it was surely not the men of Stygia, for they had a wholesome dread of Set, that strong god whose anger was to be feared, and malignant enemy of Horus, so it must have been the People of the Worm.

To and fro the stairway descended along the wall farthest from the cataract. It did not circle the shaft, but zigzagged ever deeper, its edges rounded by long use, slippery with slime in which we saw no preceding footprints. It seemed long unused.

Now I took back my mechanical arm, having first used the Words of Power. The effort was greater than ever before and I had to repeat them three times before the transformation began. Never had it been more difficult or more painful to become a man; never had I regretted more the necessity of change, never before had I so longed to remain as a carnivore or felt so weakened by assuming the human form.

Yet, I knew that while as beast I might better face Set, the Undying Worm, my only hope of recovering Sword, my only real protection from the corrupting influence of the Old Ones, was in the shape of man.

As we descended deeper, the darkness lightened. The slime on stair and walls was becoming luminescent. It crawled and shrank away from my touch as though life of a sort avoided me.

Now the plunging cataract was becoming less a column of water and more like a cloud of spray, illumined from below, as I peered into the depths, by ruddy light that shifted and wavered up at me as though it also lived.

Truly, there was life all around me, but it was not wholesome life—nor was it friendly to me or any man. My growl was feral. I raised my deadly arm. The Stygian acolyte traced a cartouche in the slime upon the wall.

We both had heard the sound which rose to us. It was a piping tune, confined in a nine note scale, repeated over and over. It seemed

XV. The Caves of Stygia

to sink into my bones, the fabric of which vibrated and shook until it seemed that every atom would fly apart and I collapse to join the slime, that now I *knew* had once been the transformed bodies of men and women, which still knew sentience, suffering and memory of the upper world.

The acolyte traced a figure within the cartouche. It was a four-legged serpent with a human head. I knew it as the symbol of the Blind Piper, Messenger of the Gods, for it was portrayed as playing upon a flute.

He pointed downward and tried to speak. The effort was vain and he scratched a single word in the slime which quivered and writhed away, but not before I read TAUT and I knew that I was within the Stygian Hell,

"Is Set below?" I asked. His neckbones creaked, as the acolyte shook his head. He drew another picture, this time of a particularly ugly creature with the head of a crocodile. He looked at me with hate, and I knew, as well as though he had been able to speak, that had this grotesque and evil demon which caused him so much dread, been in his dismal home, we would have already been perceived.

We continued to descend and the darkness continued to lighten. The piping became louder. Nausea shook my body. The spray had now become a thick cloud of mist, lit from much deeper by leaping flames.

The walls were drying with the heat from below and no longer covered with quivering slime. Instead, white worms crawled there, horribly aware of us, raising from their rear segments and turning their tiny heads and pinpoints of jet black eyes upon us as we went down. They stretched toward us to their very limits. There was little room on the stairway, but we avoided their touch, coming at last to a flat expanse of wet stone upon which I gratefully ventured, although it was but a landing and not the bottom of the shaft.

From it, a passageway led into obscurity and out of this came the dreadful sounds of the flute. I dared not enter, but crossed the landing and went down, down, down, step by weary step into Hell, and as I went, followed always by the terrified acolyte, my own fear began to lessen.

Peace came upon me. I felt that I was nearing a destination long awaiting my advent. Ythillin had said I would never know such peace. It might not last. It might never come again, but for once in my long, savage, tragic existence I was experiencing it. In a sense, I was coming home; I was returning to the womb which bore me; not to the one I hated and despised, not that of Gudrun of the Shining Locks—if she had been reborn I would happily have killed her again—but to my true mother—Gaea—who has borne in travail and sorrow all the races of Man, only to be scourged and ravaged and abused for her nurturing, her protection and her love.

Yes, love! For I felt it now, surging over me. For once in my bitter life I was wrapped in pity and affection and it was so new, so strange and so—good—that I fell upon my knees on those hard stones, covered my face with my arms and Ghor, the Mighty—Ghor, the Terrible—Ghor, the Feared One—wept and was comforted by the love of the Earth-Mother—deep, deep down below the surface of the Dark, Unholy Land of Stygia, in the very den of Set, friend of the Old Ones and Master of Mentumenen, my enemy to the death!

And a still voice echoed in my brain, saying "Beloved Son, you have faced terror and not quailed. You have done your devoir. You have earned your reward. Accept it now and set your companion free!"

I raised my head. Rising toward me up the stairway which still descended to unguessable depths an effulgence pressed aside the shifting waves of mist. It came higher, enlarging, taking shape as a giant of shimmering flame and as it rose to face me, I saw it as of human shape, its features horrifying, yet benignant, and I knew it bore me no enmity.

It had legs and arms; it had shoulders, a torso, and it had hands; and in one hand—a hand of fire, for all was flame and surging waves of flickering light and heat—it bore Sword—the mighty, powerful, Sword of Genseric—black against all that livid light of fire that was this messenger from the Land of the Fire Elementals whence Sword had been forged.

It carried Sword by the blade and proffered me the hilt. I hesitated. I would be seared to the bone, I thought, and reached out my metal hand. Sword was drawn back. The Elemental's fiery lips parted in a thin smile, denying me my desire.

Again the still, quiet voice, "Fear nothing, my Son. Harm will not come to you here, but it is on the way and you must be armed. Take what belongs to you, for Mentumenen comes, unknowing that you await and with him comes one for whom you must do battle!"

I reached out my hand of flesh. Sword was proffered. I grasped the hilt and it was cold.

The Stygian acolyte looked at me beseechingly. He took one step toward the Fire-Elemental and looked again for my permission.

I said, "Accept likewise your reward. To die is your pleasure and your boon. I need you no longer. You are free from me. You shall be free from Set forever!"

He rushed into the out-spread arms of the Elemental as though into the embrace of a lover. An acrid smoke arose as his dry body was consumed like a bundle of fagots in a furnace. Only a little white ash fell to the stones. I rubbed my sandaled foot into it, scattering it over the edge of the abyss. "To Amenti go and be judged in the Hall

XV. The Caves of Stygia

of Truth and if the balance in the Scales is weighted against you, tell them to await my inevitable coming, when I shall speak for you! The Crocodile God shall never have you now."

I was alone. I turned and began to climb upward to the heights and my own destiny, whatever that might be.

I knew now, definitely and beyond question, that Mentumenen, the Lords of Chaos, the Old Ones and Set, were allied. What more proof did I need now that I had found and heard the Howler in Darkness playing on his flute to himself, secluded in the Caves, doubtlessly awaiting the coming of Set?

I had heard that he had one enemy, the only one that he feared—Cthugha, of Fomalhaut, who would gladly come to fight with us if called upon.

As I climbed, I considered. I could see more clearly now the coming array of battle. On the one side, these terrible enemies; on ours, Cthugha and *all* humans, not merely the Nemedians whither I must next be bound, plus the Earth-Mother, who must resent this painful wound of the Caves within her body, and the Ice Gods (Lords of Order).

Debatable as to their allegiance were the Hounds of Tindalos, whom I had called, perhaps to my own dole. Could I send them back? The legend concerning them was that no man had done so without losing his own life as fee for their service!

Caught in the middle were I and Shanara, comparatively little people in this war between Gods.

Plainly now the greatest problem was not merely to save the civilization of Nemedia, but all civilization! Now I, and I alone, bore the knowledge necessary to be given the world so that feverish preparation might be made and the lines drawn for allies and enemies.

If I perished in these Caves, warning might be far too late. I must not call upon the Old Ones for help. It would be like inviting in the headsman and sharpening his axe for my own neck!

I continued to climb. It was my duty to survive. A strange feeling indeed to hold such responsibility—I, Ghor, the barbarian, who neither had friends or wanted them. Yet, I had a duty that surpassed personal feelings now. A duty to my own integrity. I intended to fulfill it at whatever cost.

I came to the landing. It was not cowardice that made me tiptoe lightly past the passageway whence issued from darkness the sounds of that obscenely gloating being that played upon the flute.

Alas, I was sensed, as perhaps we had been on the descent! Not hindered on the downward way, for who could escape Set? But to come back to upper air and safety? Unthinkable!

A ghastly ululation rose to chill my blood. A two-note call twice repeated, "*Ygnaiih! Ygnaiih!*" It was a frightful wail, but the laugh that followed was worse, as a billowing, *slopping* sound came closer and closer out of the passageway, compressing the air before that unseen body and forcing the mist ahead of it like the crowding ghosts of those who had once been human, before their children had devolved to the worm.

I stood frozen. What could Sword do against something this huge? I can only guess, for it was not necessary for me to try.

From deep below, but echoing up along that abysmal shaft, came another cry—a cry for help from the lute player's only powerful enemy—a cry in a voice I recognized. Gaea, Earth Oracle, Earth Mother, appealing for aid for Ghor her son!

"*Ph'nglui mglw'nafh* Cthugha Fomalhaut *n'gha-ghaa naf'l thagn! Iä!* Cthugha."

Thrice repeated was this cry and swiftly the answer came. Powerful wings buffeted wind down the shaft. I, a midget in the presence of giants, clung for my life to the slippery steps. Whatever it was passed me like a blast of heat. The walls and stairway steamed. Air was sucked from my lungs. My metal arm and Sword burned my flesh as I was passed by a Being which flung itself into the passageway. Foul flesh hissed there, smoke issued in clouds, screams deadened my ear drums and I ran up the stairs as though I had never been weary.

The struggle continued beneath me. Heat had dried the steps. I climbed easily and fast, my strong thews bearing me to the heights.

Then, silence below and something rising. Which? I could only guess at first, then an increasing warmth told me that the victor need not bring me fear. I shrank aside. Battering wings passed. I saw the circle of the entrance above—stars gleamed, among them distant and friendly Fomalhaut, occluded briefly by a shape so unearthly that I will not attempt to describe it. It flapped into distance.

Then as I struggled to the top, I thought that Cthugha was returning. An instant more and I knew the truth. The bat-winged monstrous shape was all too familiar. Mentumenen!

I came out upon the surface and was seen! There was a chattering shriek, a plunging, a collision! My dagger slashed once, Sword bit deep before I was felled. The mighty bat shape went wheeling out of control into the cataract in a huddle of crumpled wings and down, down it went into the shaft.

I was beneath a soft body that, insensible, weighted me heavily. I pushed it impatiently aside and looked over the edge. A glow was rising—a fiery spume of spray and fog—a fountain of sparks and cinders against the battling water that fell upon it and could not extinguish the flame!

It howled up into the night, lighting all my little world. I beheld

XV. The Caves of Stygia

Shanara at my feet. I seized her and ran, while behind me walls caved, steam hissed and voices roared in agony and dismay.

Earth trembled beneath my feet. Cracks opened. I leapt them all and ran for very life—nay, two lives, for in my arms Shanara still breathed!

I came to solid ground and looked back. The giant torch of flame still wavered and roared into the sky. Then, even as I watched, it decreased and was snuffed out like a candle.

Almost to my very feet, the ground became a concavity, the sands pouring into the shaft. The Styx rushed out over the desert like a wild living thing, seeking a channel and a new destination.

The Caves of Stygia were no more. The wound in Mother Gaea's breast was healed forever. Somewhere below, the Fire Elementals could follow their peaceful pursuits without hindrance.

But the Blind Piper? Was he—or *it*—immortal? Would we meet again for benefit or bane? Had Mentumenen risen upon that tower of flame? I only knew that, as I had sworn to myself, his blood now dripped from Sword, and I turned my face northward toward Nemedia, bearing the unconscious Shanara, soft and dear and precious to my arms.

And I knew that, if Mentumenen had survived, he too was crippled as myself. Shanara had been carried with a talon hooked into her belt. The other—the wizard's foot, in his other shape—was no longer to be seen.

My smile was tight as I strode across the desert guided by the stars. The score had been evened a little. Maybe by a lot.

And as I went upon my way, my spirits lighter than they had been for many a day, I knew that my dread allies—the Hounds of Tindalos—had not forgotten, or deserted me.

Now and again I felt a cold, scaly, sinewy brushing against my bare leg and heard a coarse panting, before, behind and at my side. Perhaps this should have brought me dismay. It did not.

True, they might not return to their strange dimension until my death—or would they, could they, be deceived by a substitute death? I felt that among my many enemies, surely one might well be spared to the Hounds!

I had coped with other more difficult problems; I, now that I cherished my love again, was confident that I could cope with this.

On then to Nemedia, the beleaguered. Beware, Hyrkanians! Ghor is coming, carrying the Sword of Genseric, surrounded by a terrible host, to bring death to your men and weeping to your women!

Chapter XVI
Doom of the Thrice-Cursed
Marion Zimmer Bradley

Out of the caves of Stygia, then, with the great river Styx bursting forth at our feet and across the desert; Shanara, still unconscious against my breast, and at my heels the dread Hounds, invisible, only a rustling and a panting and a fleeting brush against my thigh. On, Northward through the night, drawn by the northern stars that flickered cold above us; but even the giant strength that I, James Allison, wielded in those nigh-forgotten days when I was Ghor, kin-slayer and great were-wolf, was waning. From time to time my foot stumbled; and while the Hounds, creatures of sorcery, ran on unflagging through the night, I was still flesh and blood, of a kind. And at last I came crashing down on the sands of the desert, my breath going from me in a great gasp. Shanara cried out, in her stunned or enchanted sleep, then was instantly still again. I fumbled to see if she still lived; then, even in that gesture, the last of my strength went from me and I slept, exhausted, at Shanara's side. There, in the bleak desert, guarded only by the Earth-Mother Gaea, I slept . . . nay, I know not how long; but at least once the sun rolled over us and slept again, for when I came again to my senses, though it was night still, another day was breaking.

And what had wakened me at last was the weakling cry of Shanara for water. She seemed still unsurprised to see my face bending over her, only repeated her plea for water, half-swooning. Still the river Styx roared at our side, but when I looked on the water it was black and dulled, and I recoiled from the thought of drinking from that enchanted stream. I stumbled away from the sullen, boiling rivercourse, turning my back on Styx and hunting for some other source of water. At last I came to a small, muddy spring beneath the prickly desert plants, and urged Shanara thither; it was muddy and tasted of dust and the thorny astringency of the bushes, and she grimaced even as she quenched her thirst. At my waist an old dried wineskin still clung, tied there at some half-forgotten feast, and I soaked it, anew, restoring some pliancy to the leather, and filled it from the spring. It was little enough to face the desert, but better that . . . so the instincts of a wolf told me . . . than to drink from those black Stygian waters. Even now Shanara, thirsting again, turned to the river, but I commanded her away; and, though sullenly, she obeyed. As yet we had not spoken, and I regretted it, that my first

XVI. Doom of the Thrice-Cursed

words to my love after the long quest must be harsh ones.

All that day and the next, we struggled northward, finding only a little sparse water here and there, muddied and bitter. I rationed Shanara to sips from the wineskin, and went dry myself, enduring that torture rather than driving her to drink from the ominous river. On the third night the river had dwindled to a trickle running between dangerous rocks; it was torment to lie and hear the sound of water, parched as we were, but I was glad that tomorrow would put us far from that peril; the water that had flowed where the Old Gods played, and drunk the blood of the buried forces of Chaos. Even, I think, had death from thirst been my portion, nothing would drive me to wet my lips with that water.

Not so Shanara; she drank the last sips from the wineskin, chewing with her parched mouth for the last moisture, and when she slept she whimpered, dry-mouthed, in her sleep. I watched her, frowning, sleepless. What had befallen her in the Caves of Stygia, and in the hands of the sorcerer? I would never know; I wondered if she knew, herself. She seemed stunned, half-mindless at times, and, as I looked down on her, it seemed to me that her beauty had altered, with terror and privation, into a haggard, crazed, doom-laden thing. Yet to me she was still beautiful, my beloved and my mate, and I paid no heed to the taunts of Mentumenen, that she would turn upon me one day with revulsion, as if she had been possessed by a beast. Thus far, at least, she showed no sign of revulsion, but followed me, quiet and obedient, never complaining even when she stumbled at the pace I forced in our relentless march northward to Nemedia. Perhaps she, too, was eager to be at home.

But now, as she lay in her whimpering, parched sleep, I took some thought of this. How had Mentumenen handled her? If he had meddled with my woman, I thought grimly, he had paid dear— with his foot, or claw, or talon. For, however cursed, Mentumenen was flesh and blood even as I, and he had felt the tooth of the Sword of Genseric. Gaea herself, Earth-Mother, *my* mother, had warned me, too; Shanara had probably been less than faithful wife to me. Well, I thought, looking at her haggard, ravaged features, for that too she had paid. And indeed in such a world as this, a woman had no choice but to obey whoever held her body; she had become my bride by no less forceful process, and that we had come to love one another was only a single blessing showered on me amid many curses. No; I would not ask Shanara what price she had had to pay for surviving the long ordeals of capture. It should be buried, even as the caves of Stygia themselves were buried, never to come to light again.

And then, as I looked at Shanara, huddled in my cloak and the tattered remnants of her finery, I knew that what had come to her could not be forever hidden. For her body was swelling, ripening . . . and I knew that look. Even her sullenness and the persistent thirst was part of that, and it was not hunger alone set her to seeking the bitter desert herbs as we travelled. Within her breeding body the curse of Gaea was ripening.

And who had fathered this child? I myself, before she had been ravished from my arms? Mentumenen, gloating in his hate? Worse still—some nameless thing somewhere in the realms of sorcery and evil? It might well have been my own, despite the curse of Ythillin . . . *never shall you father a son for any dynasty to rule after you.* Not that I should not ever father a son; but that I should found no dynasty. Well, in these days life was uncertain and kingdoms more so, and not even the Gods, perhaps, knew what dynasties should rule; even the plans of the Gods, as I had seen in my wandering and cursed life, were prone to go astray.

And why trust the evil words of the Ice-Goddess bitch? So I pondered, and laid myself down beside Shanara, clasping her close in my arms. It perturbed me not a bit that the child growing in her womb might not be of my own seed. What was kinship to me, who had been cast out to die on the ice by the hand of the father who had sown *my* seed of life and been displeased with the harvest? What was kinship to me, who had become known as Ghor kin-slayer for the death of my four brothers and for the final doom brought down upon Gudrun of the Shining Locks? I, who had been fostered and suckled by a bitch wolf with whom I shared no drop of blood nor even a common species, resolved that Shanara's son should be fostered so by me, thus confounding the curses; I should sire, perhaps, no son to rule after me and stand beside Hialmar of Nemedia, but Shanara's son, fosterling of Ghor, should one day carry the sword of Genseric when I died, as all things must one day die, and carry the memory of Ghor down the ages.

And so, Shanara in my arms, I slept, and deeply, for when I woke she was gone from my arms, and in the sullen dawnlight I heard a sound which turned my blood to ice, for the sound was the scraping of feet on stone, and I sat upright to see Shanara, stumbling and foot-sore, making her perilous way down the rocks toward the last trickle of water from the river. I cried aloud to her, warning her back, but even while I bounded upright and ran to her over the stones, she had reached the water and stooped, taking great thirsty gulps of the water. I jerked her back from the stream, but her eyes were defiant, her face and chin dripping with moisture, and in the vacancy of her defiant stare I knew that my instincts had told me true. For there is an evil in the waters of Styx, though Shanara was the first to test that curse. The eyes lifted to mine were vacant, unknowing, devoid alike of recognition or of memory. She would

XVI. Doom of the Thrice-Cursed

have bent to drink again; I clasped her arm in iron fingers, so that she cried out, and forced her back up the stony bank. Even though it took us out of our way, we must get away from the river of Styx.

Had there been some siren call to the waters, that she, who had dwelt within Stygia for long and long, sought this return to mindlessness and darkness? For it seemed, as I gazed into her dulled eyes, that I could hear again the sound of that Blind Piper at the heart of Chaos; did I hear in it, perhaps, an echo of what lay in her mind?

Even though she struggled and cursed me, I turned our backs on the river, and by midday we were well out of the sound. And now the desert was gradually giving way to a more hospitable land. Before nightfall we found a spring of sweet water, where we could drink our fill, and a farmer, retreating before the armed hordes which had fought all over this land, had left a barn filled with corn and dried roots, and sweet hay where we slept, for the first time, in comfort.

But that single draught of Styx had wiped from Shanara's mind all memory of her sojourn below; and in that, perhaps, it had been her blessing. For she thought that she was once again in Nemedia and that we were again making our way toward the city where we had first been joined, and nothing I said could wipe that impression from her mind. Capture, terror, rape and imprisonment, all had been wiped from her mind. She looked in sore confusion at the tatters of her finery, at the metal enchanted arm I bore on my mutilated arm, at the claw-like thinness and roughness of her own hands; but when I tried to tell her what had happened, she only shook her head in confusion. It was all gone forever from her mind; and I felt in my heart that it was better so. For when she lay in my arms she was the sweet young bride she had been, long and long ago, when I was new-come to mankind out of wolf-kind, and my heart sang again at her love for me. And as the next day waned, we came again to a village of men.

• • •

And now I, in this life as James Allison who was once Ghor, Kin-slayer, fifth-born son of Genseric, must confess to a great hiatus. For some reason or other, there is a rift in my memory, like that in Shanara's. Did I drink a single draft of Styx, perhaps, despite all my good resolve? Or, kissing Shanara's lips, did some taste of that water cling to me? Or is it that the days and months which followed were meaningless, tales of struggle and privation, and thus vanished into the Limbo of lost memory? Whatever the reason, all the tale of how Shanara and I came home to Nemedia, and how we were received there, is gone from my mind as if it had never been. Somewhere, vague, in my mind, there is a memory of a great crowd cheering as I raised the Sword of Genseric, and of a great battle where the Hyrkanians fell back before us like leaves blown before an autumn wind. I know we occupied a city where high towers looked down on a barren land, at the edge of the ice-wastes. I know there was a siege, and we were driven back, into a wild country such as I, Æsir-reared, had hunted over with the wolf-pack who were my foster-brothers. And I know that one night, among the skin-clad warriors of this village, at the very edge of the ice-wastes, memory returns to me and I see a conclave of Nemedians plotting together, and I, Ghor, among them.

"Fortune has gone against us," a man with a great beard was saying, as memory returned, "but we can take all of Nemedia from here, and hold it, too. Even if that devil-spawn of sorcery bribed his way into our highest councils, we still have many supporters in Nemedia. We have our greatest leaders; Ghor, and Hialmar, and Lud here has told us of a series of caves in the ice-waste where we can conceal our stores and weapons until the remnants of the Æsir and Vanir can rally to aid us." He gestured to a great burly man wrapped in skins.

"Aye, I know, and Ghor knows too," Lud said, "for he knows this land from old. You can lead us toward the ice-caves, can you not, Ghor?"

I nodded, unwilling to speak. Reluctant I was, to return to this country where I had run with wolves and been cast out by all my kin, where, it seemed, ghosts must stalk forever at my elbow. Yet somehow the doom spoken in my youth must return to me, bringing me here, and I was covered with a fey sense of doom. When the council broke up my feet carried me, by habit, unthinking, to one of the largest houses in the village, where I had been housed with Shanara.

The gap in my memory had been longer than I thought. Her body was huge, rounding, her face haggard and drawn, though still beautiful to me. The woman who attended her draw back, and I came to where she lay sprawled on the heap of skins that was her bed, looking awkward and yet somehow happy.

"I am glad you have come back," she said, "I judge that it will not be more, now, than a day or so, when you can hold the son of Ghor in your arms; he for whom the Sword of Genseric waits!"

I smiled and stroked her hair, and blessed that single draught of Styx which had wiped from her mind all memory of capture and of the caves of Stygia. Nor did she seem to recall that once she had been hung about with silks and jewels; now she seemed content with her crude garment of skins and a little necklace of bright animal teeth which someone had found for her somewhere. But I resolved that before this winter waned I would see her once again in

XVI. Doom of the Thrice-Cursed

the ivory palaces of Nemedia, and her son, *our* son, in a golden cradle! Yes; his father had suckled at the dugs of a wolf, but the son of Ghor should have handmaidens and wet-nurses and playthings, and be reared as a king's son in the Southlands!

But now we were to move northward again, into the ice-waste; and as I led the horde across the frozen lands, Shanara carried in a litter between four hearty men (for I would not leave her), it seemed to me that ghosts stalked me across this ice. Ever and anon, at my heels, it seemed that I was brushed by a slinking form whom I half-recognized as one of my erstwhile wolf-brothers, those who had suckled with me at the wolf's teats, and with whom I had clawed and fought for a dripping bone. I knew the invisible Hounds of Sorcery were with me, but at times they seemed to appear, haunting me, and other faces appeared and disappeared in the frost. Whenever I touched the hilt of Sword, I seemed to see again the great broad red face of Genseric as it was before I slew him; and from time to time, in the freezing mist, the faces of my brothers whom I had known only at their death-hour; again I numbered their names in the old, obsessive way:

Raki the Swift. Sigismund the Bear. Obri the Cunning. Alwin the Silent.

Ghor . . . the Kin-Slayer! Ghor, the Accursed!

And then, through the dazzling frost and sun, it seemed to me that a woman's face shone before me, but changing and shifting, as I myself had shifted into man from wolf and back again to wolf. And the face in the frost was that of Gudrun of the Shining Locks, for a moment; and then, merging and changing, it was the face of Ythillin, the Ice-Maiden; and then again the face of Gudrun.

"Hi! Ghor, man, what's come to ye," the voice of a companion broke in upon me, and in a daze I clutched at my sword, for it seemed to me the very voice of doom; and then I caught at remnants of sanity, for it was the face of Lud. Brushing ghosts and rime from my eyes, I blinked at him and he said "What ails ye? Ye look half-dazed; fey!"

I made some muttered excuse. Indeed, I felt fey, accursed, a sense of doom, as if, coming back to the place of old curses, I should have picked up the sense of doom I had shed in the long trek southward. I should never have come back here; above all, I should keep clear of the ice-wastes, where Ythillin's curse lay waiting for me, the curse I had forgotten in the warmer southern lands! And Ythillin's curse lay not only on me, but on my son . . .

Well, it might be that he was not my son. And so he should escape my curse. But there was an ancient, fierce ache clawing at my leg, half-forgotten since the days when I had scrambled, a naked and crippled babe, upon the ice in the wake of my wolf-brethren.

We slept that night in an even cruder village, eight or ten buildings, only piled blocks of ice stacked against a foundation of ancient bone; the villagers in years past had preserved the bones of their prey, walrus and whale, having no other building materials. Shanara was quiet and queasy, eating little of the fatty meat which was all our hunters could find, and soon after dusk, which came early at those latitudes, the woman who tended her was summoned by a cry, and told me that her pains had begun. I had grown accustomed, in my years among mankind, to knowing that women made much more of the matter than the easy whelping of the wolf-years, so I left her to the woman's tending; but shortly after midnight, the woman summoned me back from where I sat among the chiefs, drinking sullenly and growling at their jests, to where Shanara lay in the straw with the red-wrinkled child at her breast.

He seemed very small, and wrinkled, and ugly; hairless, not so pretty as a newborn wolf-pup, but she held him and crooned to him, and I suppose, as women do, she thought him very nice. So I stroked his bald head with my thumb and kissed her, and she smiled up at me, a tired smile, and whispered, "I have heard . . . .that the men of the Northlands . . . .cast their babes away if they are ill-formed. You will not cast this one away, will you, my beloved Wolf?"

And she took away the skin wrappings of the child, and showed me the warped and twisted little foot.

For a moment the words stuck in my throat. So the child was mine, and the curse upon him! But then I said, summoning calm, "My own foot was twisted at birth; but it grew straight with exercise and running. When he is big enough to run we must be sure he is well taught and not over-pampered, my love," and stroked the small crippled foot, so tiny that it was lost in my big hand.

That night as I slept at Shanara's side it seemed that ghosts rooted at my pillow. The face of Genseric seemed to hang in the air above me, and it seemed that I could hear the mocking words of my mother, Gudrun of the Shining Locks, as she doomed me to be cast out to die.

Like Father, like Son! But this one will die on the ice and not return to haunt or kill! And the faces of my brothers, circling around me in nightmare, riding through my uneasy sleep.

And then the face of Ythillin, slowly taking shape amid the ice-crystals that seemed to fill our sleeping-place, white and shining, as I lay paralyzed; the shimmering Ice-Goddess, hovering over Shanara and the babe; beckoning to her.

Come, whispered a soundless voice, *come, the doom is on you, Shanara, who chose to share the curse and the doom of the kin-slayer! Come; you cannot resist my call, you who have drunk of the waters of darkness, I*

XVI. Doom of the Thrice-Cursed

bid you remember what you have forgotten . . . . and the frost-rimed figure of the Ice Goddess leaned forward, touching Shanara with a cold fingertip, breathing upon her in a shimmering cloud. I tried-to spring up, to shout at her:

"Leave her, Ice-Bitch! I alone incurred your curse! My bride and my son, they are guiltless!" And, as a dog-wolf will fight, tooth and claw, so I struggled to come at my sword and leap to my feet; but her cold breath was like a freezing cloud over me, and I lay paralyzed, and it seemed to me that I saw Shanara, the child in her arms, rise from the bed and glide after the retreating form of the Ice-Goddess; and Ythillin turned back to glare at me, triumphant, and her face merged into the sneering, gloating face of Gudrun of the Shining Locks, whom I had slain, laughing exultantly at the coming of her curse . . . .and I awoke.

I awoke, gasping a prayer of thanks to Gaea that this had been but a dream, and turned on the skin-bed to clutch reassuringly at Shanara; but my hands felt nothing but emptiness. She was gone!

Had it—Gods! Had it been real, then? No; the Gods do not walk in mortal rooms, nor do the dead come forth to gloat over their slayers. Yet I could still see the mocking eyes of Gudrun of the Shining Locks, hear the curses she had flung at me. I sprang out of the bed and hastened to the door. Before me a full moon shed cold radiance on the ice, with blue flickering aurora springing up in the north, and shadows everywhere; but it seemed to me that I could see a paler shadow, flickering in the wake of the aurora . . . or was it the shimmer of Ythillin, leading the dreaming Shanara after her to death on the ice-waste?

Ah! The curse! Crying out like a wounded wolf, I clutched the Sword of Genseric in my hands and ran; half naked, barefoot across the icy waste, howling Shanara's name. *The curse, the curse of Ythillin, that I should father no son to found a dynasty* . . . . was my son to perish with Shanara on the icy wastes here and now? I was fleet of foot; it might still be given to me to find them before they perished . . . .

So I ran, and so I gasped and cursed and prayed, when I could begin to see the form of Shanara before me. I cried out to her, but she did not seem to hear. Had she recalled all that had befallen her in the hands of the sorcerer Mentumenen, and had the memory driven her to madness? Had the breath of Ythillin restored to her the memories mercifully vanished in the waters of Styx? What horrors of sorcery, ravishment, despair had surged through her mind, while I lay in my fey nightmare?

Yet she was faltering, a woman weakened by childbed, while I was strong and powerful, and I was gaining on her retreating form.

And then, when it seemed that I was about to grasp her in my arms, a great darkness came before my eyes, and a huge wavering form, in the shape of some evil bird, wings flapping, foul breath of carrion, evil beak darting at my eyes. I whipped out Sword from my hand, thrust wildly upward; the evil bird wheeled, regarding me with glittering eyes in which dwelt pain and a rabid malice. Even in this form I knew him; the sorcerer Mentumenen! Mentumenen, wounded by this blade, come on the wings of sorcery to thrust himself between me and my fleeing, crazed woman!

"Let me pass," I said, between my teeth, "I swear on this sword that I will face you, bare of hand and tooth if you will, when Shanara is safe!"

The great bird-form dwindled and Mentumenen, man-form, halting on one leg, stood before me, shimmering with the green fires of sorcery. "Oh, you would like that," he taunted, "but let her dispose first of the crippled wolfling she bears . . . let her throw it to the wolves as you were thrown, this time without salvation, and your accurst line will be gone forever with the dying Æsir! You cleaved away my foot, so that for all my sorcery I shall go halt and lame till the far day of my dissolution; but your son shall pay for my laming! Ghor's son to the wolves, and Ghor to my vengeance, and Shanara—Shanara to my throne in hell!"

"It is to hell indeed that I shall send you, hell-spawned," I cried, and fell upon him with the Sword of Genseric. He seemed unarmed; but as he thrust out his hand a weapon appeared in it, a mirror-image of my own sword, rising and parrying the strokes of Sword as if by some mirrored sorcery. Damn him, was he there at all, or was he another image, another illusion, was this all some frightful nightmare born of terror and fear and my dread for Shanara and the babe?

Now indeed I called out in my frantic need to Gaea and the Gods of the Law who had set me to serve them against Chaos; for here before me stood no man, not even a sorcerer, but a very demon out of Chaos, come to rob me of the last thing I held dear. But no Goddess sprang to my aid; I had nothing but the Sword of Genseric, and my own strength. And, try as I might, I could not get through the flickering barrier of the mirrored sword he bore; shielded by magic, Mentumenen held me there, delaying, while Shanara fled further and further into the icy wastes, with our newborn son.

How does a mere mortal slay a demon? The answer to that is that he cannot. A sword cannot stand against magic; and I bore my sword only against magic. While I was armed with Sword, he was armed also . . . . and suddenly I knew this was the answer. He could bear only such arms as I bore, only the echo of my own. I whirled and cast the Sword of Genseric far away from me—and even as I turned back I heard Mentumenen cry out in dismay, for as I had guessed, he was armed only with the mirror image of the weapon I bore; I unweaponed, he must face only with his own strength!

XVI. Doom of the Thrice-Cursed

Snarling, all the memory of my wolf-years surging in me, I cast myself upon him; my teeth met in his throat, and I felt the black, foul ichor of his blood breaking forth. He clawed and spat and I felt his nails tear at my eyelids, but I held on, relentless, teeth fast in his throat, iron fists clutching his hands. And he had only one leg. I forced him relentlessly back; his magic was no good to him here; back and back, his blood spouting, his grip weakening.

I broke his back across my knee.

Letting his limp form slide from my arms, shrunken and broken as it was, I stared in horror as even the corpse dwindled and vanished, until only the broken body of a raven lay on the ice before me. To this had Mentumenen the sorcerer come! And it seemed to me that the head of Set Himself wavered in the frost, and was gone; the gods of the southlands could not survive, here in the frozen wastes, without the strength of their worshippers! Oh, Mentumenen had done ill, when, guided by his lust for revenge, he had taken shape-shifting form and flown northward, out of the lands of his own God! Set might indeed return to the Southland; but he would do so without his tame crow, Mentumenen!

I came to myself from the frozen trance of horror, snatching up the Sword of Genseric, and fled after the disappearing tracks of Shanara. Somewhere a wolf howled, and the face of Gudrun of the Shining Locks seemed to waver and disappear before me in the ice. Far on the horizon, the day was breaking. And far, far away, it seemed I saw Shanara . . . .

I ran on, my heart pounding, the Sword of Genseric clutched in my one hand. Somehow, somehow, I must reach them in time to drive off the wolves! My breath stumbled like my gait, for that desperate fight with the sorcerer Mentumenen had taken the last, or near to it, of my strength, but I would fight, tooth and claw, if I must, for bitch and whelp . . . I was no man, but a besieged wolf, howling, and somewhere other howls answered mine. Wolves! Wolves had gathered, somewhere, and where they snarled and fought, something screamed, a human scream, at their midst. I plunged into the pack, the Sword of Genseric flashing and dripping blood, and the wolves scattered before the flailing steel.

On the ice before me lay Shanara, her son still clutched in her arms.

But the wolves had made Havoc of them both.

And then I howled like a wolf to the sky, and cursed. For the curse had come down upon me indeed; I, kin-slayer, had in turn been robbed of my kin.

"Ythillin!" I howled. "Behold your curse! Now, Ice-Bitch, and all you Gods who have betrayed me! Ghor the Wolf will meddle no more in the affairs of Gods or of men' I will be no more a pawn of

Order or of Chaos, but I will be a wolf of wolves, as I was intended to be when I was cast out!"

I flung the Sword of Genseric to the ice.

"I shall carry no more the sword that slew my kin and could not save my beloved nor my son!"

I ripped the skins from my body.

"I will wear no more the trappings of a man! Come to me, ye Hounds! A Wolf among Hounds, I shall run forever on this ice, and die at last like the beast I was made upon the day of my birth! And cursed be all Gods and all men and all civilizations!"

The human form flowed away from me like water. Dropping to all fours, I fled northward, running hour after hour, tireless, toward the cold northern stars.

But behind me I could hear the laughter of the Ice Goddess, maddening me.

And at my heels ran the Hounds.

Chapter XVII

The River of Fog
Richard A. Lupoff

"You bastard, James Allison!"

I turned from the window where I had been staring down from my suite atop San Francisco's Nob Hill, watching the fog like a river of ice flow through the Golden Gate. I faced my three guests. They were all seated in deep Moroccan-leather chairs, surrounding the jade-inlaid table near my fireplace.

A fragrant back-log had burned low, but still cast enough of a glow that no artificial lighting was required in the room.

The speaker had been Yuriko Yamash'ta. She was probably the most beautiful woman alive, and the low flames reflected from deep in her dark eyes, her long glossy black hair and the matching costume that did little to conceal her elegant figure. She was also the only human being to climb the perilous north face of Everest alone. And she was known to have killed no fewer than five armed men—three of them on one occasion—with her bare hands.

"Bastard, my dear?" I smiled at her. "In fact, I am not that. Not as James Allison. Although I'm certain that I was indeed a bastard in most of my prior incarnations. Most of us were."

"You really believe in that reincarnation business?"

The speaker now was Abraham Steinman. His wheelchair lay folded in the outer vestibule of my suite. A cursory glance at Abraham as he sat near the hearth would never have suggested that he had been a paraplegic from early childhood. Nor had the injury to his spine that had turned his body into a passive appendage interfered with the development of the most innovative mind since that of Edison.

Steinman's greatest invention to date—the one that had freed the industrialized world of its bondage to OPEC oil and that had made Steinman the world's first self-created billionaire since the original Rockefeller—was the Steinman Universal Conversion Engine. That engine, in sizes anywhere from the dimensions of a wristwatch to those of the Grand Coulee Dam—could convert energy from any form into any other form, including solar, wind, or thermal power into electricity. And it could do that with an efficiency of 99%+.

Abe Steinman maintained a giant technological and administrative apparatus to manage his inventions, but he kept a private laboratory in a wooden shed for himself. And from that wooden shed, he had sworn, he would bring forth a set of neural-controlled miniaturized servo-motors by means of which he would walk within three years and would play third base in the American League within five. If he had to buy his own team to get the job, he said, he would do it. And he would hit for .300 or better!

I answered his question. "I don't just believe in reincarnation, Abe. Any more than you 'believe in' rainstorms or the element oxygen. They *exist*. You know they exist, but that isn't what makes them real. There would be rainstorms whether you believed in them or not. There would be oxygen molecules, pairs of atoms with an atomic weight of eight and a valence of two, whether you believed in them or not. We're all reincarnated, time after time after time. Belief has nothing to do with it."

"Not so." He moved his head slowly from side to side, one of the few actual motions he was capable of. "Belief is all important. If we all believed in reincarnation, there would be no reason to struggle for anything in this world. We might as well lie back and wait for a better life if we weren't happy with this one. No, Jim, it's the belief that this life is our one chance at the brass ring that makes us try for the ring—and some of us actually snag it!"

My third guest made the kind of loud, inarticulate sound that writers render as *hmph*! He reached an elegantly-manicured hand for the small cobalt-blue glass-lined silver dish on the jade-topped table, lifted it and an even tinier silver spoon. He filled the spoon carefully with fine white powder and offered it to Yuriko and Abraham, then carefully took a spoon for himself.

After a few seconds he said, "I agree that belief is all important, but belief in reincarnation isn't necessarily as debilitating as you suggest, Abe."

"Come now," Steinman rejoined. "That belief has been the greatest impediment to the development of India. One of the world's great cultures—gone stagnant and flat. Why work?

"Why bother to advance oneself or society, when there's always another chance and another chance and another chance to come? Someday we'll all be kings if we keep our karma right, so why bother to improve the lot of peasants, even if we're all peasants in this turn around the wheel?"

"Ah, Abe, Abe, Abe," the other said. "You ought to get your nose out of the laboratory once in a while and observe the way the world works. It wasn't reincarnation that set India back, it was the British East India Company! And India's still working to undo the distortions in her character that Britain brought about."

Steinman grimaced. "Very well. I certainly bow to your greater understanding of politics, Senator."

XVII. The River of Fog

Senator McPherson smiled in mock gratitude.

Gardner Hendricks McPherson had been the most brilliant cadet to graduate from West Point since Douglas MacArthur, and had broken even MacArthur's record for a speedy rise from second lieutenant to brigadier general. His star continued to rise in the military firmament until he startled the nation by resigning his commission to run for a seat in the United States Senate.

He had won, had performed with similar brilliance in the Senate, becoming Minority Leader before the end of his first term—another unprecedented achievement for McPherson. It was now a foregone conclusion that he would be President of the United States one day, whether four years hence, or eight, being the major question that remained.

He placed the cobalt-blue dish back on the table, selected a slim, hand-rolled stick of Thai gold from a filigreed tray, and lit it with a solid gold lighter. He exhaled slowly, nodded and passed the stick to his right.

"Surely you didn't mean to direct the conversation onto abstract philosophy, Yuriko, when you called our gracious host a bastard." McPherson inclined his head toward the mountaineer. "But what *did* you have in mind?"

"I had in mind that James was a bastard for leaving his story hanging there. Whether it's gospel truth or whether it's all a cock-and-bull story, I don't even care. With due respect to your convictions, Abraham and Gardner. But James . . . ." She shook her head despairingly. The back-log hissed and flared briefly, throwing golden lights dancing across Yuriko's hair.

I crossed the soft Kermanshahan carpeting and stood before the hearth. Yuriko held the Thai toward me, as if to say, *Never mind my words, everything remains between us as before*. I nodded my understanding, inhaled the fragrant gold, held the Thai for Steinman and passed it along to Senator McPherson.

The strains of a Mozart concerto emerged from speakers whose baffle-cloths were indistinguishable from priceless centuries-old tapestry for very good reasons.

"What further did you wish to hear?" I asked.

Yuriko laughed. "James, you're fortunate to have inherited your fortune. You'd never be much good at earning money—at least not if you tried to do it by writing novels."

"I never claimed to be a businessman *or* a novelist," I responded. "But just what is your complaint? I've simply told you the story of Ghor, fifth-born son of Genseric. As I lived it. Yes, my dear, as I lived it, unmeasured millennia ago. You might quarrel with the structure of a novel, but how can you complain about the truth?"

"Well, James, let's see where you left yourself. That is, Ghor."

Her startlingly slim and graceful hands flowed through an arresting gesture. "You started life as an abandoned cripple, suckled by a conveniently lactating wolf-bitch. Certainly a familiar touch, that!"

I agreed.

"You survived your infancy, overcame your twisted leg, were raised as a wolf, returned to human society and took rather sanguine vengeance upon the family that had abandoned you."

"Yes."

"And then you launched yourself on the most extraordinary series of adventures. Including, as the expression has it, arson, rape and bloody murder."

"But what is it that you find so objectionable in my tale?" I asked her.

She smiled at me.

"I'll accept all of the improbabilities, James, and I'll even write off the seemingly supernatural interventions that seem to occur so often. Let's just say that they were the barbaric mind's interpretation of events that we would find other explanations for, today."

"Such as?"

"Well," she reached and touched my hand lightly. I felt the electric thrill that never failed to come with her touch. "Well," she said, "just for one example. That strange incident on the island. What happened? A volcano opened, bronze robots emerged from its molten bowels, wiped out Ghor's followers, then flew away into the sky. Now really!"

"It happened," I said angrily.

"Of course it did. But was it magical? Might there not have been a more advanced civilization in the world at the time? Maybe they were geologists, sent there to study that volcano. Once it blew, they took their findings and left. They weren't robots. They were wearing protective suits."

"Still, Yuriko, why the 'You bastard' treatment?"

"Because, James, at the end of your whole incredible saga, you just left it hanging. All of the blood, all of the suffering, your wife and child dead, your arch-foe Mentumenen dead. You'd been, literally, to hell and back. And there you were, living with the wolves once again. What happened?"

Before I could answer her, Abraham Steinman raised another objection. "I find it hard to reconcile your pantheon, Allison."

I stood with my back to the guttering fire, waiting for Steinman to elaborate.

"At the start of your tale you made reference to some Scandinavian deities. Ymir, of course, is a familiar figure. Ythillin is less so, but your description of her fits into the Norse concept. But then you

XVII. The River of Fog

bring in Mitra, who was worshipped for some centuries as a sort of alternate Jesus. Ishtar, who was the great Babylonian goddess. Set, the Egyptian devil-god who murdered his brother Osiris. Gaea, the Greek earth-mother. And the Hounds of Tindalos, creations, I believe, of the modern genius Belknapius. Not to mention Cthulhu, Yog-Sothoth, Cthugha of Fomalhaut."

He clucked his tongue like a nursery school teacher who had caught a five-year-old in a fib. Compared to that great intellect, I suppose we were all on the level of five-year-olds.

"If all of this took place those untold thousands of generations ago," Abraham resumed, "how to account for the admixture of deities and beings from so many cultures and such widely separated periods?"

"I do not account for them," said. "What I have told you is the baldest outline of a life I lived long before this one. What happened, happened, and I make no effort to defend or justify it. This is not a courtroom. If you choose not to believe me, then consider it all just a tale. I hope that I have amused you, these past hours. You are surely not obliged to believe me."

"Well," Steinman considered, "I suppose that's fair enough."

Now Senator McPherson spoke. "Suppose, though, to satisfy Miz Yamash'ta, you do tell us what happened after you rejoined the wolves. Surely your memory doesn't just fade out at that point?"

"Surely it does not," I said.

• • •

And so I found myself a wolf once again, a beast in my heart and largely, even, in my body. It was as if I had reverted to the days of my childhood—or cubhood!—in that terrible time after Gudrun of the Shining Locks had rejected me and Genseric the Sworder exposed me on the ice to die.

Werewolf, wolf-man, man-wolf, what difference did it make? I struggled not to think, not to deal with the terrible events that had overtaken me and the terrible deeds that I myself had performed since my first encounters with the Æsir and the Vanir.

Did I change? Did the weird Lycanthropic alteration come over me, there in the snow-riven waste? Did I mutter those few simple syllables that I had learned from Telordric the White Magician, going now on two legs, now on four, fighting now with fist or the metal arm made for me by Dar'ah Humarl, now with the fangs and claws of my animal form?

I knew not, neither did I care.

At times I think I switched back and forth between my Lycanthropic form as a werewolf and my human form as a wolfman. What difference did it make?

The anguish of my life was forgotten, and that was all that mattered to me. None of the fighting, none of the killing—nor any of the wounds, the pain, the injury that had been inflicted upon me—mattered. It was all like a grand game in which the winning of a battle, the conquest of a nation, the overthrow of a dynasty meant neither more nor less than the gain or loss of a marker.

I had seen enough of death to know both that it came inevitably to all men and indeed to all living things, and that it was to be fought off and avoided only for the purpose of prolonging this game of warfare that we chose to call life. There with the wolves of the ice-pack I could forget the one memory that it had been impossible for me to accept—the memory of my wife Shanara and my nameless infant child, dead in the northern wastes.

Surely this was a rich irony. I who had slain parent and brother with never a moment's hesitancy, who had gloated in their dying agony, had been brought low by the loss of two loved ones of my own.

The Ice Bitch Ythillin laughed her cold and bitter laugh, I am sure, at the irony of my grief! And it was my life with the wolves of the ice-pack, my deliberate and willful abandonment of human identity, human consciousness, human recollection, that alone made it possible for me to live on.

With the wolves I hunted elk, exulting in the acrid stench of fear that emanated from our prey when some great ruminant realized that it was trapped, doomed. I lusted for the feel of living flesh between my fangs, the taste of hotly spurting blood on my tongue.

As a wolf I became respected as a sharp-nosed scout, a peerless and tireless tracker of our prey. In the moment of attack none was more fearless and none more ferocious than I. At the moment of the kill, no wolf was more savage or more terrible than I.

And I rose, not by design but by the inevitable competition of courage and strength and skill that settles the social order of the wolves, to the moment when I was the second leader of our pack. And then one day I felt myself overcome by strange urgings, irresistible urgings. I felt my hairs stiffening, my tongue lolling, my nostrils twitching to the stimulus of a scent like none other: that of the wolf-bitch in heat.

I rose from my place and trotted across the glittering ice. Soon I found the source of that all-powerful stimulus. It was the mate of the leader of our wolf-pack. He was an old and wise wolf who had seen many winters. He had mated as a young hunter, and as do wolves, he had mated for life. But after years of companionship and litters of whelps, his bitch had died, and after a period of mourning—yes, wolves mourn!—he had mated again, this time with a young female of glittering eyes and long, luxuriant fur.

But now her scent called to me and I could no more resist that

XVII. The River of Fog

call than a fir can resist the call of the springtime sun. I trotted to her side. She lay on a bank of soft snow, looked up at me, licked the fur of my muzzle.

I issued a challenge, a mighty howl that said as clearly to the wolves of our pack as ever human speech said to human ear, that I was claiming the mate of the leader. With her, I claimed the leadership of the pack itself.

By the law of the wolves—and, yes, the wolves have law!—the old leader could choose one of three courses. He could accept my challenge and fight me, fight me to the death. He could yield to my claim, yield to me both his mate and his leadership of the wolf-pack, and become a submissive follower. Or he could leave the pack to wander the ice-floes, a loner, a rogue wolf, hunting such small prey as he could bring down alone, picking at the offal left by others, perhaps attacking the despised Man.

He chose to fight.

There are few preliminaries in the life of the wolf-pack. The challenge had been issued. The old leader had accepted. The rest of the pack assembled, ringing us, the leader's bitch settled to one side of the circle of wolves while the old leader and I stood glaring and snarling at each other in the center.

He was older than I. Larger. Immensely strong. But he was an old wolf, his reflexes not as rapid as once they had been, his stamina less than it had been years gone by.

While I was—ageless.

He must, somehow, have sensed that difference between us. He knew that his sole chance for triumph was to carry a rapid and decisive attack.

He charged across the hard-packed snow until he was a half-dozen strides from me, then launched himself into a flying lunge, his bared yellow fangs directed at my throat.

I timed my response, ducking my belly onto the snow and lunging forward just as he descended to complete his attack.

He missed my throat, skidded across my body, his belly sliding over my hind-quarters as he tumbled onto the snow.

In a flash I reversed myself and caught him from the rear, nipping him on a hind haunch as he scrambled to recover from his failed attack.

With a coughing growl he came back to his feet and stood glaring at me. He was hardly injured by the nip I had taken from his haunch. A tiny dribble of blood trickled down his fur. He edged sideways, trying to circle into a more advantageous position to use against me. He had been humiliated, and he did not wish to be humiliated again.

He growled a challenge to me, urging me to attack, but I refrained, taunting him. I edged myself into position before his bitch and urinated into the snow beside her, marking her as my possession with my spoor. With one paw I cuffed her gently, not to hurt but to show that she was my mate now.

The old leader almost choked on his snarl. He charged across the circle at me, this time making a low approach so as to lunge upward at my throat. This was a far more dangerous attack than his earlier, almost contemptible, flying leap.

I skipped sideways with my hindquarters, backing a halfstep so that the trajectory of his new attack lay at right angles—what men would call right angles!—to my own position.

He tried to correct his attack, and partially he succeeded.

We lunged and snapped simultaneously, our very fangs clashing as we collided. We both went sprawling; I rolled onto one side as he skidded to a halt. He was on me before I could regain my feet, and his teeth would have closed in the soft flesh of my neck ending the challenge—and my life—save for the thickness of my heavy coat and the force of our previous clash, which had badly hurt his lower jaw.

So instead of my gushing jugular, his only trophy of the attack was a mouthful of thick fur and a single gobbet of my flesh.

This time I growled my fury and resentment, and backed away, belly down, trying to regain my lost advantage.

My opponent spat and sputtered, clearing his mouth of the fur he had ripped from my throat. I uttered a snarl of fury and circled. My opponent had placed himself before the bitch who was both the symbol and prize of our combat. He stood over her, growling his warning to me.

At that moment I almost uttered the brief syllables that would turn me into a man, armed with the bronze mechanical arm of Dar'ah Humarl, prepared to aim some spring-driven blade or spiked ball at my foe, to destroy him as a man destroys a wild, dangerous animal. But no, I was myself an animal, as wild as my opponent and, if anything, even more dangerous.

I resisted the urge to snarl those syllables, and instead threw my bulk into a murderous charge against my opponent. Not ten paces from the bitch I feinted as if I would leap past my opponent to the left. Instead I shifted my course to the right as if I intended to pass him on that side and seize the prize, the bitch, for myself.

The old wolf spun first one way, then the other, trying to compensate for my feint and my change of direction.

Another calculated movement and I had my opponent trying to maneuver in three directions at once. He reared above me, forepaws flailing for balance, hind feet scrambling on the snow for purchase.

XVII. The River of Fog

I launched myself with all the power of my iron-hard sinews. I aimed my attack not at my opponent's throat nor at his unprotected belly, but at his mighty chest.

My jaws were opened wide, my head twisted to one side to bring my upper and lower jaw together on the two sides of his ribcage. My razor-like fangs cut through the thick fur and the muscular flesh of the old leader as if they had been the soft wool and tender flesh of a newborn lamb.

As the mighty muscles of my jaw snapped shut I felt and heard the brittle bones of his ribcage snap. My teeth met in the middle of his chest. I wrenched my head, tearing away the prize of my successful attack. I had ripped the very heart from my opponent, and as I tugged it away, his body fell, lifeless, to the snow.

He did not even twitch.

I dropped my prize on the snow and pawed at it. I stood over the body of my defeated opponent while the rest of the tribe stood or sat in their positions around us. I made a little summoning whimper to the leader's bitch and she minced temptingly toward me. She licked the little wound on my neck. I made the low, whimpering sound that gave her permission to sample the fresh carrion before her.

She sniffed at the flesh of what had been her mate, pulled away a gobbet of steaming bloody flesh and carried it to her place to be consumed.

One by one the remainder of the wolf-pack advanced to make obeisance to me, their new leader, and to receive their share of the flesh of my defeated predecessor.

Once my dominance of the pack was formalized and accepted by all I strode from the circle, growling to the others a warning that none might follow me.

I walked alone across the snow and ice until darkness fell. The sky was black but clear, the stars and moon bright in the crisp, almost polar air. They cast a bright glow that was reflected from the white surface, giving the world a ghostly semblance of daylight.

Now I muttered the syllables I had learned from Telordric before I killed that white magician. They were brief and simple; they must be, to be made by the vocal apparatus of a wolf, apparatus designed for the making of growls and snarls and whines and eerie howls but not for the making of human syllables.

I felt my body shifting, my hind legs growing longer, my forelegs turning into arms and my forepaws into hands. My muzzle shrank to the nose and jaws of a human. My pelt was absorbed, leaving only the poll and beard and coarse body-hairs of a normal if hirsute man.

I threw back my face and glared into the sky, shouting my challenge to my enemy, mentor, patroness and tormentor, Ythillin the first daughter of the Ice Gods.

"Bitch," I shouted. "Bitch! I have won the leadership of the wolves! I have won the beautiful wolf-bitch for my prize! Is she not a token of yourself? What more must I do? Whom else must I conquer? Why can I not die, Ice-Bitch!"

A terrible wind rose and spun glittering crystals of snow and ice around me. Prism-like, they broke the spectrum of the moon- and starlight into a shimmering rainbow that bathed and burned me until I felt like a living, chromatic flame. I was swept from the ground, raised by that icy whirlwind like a sailor caught up in a waterspout or a dirt-grubbing farmer snatched from the earth by a cyclone's whirling black funnel.

I was carried high into the air, spun topsy-turvy until I could not tell whether the glaring white disk and the twinkling specks that whirled past my eyes were the true moon and stars or their icy reflections glittering at me from the frozen slopes beneath. The wind howled in my ears and in it I heard the voices—I thought I heard the voices—of those gods and mortals with whom I struggled these terrible, toilsome years.

Gudrun and Genseric were there, old Bragi and the four brothers I had slain, Raki and Sigismund, Alwin and Obri. Harolf was there, the Æsir chieftain and Hetlund his son, Tjarvakka the Æsir priest and Hialmar my companion in arms. Oderic and Guthric, Nald and Cudric, warriors all, of the Vanir, and Hengist Ironarm my uncle and Tostig Bearslayer my cousin.

Gl'erf was there, leader of the half-human Mi-Go, and Klu'do the she with whom I had tried—and failed—to mate.

Agha Junghaz, king in Turan, and the beauteous Jahree the chiefest of his wives. Ushilon and the Stygian sorcerer Mentumenen, Kaius Valkonnus of Aquilonia and Lamaril the Invincible—who had proved, before my attack, to be anything but what his title claimed.

And Lord Garak, king in Belverus, capital of Nemedia, and his sons Tashako and Yashati and his daughter, my wife the Lady Shanara of Jelah and our child.

The wind howled and howled. Somewhere wolves howled. And somehow the howling turned to a terrible baying, the baying of the Hounds of Tindalos.

They were around me now, their eyes shining redly against the black of the sky and the white of the snow and ice. The Hounds who came, once they were summoned, through the very *angles of space*.

I could see the Ice-Bitch Ythillin, and for once she gazed upon an earthly scene—no, upon an unearthly scene!—not with her expression of detached and supercilious amusement, but with one of

XVII. The River of Fog

concern, of alarm, of—I could not believe my own perceptions—fear!

"Ghor!" she cried. "Ghor!"

"What is it, Bitch?" I replied.

"Come with me! Flee, flee the Hounds, for we are not finished, you and I! We are not finished!"

I laughed and laughed. I tugged at my wondrous arm of bronze that had been made for me by Dar'ah Humarl of Zaporakh, tugged at it and hurled it from me to tumble and tumble onto the ice-fields below.

"Escape with me, Ghor!" Ythillin cried again. "Mortal man, beast, Lycanthrope, killer and king! I will make you one with the immortals, one with the very Ice Gods themselves! Come with me!"

She swept toward me, rushing through some transdimensional realm that neither ancient man nor modern scholar can ever hope to comprehend. In some inexplicable way she seemed to move through planes of existence, to approach me without traversing the finite loci that separated us.

She did not move through the volume of space, but through its angles.

The baying of the Hounds rose in triumph, and before me I saw Ythillin the Ice-Bitch surrounded by their panting, slavering throng.

Too late she turned to retreat.

The Hounds had her, dragging her down by the long shards of her raiment, rending her flesh, spilling her blood, blood that flowed not red like that of any earthly creature I had known but an icy pale blue. A drop of that blood—a single drop!—spattered on my flesh.

Here, right here, where you see the scar.

It burned me and froze me, tormented me with unbearable anguish at the same instant that it transported me to realms of ecstasy indescribable.

I lost consciousness. I lost life. All was over. All.

All.

All.

• • •

The back-log in my fireplace above San Francisco's streets hissed softly. Through the nearest window I could see the river of fog flowing weirdly back through the Golden Gate, to disperse with the morning's warming sun onto the gray Pacific waters.

"And that was all you remember," Abraham Steinman asked me, "until your present life as James Allison? Ghor?"

I realized to my own surprise that I was panting and disheveled, drenched with perspiration that soaked my formal shirt and dark tuxedo jacket. Like a man bewildered—or, I thought, like a wolf emerging from an icy stream—I shook my head and gathered up my wits.

I looked around the room. Steinman and Senator McPherson and Yuriko Yamash'ta sat in their Morocco chairs, waiting for me to answer Steinman's question.

I drew in my breath and mopped my sweat-laden brow with a silken handkerchief.

"By no means, Abraham," I answered him at length. "Oh no, by no means is that the last I remember. Long after Ghor was dust and dried parchment, I lived the life of a warrior-priest in Atlantis. I was a Pict in ancient Britain. I lived in Khitai—you remember fabled Khitai in the East, surely! Ah, there I witnessed events and myself committed acts that you would never believe, had I the temerity to tell you of them.

"Yes. I dwelt in Shem. I know the true origins of the legend of Eden. I trekked across the Bering Strait when the land-bridge stood between this continent and that which we please to call Asia. I was of the Mixtecs of high Middle America, and of a people who dwelt near the South Pole in a city you would not wish to call a city, and had a form you would never dream to call human.

"All of these. All of these, Abe, and as many more, and as many more again! These lives I have lived.

"And after this one, this little life of James Allison, is over—there will be as many more to follow. I do not *believe* this, Abe. I *know* it!"

He snorted.

"Some time I will tell you of these other lives," I resumed. "That is, I will do so if you wish. Otherwise—let us discuss the politics of nations, or the strategy of the Oakland baseball club, eh? Or amuse ourselves, perhaps, with a quiet game of chess?"

"I think we should be going now," Senator Gardner Hendricks McPherson put in. "Can I give you a hand, Steinman?"

Steinman accepted the offer.

Steinman, I knew, would achieve all that he had set himself to achieve. I *knew* that he would walk again, within three years. That he would play third base in the American League within five. I didn't tell him so. It would spoil the fun.

And so he was helped to his wheelchair and wheeled to my private elevator by Senator, ex-General, Gardner Hendricks McPherson, who confidently expected to be elected President of the United States in four years, or perhaps in eight. He would not be, that I also knew, but I did not tell him either. It would spoil the fun.

The elevator door hissed shut behind the Senator and the brilliant paraplegic engineer.

Behind me, the soft voice of Yuriko Yamash'ta blended perfectly with the strains of a Mozart quintet. "I do not wish to leave, James."

XVII. The River of Fog

I turned and saw that Yuriko had lighted a stick of Thai gold. She held it toward me.

"Thank you," I said.

"And again, my dear, I thank you."

Publisher's Note

Ghor, Kin-Slayer was conceived in the late 1970s by Jonathan Bacon, editor of *Fantasy Crossroads*, a popular fanzine during the Robert E. Howard "boom" of that period. At the time Bacon had been presented with an unfinished story by Robert E. Howard, "Genseric's Son", which he quickly recognised as having strong possibilities if completed not by one, but a whole series of authors.

Beginning with *Fantasy Crossroads* in March 1977 Bacon lined up top authors in the fantasy field to each contribute a chapter until the novel would be completed some 17 installments later. Each issue of *Fantasy Crossroads* would include two or three chapters until the saga was finished. Unfortunately, though, after only 12 chapters saw print with the January 1979 issue, *Fantasy Crossroads* was no more, and for all intents and purposes, *Ghor, Kin-Slayer* was lost forever.

Now, more than 20 years after the story began, it is with great pleasure that we at Necronomicon Press can present the entire novel in one volume, including all of the concluding chapters which were thought lost long ago.

Producing this project was not an easy chore. It was only by sheer luck that Glenn Lord owned a complete copy of the novel's manuscript, including all of the unpublished chapters. Without Glenn, this book would not have been possible, lending yet another item to the long list of contributions he's made to the field over the many years.

Special thanks are also due to the many contributors who have granted permission for their chapters to be reprinted. Unfortunately, a number of the authors involved have passed on since *Ghor, Kin-Slayer* was first written; thanks are given to their estates for cooperating with us in this project.

Finally, a number of people were involved in the research and production of this book. Our thanks go to David Drake, Carol King, Kevin D. Shields, R. Dixon Smith, and Robert Weinberg for their help in tracking down authors, and to Rusty Burke, Susan Michaud, and Chuck Morgan for their efforts with copy-editing and proofreading.

Whether *Ghor, Kin-Slayer* succeeds as a novel is left to the reader. Its premise is certainly unique, and there can be no question that the contributors' list to this book reads like a who's who in the fantasy fiction genre. Our appreciation goes out to Jonathan Bacon for starting this project, and while we were unable to contact him (not without trying, though), we trust he'll approve of our efforts in bringing this endeavor to fruition.